A tall man stood in the arc of bright light thrown by the torch, and although Catherine hadn't seen him in years, there was no mistaking Devon Macgowan.

She tried to shrink back into the darkest corner of the chamber, but he lifted the torch, ensnaring her in a shaft of yellow.

"You will come to no harm. I'm not here to slay you," he exclaimed.

Catherine jerked her head out of the light and strained to see his expression, but his face was in shadow.

"If you meant me no harm, why do you carry a sword into my chamber?"

"I need you," he said into the darkened room.

"Why?"

"As my prisoner."

Dear Reader,

We, the editors of Tapestry Romances, are committed to bringing you two outstanding original romantic historical novels each and every month.

From Kentucky in the 1850s to the court of Louis XIII, from the deck of a pirate ship within sight of Gibraltar to a mining camp high in the Sierra Nevadas, our heroines experience life and love, romance and adventure.

Our aim is to give you the kind of historical romances that you want to read. We would enjoy hearing your thoughts about this book and all future Tapestry Romances. Please write to us at the address below.

The Editors
Tapestry Romances
POCKET BOOKS
1230 Avenue of the Americas
Box TAP
New York, N.Y. 10020

Tangled Vows

Anne Moore

A TAPESTRY BOOK

PUBLISHED BY POCKET BOOKS NEW YORK

This novel is a work of historical fiction. Names, characters, places and incidents relating to non-historical figures are either the product of the author's imagination or are used fictitiously. Any resemblance of such non-historical incidents, places or figures to actual events or locales or persons, living or dead, is entirely coincidental.

An *Original* publication of TAPESTRY BOOKS

 A Tapestry Book published by
POCKET BOOKS, a division of Simon & Schuster, Inc.
1230 Avenue of the Americas, New York, N.Y. 10020

ISBN: 0-671-52626-X

First Tapestry Books printing January, 1985

10 9 8 7 6 5 4 3 2 1

POCKET and colophon are registered trademarks
of Simon & Schuster, Inc.

TAPESTRY is a registered trademark of Simon & Schuster, Inc.

Printed in the U.S.A.

To Maura Seger

Tangled Vows

Chapter One

Ireland, December, 1602

"CATHERINE, WAKE UP! YOU MUST FLEE!"

Catherine Craig heard the words dimly and cried out at the nightmare. It was always the same one, a dream which was not really a dream so much as a reliving of a terrifying memory. Men stormed their castle, and she and her family had to flee.

She woke up with a start. Tears had streaked the smooth curves of her cheek, and her nightsmock had knotted into wild, damp coils about her legs. Blinking into the darkness of her room, she realized that someone else was in the bedchamber with her. Sister Brigit stood over her. The small, elderly nun had grabbed her by the arm and was shaking her.

Sister Brigit cried frantically, "Get up! There are soldiers outside. Scotsmen. They've come to find you. Quick, you must flee!"

"Soldiers? What do you mean?" Catherine brushed aside the sleep-tumbled strands of her mahogany hair. Her hazel eyes swept over the small, chaste room but nothing seemed amiss. "Do you mean my father is here?" The last she had heard from him, her father had gone back to their native country of Scotland to try to retrieve their stolen lands. He had placed her at this small Irish convent for protection while he was away.

"No!" Sister Brigit's frail, translucent hands trembled from some violent emotion. Her wimple had fallen off, letting grey hair fly in agitated wisps about her face. "Strangers—I've never seen them before. They woke up all the sisters in the abbey looking for you. They have weapons. I—"

Catherine scrambled from her narrow cot. Heedless of the icy floor and her bare feet, she darted to the window and pressed her cheek to the pane of leaded glass.

Helmeted soldiers strode up the cliffs from the beach, their torches sending incandescent beams into the night-darkened fog. Doubtless they'd landed a ship at the cove beneath the cliffs. A number of the men appeared to have already entered the convent walls, for she could make out faint sounds coming from the direction of the dormitory—door hinges groaning open, heavy boots scraping against stone floors, and a more ominous sound—the clanking of swords.

Dread prickled down Catherine's spine like a spider. There could be only one Scotsman, other than her father, who could have any interest in her. That was the same man who had razed their castle, stolen their lands, and driven them from their native country. Her husband, Devon Macgowan.

It was her nightmare come to life. And, for the

second time in her twenty-six years, she would have to flee. "How can I get out? Are the soldiers outside?"

"So far, they have only entered the convent bedrooms. I don't think they understand that since you are not a nun you must sleep in a chamber kept for visitors."

Catherine considered quickly. The abbey was surrounded by a tall, ancient wall. The only way to leave, judging from what she saw at the window, would be by way of the refectory, where the nuns took their meals. Once she was through the door there, it was only a short run to reach the stables where the farm horses were kept. "I'll have to leave through the refectory."

Sister Brigit gave a sharp nod. "Yes, that would be best. Let me see if the cloisters are empty." She half turned toward the door, and then stopped, and looked up at Catherine. "I must say something." In the oppressive darkness, the nun smiled at her. "I've come to care a great deal for you during the years that you've been with us."

Catherine flung her arms about Sister Brigit. There was fourteen years of affection in her gesture. "I hope I've never given you any cause to regret taking me in."

The nun shook her head at Catherine's words. "You worry about everything, about silly things."

Catherine was unable to speak. In truth, although she had done her best, she didn't think that she had fitted into the life of the convent very well.

Certainly she had never managed to achieve the inner serenity that the nuns strove for. It simply didn't seem to be in her nature to be passive. Whenever Catherine cared, she wanted to care about something with all of her heart and mind and body. And as much as she loved the sisters, she hadn't been content at the abbey. She'd secretly longed for something other than the endless round of prayer and fasting and retreat.

At times it seemed as if her entire life had been spent in yearning, of imagining a life that included love and adventure. Dreams that would hang in the air, insubstantial as woodsmoke, and then vanish. For none of it would ever happen. There could never be any handsome man for her to love. She was already married. Nor could there be adventure, not in the convent.

At least not until now. Her abdomen went weightless in sudden fear, and Catherine struggled to control her terror. "Sister," she announced at last, "let me see if the way is clear." Her nightsmock looked like a white candle in the black night as she slid up the latch and opened the door.

Outside, a torch had been thrust into the ancient iron ring in the cloister wall, and bright yellow light arced over the rows of grey columns and down the long, stone walkway. And fell, also, on the backs of a dozen soldiers. Catherine shut the door silently.

The two women stood for a moment, holding their breaths, staring at one another. Catherine was the first to speak. A little shakily, she stated, "We'll just have to wait for them to leave." There was no point in adding the obvious: that the men might not leave in time, that, in fact, the soldiers might well realize how close they were to finding her room.

"Yes." The nun whispered as softly as Catherine had done. "Do you know who has come for you?"

"My husband." It felt odd using that word. Their marriage had taken place so long ago it hardly seemed real. She'd been twelve years old, and the wedding had been forced on her and Devon Macgowan as a way to end a clan feud.

"But why would he be here to seek you out?"

Catherine shrank back against the grey stone wall, feeling its cold roughness against her fingertips. She said in a low voice, "I can think of only one reason. My father has been disgraced, and my lands and money are gone. Doubtless my husband wants to end our sham of a marriage so he can wed some other, more advantageous, woman." She swallowed. "He's come to slay me."

The room was shrouded in shadows, dark, cold, and flat. Catherine shivered. What better place for murder than this lonely, isolated Irish abbey, with only a handful of nuns to protect her or to give witness? There were no other settlements for miles. Ireland was a country torn by war, and, like Ireland herself, the abbey had long since fallen into near ruin.

An icy wind leaked in under the door and made the edge of her nightsmock tremble. She yearned to go over to the iron casket which held her clothes and shoes, but didn't dare. It shrieked as if wounded whenever the lid was lifted.

She was far too frightened to do anything that might cause the soldiers outside to notice this room. Catherine's eyes closed. Her father had drilled the need for courage into her. He thought bravery and loyalty and pride in one's clan were everything. He himself charged through life, never able to believe in his mortality or in the possibility of defeat.

It hadn't been that way for her. She was far too imaginative to have his sturdy, unthinking bravery. She'd had to force herself to do the things he wanted. With a gritty persistence, she'd learned to ride, and to hunt, even though she hated it. In doing so, she'd developed a way of dealing with daunting situations, a trick of brazening things out, of facing up to danger by pretending not to be frightened.

Catherine looked up when Sister Brigit said softly, "I think enough time has gone by. I am going to look out the door again." She walked softly to the door and drew it open the merest sliver. After closing it again, Sister Brigit whispered. "The way seems clear. I am going outside to make certain."

Catherine put a hand on her arm, preventing her from leaving. "No!" she whispered vehemently. "Let me go. I couldn't bear it if you were harmed for my sake."

Sister Brigit gently shook off her hand. "The soldiers have treated all the nuns most circumspectly. Truly, I will be in no danger, even if they do spy me." Before Catherine could protest again, Sister Brigit's fingers pulled open the door, and she slipped outside.

The small chamber seemed much emptier without her. Catherine's teeth started to chatter, and she rubbed her hands over her shoulders in an attempt to warm herself. She wondered how long Sister Brigit would be gone.

A violent burst of noise near her door made Catherine freeze in terror. What was it? Had a soldier come upon Sister Brigit?

Catherine jumped into motion. She had to help! Her nightsmock billowing around her, she flew to the door and thrust it open.

A mistake. For outside, past the cloisters, Sister Brigit was already being led away by a dozen soldiers. Only one man had remained behind; but at the noise she'd made, he turned and stared in her direction. Catherine slammed the door shut again and fell back against the wall inside.

The door burst open. A tall Scotsman stood in the arc of bright light thrown by the torch. He brandished a claymore high, in a menacing gesture. Catherine stared up into blue eyes which held a wary intelligence. Her heart seemed to stop in mid-beat.

Even though she hadn't seen him in years, there was no mistaking Devon Macgowan. The sun-washed brown hair, the face of austere, severe beauty, and the tall, well-honed body were unmistakable. He radiated a tightly controlled authority and disciplined power. From the slashed doublet of the finest silk to his high Russian leather boots, he looked, and was, a man who had long been accustomed to commanding others. She knew that he had become leader of his clan when he was only sixteen. By now he was thirty-four, and through his skill and strength of personality, his family had become the most important clan in the Highlands.

She had tried to shrink back into the darkest corner of the narrow bedchamber, but Devon must have been able to see at least the outline of her, for he turned his head toward her. "Cat?" He used her childhood nickname.

His tone held no threat, but she could hardly talk, she was so frightened. Nevertheless she forced herself to try and brazen things out. Through stiff lips she said querulously, "You've made a mistake. My name is Alice."

She watched his eyes narrow slightly as he studied her. Was it so dark that he wouldn't be able to make her out? The shadowed corner where she stood seemed as black as tar. But even if he could see her, perhaps he still wouldn't know who she was. He hadn't clapped eyes on her in over a dozen years.

"I tell you, sir, my name is Alice." She tried to add an irritated whine to her voice. "Alice O'Rourke. My parents left me here while they went to trade cloth at

7

Donegal Castle. They don't like to leave me alone in our cottage."

In response, he reached outside the room for the torch, then lifted it, snaring her in a shaft of yellow. It happened too quickly for her to move away.

The light fell over her, revealing a young woman whose hazel eyes were wide with apprehension and whose rounded breasts were barely concealed by the linsey-woolsey nightsmock. Catherine was not beautiful, but her face held an aliveness more compelling than mere beauty. Her lips were soft and red, and there were glints of crimson, like captured threads of fire, in the waves of mahogany hair that cascaded down her shoulders.

Devon exclaimed, as if the words were dragged out of him, "By all the—"

Catherine jerked her head up out of the torchlight. She breathed in the chilly night air in heavy gulps. The look she had seen on his face didn't show recognition, but it did reveal something else. For a fraction of a second, before Devon had supressed it, she had seen a flare of passion in his face that alarmed her almost as much as his being here. She grew aware that she was alone in a bedchamber with a strong, virile man, and that she had no protection. "Go away! As I told you, I am Alice, not the one you seek."

And then, horribly, she realized that when she moved, she had allowed his torchlight to slant over her hand. The yellow finger of light pointed straight at her wedding ring. If it had been the ordinary thick gold band that most men gave their brides, that might not have been so disastrous. But the one Devon had given her had a large and very distinctive ruby set in it, and the gem glittered in the streaming light. She saw his

8

face tighten as he spotted the ring, saw knowledge hit him like a blow.

He bent to lay down the torch. He would be at her in a second. She screamed, "Don't come any closer! I have a knife!" In the meantime, she scrambled frantically on the dark floor for a weapon, any kind of weapon. Her hands scraped over an iron box. The shape was awkward, but it was heavy and hard.

She jerked it up and hurled it at him just as he made a move for her. It slammed into his shoulder with a sickening thump. Devon gave a cry of surprise, and stumbled to the floor.

This was the only chance she would have. Plunging past him, she fled through the open door.

Beyond her room, she found the walkway empty of people. She took the quickest route to the stables by dashing through the cloisters and then running into the refectory.

Devon called to her. She guessed he was now on his feet and out of her room, but she didn't dare turn around to look. The refectory wasn't lighted, and in her haste she crashed into the legenda sanctorum. The book of meditations, which was read during every meal, clattered into the greenery left out for the Christmas celebrations.

Pain jarred through her upper leg where she had bumped it, but she paid no heed to that. All her thoughts were concentrated on one terrible realization. She was taking too long. Devon would catch up with her if she didn't hurry.

That knowledge spurred her. When the door that led outside stuck, she yanked on it so hard the latch nearly broke off, and small stones and plaster tumbled down from the ancient walls. Please, she prayed desperately, please let it be unlocked! She gave one last jerk, and it gave way. Cold air and damp curls of fog rushed into the room.

Shivering, Catherine dashed out to the meadow. From here, there would be miles of low, rolling hills covered in grass and bracken, and, behind her, fissured cliffs that fell down to the sea. She could hear the distant thunder of the waves, and taste the salt in the moon-struck mist. Whatever happened, she must not lose her way and head toward the cliffs. It would be far too easy in the fog to miss a step and tumble over.

She set off into the dark, running out into the wide meadows. The blackness was so total she felt blind. Already, the convent behind her had dwindled into a huddled shadow on the horizon. Gasping, she ran with her hands extended, expecting at any moment to slam into a tree.

The grass was wet and slick, and her nightgown soon slapped soggily against her legs. But her legs moved relentlessly, pushing her forward. She stumbled into a wet, spiny bush, the leaves and branches snapping and flaying about her, and got up, shaking and scratched, and went on to run some more. Her heartbeat pounded in her throat and there was a band of tightness across her chest.

Her feet had become cut and bruised and her lungs ached from the exertion. She hurt all over. But she knew Devon would be behind her, perhaps only a few feet away. Any second he could be upon her, so she kept on, helpless to do anything else.

And then, in back of her, came a phosphorescent moon which bobbed and weaved in the dark fog. It was a man carrying a torch. Devon.

She could imagine him raising that huge claymore, imagine the cold, slashing hiss it would make as it cut through the air. Could feel its sharp bite into her back. A scream built in her throat, pulsing and shrill, but she knew she couldn't scream, mustn't draw his attention to her.

Frantic now, she pushed her legs mercilessly, racing in what she hoped was the right direction. Had she lost her way? Where were the stables? At last she saw the silhouette of the stables, a black etching against a black sky.

But Devon was nearly upon her. She just couldn't seem to move any faster, even though she strained her legs unmercifully. He was so close now she could see him, hear the stridency of his breathing and the steady drumbeat of his boots slamming against the ground. She cried out when he made a flying leap at her.

He caught her, and they fell back together onto the wet grass. Catherine struggled against Devon but he was heavier and far stronger than she. They rolled over and over, crushing the breath out of her, tangling her legs and arms with his. The point of his dirk and the cold spine of his gold neckchain dug into her skin. She was barely aware, as she flailed at him with clenched fists, that she was screaming.

At last he managed to grab her about the wrists, clasping her hands as tightly as any manacle. He sprawled on top of her, a heavy, unyielding weight. "Have done, woman," he said on a breathless laugh.

Catherine dissolved into panic. Certain he was going to raise that sharp sword and cleave her head from her body, she became completely hysterical, thrashing and bucking against him. "Murderer! Let me go!"

"Before God as my witness, I mean you no harm." He pinned down her legs with his, forcibly stilling her body.

She couldn't move beneath the mastery of his hands

and legs. There was no longer any hope. Her heart tolled like a bell, but now that she knew for certain there was nothing more she could do, Catherine had at last gotten some measure of control over herself.

She snapped, "If you're planning to kill me, do it quickly. It would be slow and dull to be crushed to death by you." She shifted under his heavy body. "And I certainly don't care to spend much time in your company, Macgowan!"

Catherine tensed because she expected to be hit. But to her surprise, Devon laughed again, a pleasant, round laughter, as if he'd enjoyed their violent flight from the convent, as if she'd given him a fine time and put him in a good mood. "Truly, you will come to no harm. I am not here to slay you."

Devon's torch had fallen onto a large, flat slab of rock on the ground next to them. From its flickering light, she strained to see his expression, but his face lay in the shadows. "If you meant me no harm, why did you carry a sword when you came into my chamber?"

He shrugged. "In these times, need you ask? Every turn, every shut door can mean danger. My sword was not meant as a threat to you. On the contrary. I need you."

"Why?"

"As my prisoner."

Her breathing slowed. His flat, even tone had been curiously convincing. Nor was he making any move to harm her, even though he could easily do so. Catherine closed her eyes in relief, hardly able to believe that he was not going to kill her.

Devon rose suddenly, dragging her to her feet by the vise-like grip of his hand. "I'm taking you back to the convent now. Would you like my cloak? You must be cold."

She nearly laughed aloud at his being thoughtful of her. Instead she said crisply, "I want nothing of yours." After a few moments of walking, when her pulse slowed a little, she added, "I can't imagine what good I would be to anyone as a prisoner. My father has lost everything. As you should know, since you stole his lands. He cannot pay any ransom for my kidnapping."

"I'm not interested in a ransom."

She glanced up at his face, wondering what he meant to do with her. But she could read nothing in his expression.

She wished she knew more about him. Their wedding had taken place so long ago it felt like a dream to her now. They had been forced into the marriage because the king had grown angry at the unending feud between her father's clan and that of the Macgowans. So angry that he'd insisted that Catherine, the only daughter of the laird of the Craigs, marry Devon, the laird of the Macgowans. She and Devon had scarcely met one another before the ceremony. And afterwards, Catherine had returned home to live with her parents, still a virgin. As was customary for such a young bride, she was to be returned to her new husband when she was deemed old enough to be bedded.

That never happened. Although the marriage was supposed to mend matters between the two clans, about a year after the ceremony Catherine's father raided the Macgowan castle. The raid ended in disaster. Six people had been killed. Devon Macgowan's retaliation had been . . . no, she didn't want to think about it!

Instead she tried desperately to think of a way to escape him. Devon held her by the arm loosely. Perhaps . . .

In a sudden flash of movement, she used her leg to

13

try and trip him, at the same time jerking with all her might to free herself. She must have caught him unawares, for he dropped her hand. But he didn't stumble, as she had hoped. In a movement that was quick, quicker than she would have believed possible, his fingers closed over her shoulder.

"Very foolish," he said silkily.

She tried to struggle, hitting at him with her free hand. Devon grabbed her flaying arm and, in the process, accidently snagged the top of her gown. Catherine struggled, and they were both flung back to the ground. There was a sharp ripping sound. He had rent her gown down the front, baring her breasts to him.

"Oh!" She was so mortified she could only think to reach out and pull him down against her. They lay sprawled again on the wet grass, with Devon once more on top of her. This time she pressed close to him so that he couldn't see her naked chest.

His voice against her ear was rich with amusement. "What are you going to do now? If we get up, I'll see you. If I stay here wrapped in your arms, I may well get the very ideas you're so valiantly trying to keep from straying into my mind."

Catherine assumed he was joking. Then she recalled the hot look Devon had given her when they were in her bedchamber, and a new uneasiness gripped her. She stated in a rush, "Let me up. You're crushing me. Only please do it so that I can pull my gown across my chest."

His mouth was very close to hers. "I like you in this position."

He sounded as if he were teasing her, but she wasn't certain. Devon was close enough for her to feel his warm breath on her cheek. He was breathing evenly, to

14

her annoyance. Catherine could scarcely draw in air, with her chest still jumping from their run. "Don't you dare to so much as—"

"What? Touch you? But I'm already doing that. And do you always bluster and threaten when you've already lost?"

She prayed her teeth wouldn't start chattering again. "It isn't bluster. I will make you sorry if you do anything to me!"

"How?"

He would ask that question. In truth, there was nothing she could do. He was stronger by far than she was, he was in control of the situation, and she had no weapons. "Let go, please. This isn't decent."

"Not decent?" He laughed. "With my wife?"

An hour earlier, Catherine would never have imagined she'd smile at anything Devon Macgowan could say, but now she found herself smiling. Then she realized what she was doing and the smile faded from her face. Yet her gaze remained locked with his. Before heaven, she thought, his eyes are blue! The grin had vanished from his face, too, to be replaced by some other, stronger emotion, and in the sputtering golden light from the torch, they stared at one another. Catherine had the strangest feeling they were sharing some sort of moment apart from the ordinary, a timeless moment that bound them together in some mysterious way.

She watched his stern face lighten a little and the harsh lines on the edge of his mouth melt away. His gaze wandered over her face as if he were assessing her. And there was something else, too, some other emotion, something she couldn't name. An acknowledgement of attraction, perhaps.

15

An attraction that must not, could never be. All their past lives stood in the way of it, their families and their backgrounds. And yet it was there, and real.

She said quickly, "We're not really married."

"If you mean we have never consummated the marriage, I had just recalled that fact."

He gazed down at her, while Catherine tried to think of something, anything, to say to make him leave her alone. "My father claimed you were the most dangerous man he'd ever met."

"Did he?" Devon's elegant, educated voice was laced with mockery. "Very odd, considering that he was the one who was forever raiding my family's lands.

"He said you are as ambitious as the devil. That you'd gone to the university in Geneva and the court in Edinburgh and learned to be eloquent and cunning. That you could talk anyone into anything you wanted."

"At this moment, I wish that were true." Then he stated, in a more forceful tone, "I want to see what you look like. All over." It was the voice of a man accustomed to authority, a voice that brooked no opposition. Before she could utter a word, he rolled aside to stare at her.

She glanced down, stunned, at her bared chest. An Irish mist of curling fog and soft, dancing points of water spangled her with droplets that gleamed like jewels. The yellow torchlight clearly illuminated the glittering expanse of her chest. Her breasts were round and full, and, in the cold night air, the pink tips had tightened into small rosettes.

Quickly, frantically, she dragged the torn halves of her nightsmock together, covering herself. Devon couldn't have had more than a second or two to study her, but in that time his eyes had swept over her thoroughly. She'd felt almost as if his hands were on

16

her, stroking wherever his gaze fell. Before, she'd never been able to imagine how it would feel to have a man caress her. Now she could picture it all too well, could picture it because she knew that was what he had been imagining.

He desired her. She could sense it, feel it in the clasp of his hands on hers, in the sudden tenseness of his lean body. What would he do? Possess her here, on the soft, springy grass? The thought horrified her. She wouldn't let him!

Yet when Devon finally spoke, he only said mildly, "You're shaking. You don't need to. I've never ravished anyone, and have no intention of harming you."

"I wasn't shaking," she lied.

He pushed back a curl from her forehead, and said absently, "I remembered you as being a little girl. A very skittish little girl with large hazel eyes, who was pretending not to be scared during the wedding ceremony."

She remembered, too. At the age of twelve, Catherine had looked like a slender young boy, all skinny arms and legs that refused to stop moving. Her chest had been uncompromisingly flat, her hips without curves. Doubtless when Devon came for her, he'd carried that picture of her in his mind. Hadn't it occurred to him how much she might have changed?

But mayhap he'd thought of her only as his hostage, a faceless part in some plan of his. That knowledge brought her back to reality in a cold, uncomfortable rush.

"Girls do grow up," she pointed out dryly. Her body felt warmed by him, strangely glowing. She told herself she didn't like it. "Will you let go of my hand again? I want to tie the two ends of my smock together more tightly."

17

"And what if I say no?"

"Why wouldn't you? I thought you only wanted me for a prisoner."

The amusement was back in his voice. "That was before I had a chance to truly look at you."

"What are you going to do?"

"I'm considering kissing you. Tell me, have you been kissed often?"

"That is none of your business."

"Once again, you've forgotten we are married. Perhaps you need some schooling in what it means to be husband and wife. Do your lips taste as pleasant as they look?"

He leaned forward to kiss her, and his chest pressed against hers. Every pore of her skin seemed to tickle with life. Behind his shirt, she could sense the flat, broad chest. His lips came down slowly, moving ever nearer.

She jerked her head to the side. "Don't touch me! I'll fight, I swear it. By my troth, you will never have me." She started to squirm against his chest.

"Continue to writhe under me like that, Cat, and you will get me to make love to you, just as you apparently expect."

She sniffed, "What conceit. And so totally unjustified, too. I have seen handsomer snakes." It was a patent lie. There was no denying that he was attractive. Even without the severe perfection of his face, or those broad shoulders and narrow hips, the sheer presence of him, the masculinity of him, made him handsome.

Devon gave a little sigh and moved away from her. There was a moment of silence and then he drawled, "Come, wife."

Her brows drew together. "I don't want you to call me that."

18

He climbed up from the ground in a single easy, lissome movement. His hand still held hers by the wrist. "It's time to leave," he said. "Whoever you are."

By the time they reached the convent again, Catherine's teeth had once more started to chatter and her toes had gone numb, even though Devon had forcibly wrapped her in his fur-lined cape. There hadn't been anything he could do about her bare feet, however, since she could hardly walk in his large boots. He did offer to carry her but she refused to let him do so.

The first person Catherine saw as she walked up the path to the convent was Sister Brigit. The nun stood in front of the convent, a wool blanket wrapped about her thin shoulders.

Catherine walked toward her. For a moment, she recalled the day her father had brought her to the abbey. Catherine had been frightened that the nuns wouldn't take her in. Convents did offer refuge to widows and hospitality to visitors, but Catherine was a married woman, and a Protestant.

Luckily, she had had an Irish cousin, an earl, who could add his pleas to her father's. The family connection was not unusual. For centuries, many Scot lairds had held land in Ireland, or had married into Irish families. In the Highlands, Gaelic was spoken, just as it was in Ireland, and the cultures were similar. Only in the last few years, with Ireland beset by war with the English, and with the change in religion in Scotland, had the ancient ties between the two countries loosened.

Catherine sighed. She'd been at the convent for so many years it seemed strange to imagine she might never see it, or Sister Brigit, again. She hurried forward.

The fog wound about Sister Brigit in affectionate

19

spirals of grey vapour. As soon as Catherine was near enough, the nun asked anxiously, "The soldiers claimed your husband means to take you aboard his ship. Is this true?"

Devon answered for Catherine. "Yes. Would you help her with her packing? Put in anything she ever wants to see again."

"Why?" Catherine wondered. "Why are you taking me?"

Devon's face was a mask. She could read nothing in it. He said only, "I'll explain when it is necessary for you to understand. For the moment, the only thing you need to know is that you should be packing. We leave with the tide."

While Catherine stood rooted to the ground, a hundred questions hammering at her, Sister Brigit plucked at her arm gently. "Come, child, we have no choice. We must do as he commands." Before she left, the nun glanced in the direction of Devon. She said fiercely, "I shall pray that you treat Catherine with care. She is worth—" The nun fought to find words, but appeared too upset to do so. At last she ended lamely, "She is a fine person."

Devon's eyebrows rose. "I will not harm her."

But Sister Brigit looked at Devon as if she didn't believe him. Her hand quavered a little as she opened the door to the convent.

Chapter Two

"I WANT YOU TO STAY PUT."

Catherine raised her chin in a defiant line. She and Devon stood on the forward deck of the *Evening Star*. The vessel shuddered through wind-troubled, darkly rolling waves. Before them, on the eastern horizon, the sun was a red coal blazing against the midnight sky.

"You want me to stay put," she repeated. "Why? I can't escape from the ship now unless I sprout wings and fly."

Devon had half turned from her, as if to leave. His rich brown cloak, caught by the fresh sea wind, swirled restlessly about his legs. "I need to know where you are for one thing. And I don't care to have you wandering through the vessel."

Apparently having said his piece, he stepped away from her. Catherine put a hand on his arm to delay him. Devon glanced down at her as soon as her fingers came into contact with his forearm. She realized uneasily that the touch of her hand had created some sort of reaction in him. The knowledge added a certain wariness to her voice when she asked, "Why can't I wander through the ship? What trouble could I cause?"

"You're pretty," he pointed out. "And the only woman on board. I think that should answer your question."

She jerked her hand away. There was no reason to think he was remembering the moment in the meadow when he had looked down at her bared breasts. No good reason at all. She couldn't even see his face very clearly in the damp, colorless morning air. Yet every feminine instinct within her screamed to beware, told her that her touching him had been a mistake and that he was aroused.

Catherine watched him walk away from her, his shoulders broad and startlingly straight. He spoke for a while to a group of his men and then returned to her.

Devon said, "In spite of my careful warning, I realize you might forget and try to roam off. To make certain that doesn't happen I am leaving Mouse here to guard you."

She frowned. "I see no point in having a guard. Why can't I go below to one of the cabins?"

"Indeed you can, at least in a while. I sent two of my men to clean out a room for you. It should only take an hour or so before it's prepared." Just then, a redhaired sailor with a chart asked for Devon's attention, so Devon made a small bow to her and strolled off.

Left alone, Catherine stared owlishly at the man her husband had ordered to guard her. An ordinary human being like herself had difficulty standing on the pitching deck. But not the giant Devon had asked to watch over her.

Even though the *Evening Star* shuddered through

metal-grey waves, waves that hissed and seethed against the bulkhead, Mouse remained stock-still. Occasionally, a spray of sea water would furl across the deck. It left flecks of foam and glittering drops of water clinging to the planks and the man's legs, which were bare from his boots to the end of his kilt. The giant didn't seem to notice.

Whoever had named him Mouse must have had a rollicking sense of humor. Mouse appeared to be over seven feet tall. He had a ferocious black beard, a long plaid hanging around his tree-like legs, and the kind, mild eyes of a rabbit. He had not spoken a word to her.

Catherine wondered if she couldn't use him as a source of information. There were dozens of questions she needed answered. Tipping her head toward him in a friendly way, she asked, "Where are we going to land? Glasgow?"

"I canna say, lass."

He must have been warned not to tell her anything. Slyly, she tried a different tactic. "How long do you think the journey will take?"

"I canna say, lass."

"I don't suppose you'll tell me why the Macgowan wanted to take me captive."

"I canna s—"

She all but ground her teeth. "Don't you know anything except that one phrase? Never mind. Will you go tell the captain of this vessel that I want to speak to him?"

The giant rolled his soft rabbit eyes at her. "No."

Catherine gave up. Frustrated, she turned her head and watched a sailor in a black cap perform mysterious tasks with the swooping rigging. The sailor worked in the half-dark, yet he performed quickly, efficiently, with an ease born of long practice. Pleasant daydreams filled Catherine's mind, ones in which she performed as perfectly as the sailor, ones in which she escaped Devon by being brilliantly heroic.

Then she realized there was no use plotting escapes when she had no knowledge of where they were going, or why. If only she had some idea of what Devon wanted her for! Everything he had said about the matter only confused her more. If he had no intention of ransoming her, why had he taken her captive?

To be his wife? Before she could even consider the idea, a mental image of that flat, broad chest of his flew into her mind. It sent an odd jolting rush to her abdomen. Her reaction surprised her so much she nearly cried out. Half frightened, Catherine shook away the idea that Devon might want her as his wife. He couldn't have come for that reason. No man would want his enemy's daughter as wife.

Then could she be important to someone for a reason unknown to her? But the only people who would be concerned about her were her brother and father. Her brother was back in Ireland, and her father was an outlaw, impoverished, landless, and living under threat of death. What would anyone want from either of them? None of it made any sense.

Her hands tightened on the rail. Whatever his excuse for finding her, she had no doubt at all that Devon desired her. That had been obvious last night and then again this morning when she touched him. She had no skill with men. How could she, having spent all those years in a convent? So how would she deal with his interest in her?

It might be easier if she had some idea of what Devon was like. But all she knew about him was that her father had called him an ambitious and clever man, one who cared nothing about hurting people who stood in his way. According to her father, Devon was utterly evil, a man whose thoughts you could never guess because he knew how to disguise them behind a barrier of amusing conversation. But what of his inner self? Was he as wicked as her father had claimed?

Her only certainty was that Devon had been the cause of her having lost everything of value she could have ever had—the chance to live with her family, to stay in her native land, and have a real husband and children. Now he was taking her to some unknown fate. She was helpless and alone and she had no idea why Devon needed her, or what he meant to do with her.

Catherine stared sightlessly out in the direction of Ireland, which had been lost in the swirling mist that the sunrise had not been able to burn or blow away. The future seemed to be full of traps and mysterious blanks. She shivered as she raised her head into the wind, and let the salty wind sting her face.

It was midday before the sailor announced to Devon that Catherine's cabin was ready.

Devon supposed he should tell Mouse to take her below, and let it go at that. Yet he was filled with a desire to see her again, to talk to her, to learn more about her.

He found his wife standing where he had left her. Tendrils of mahogany hair escaped from under her cap and circled her face. She had turned to look up at the thick, brown ropes and the white canvas swaying near her. The hard northeastern wind made sounds like distant thunder when it hit the white canvas, first cracking the stiffened material, and then swooping it out, booming loudly. The masts creaked and the ropes tightened, and the night lantern shook giddily under the force of the driving air. Far above the sails, the *Evening Star* flew her colors, a bright flag flashing against a white crystal sky.

While Catherine studied the ship around her, Devon gazed at his wife. Everything about her intrigued him. The way she leaned forward tightened the moss green material against her chest. His gaze wandered there and lingered, and he found himself remembering the rounded breasts he had so briefly glimpsed. Her over-skirt of moss green was occasionally tossed up by the breeze, revealing an underdress of mint trimmed with small sewn yellow roses. It was not an expensive dress. It lacked seed pearls sewn on the bodice or extensive embroidery done in threads of gold and silver. Nevertheless, it flattered her.

He walked over to her and said, "You are a bonny sight this morning. I daresay you have been making poor Mouse fall in love with you."

She glanced over at Mouse, who had discreetly moved out of earshot. "The loyal mountain? I am afraid not. In truth, I could not get a single fact out of him."

"Have you been plying him with questions?"

"Of course. You," she pointed out, "haven't deluged me with information."

"I shall tell you whatever you wish to know. In time."

"Aye, as soon as it is too late for me to do anything about it," she said gloomily.

"Yes." He enjoyed her expression of hostility mixed with amusement. Catherine must be too innately honest to conceal her emotions, for he could read her thoughts easily by her face. It was curious to meet someone like her. He'd grown accustomed to the manners of men and women at court, of people who had to weigh their words with care, of people schooled in deception. "I came up to ask if you had been given breakfast."

She tossed her head, and the feather in her green velvet cap bobbed. "No one has offered me so much as a sip of barley water. I was beginning to think your plan was to starve me to death."

"I am never so crude. Follow me and I'll find you some food." Devon led her down the narrow stairs to his cabin. The stairway reeked of a yeasty combination of fish and men and wet ropes, but he had arranged for the cabin to be comfortable and almost clean. Fresh linens were on the bed, and the table had been scraped of all its dirt so that the meal he had ordered could be set out on it. The breakfast turned out to be plain fare: haggis, boiled cod, oatcakes, and, to drink, sack served English fashion with brown sugar. As soon as they entered, Devon moved to the lantern, struck a flint, and lit it.

Catherine remained in the middle of the floor. She eyed the table set for two as if she found some fault with it. He guessed shrewdly that she didn't like the idea of being alone with him. At last she said, "I hadn't realized you meant to eat with me."

"I, too, get hungry," he said, a little dryly.

"Mayhap you'd like to eat, then. But I don't feel like eating at the moment. I'd much rather go upstairs."

"I doubt that. You just don't want to be alone with me. And the reason has to do with what happened to us out on that meadow. I was aroused, and so were you. And that's what alarms you."

She said nervously, "Nothing about you frightens

me, Macgowan. And as for arousing me—the very idea is repulsive." She walked to the chair. "Very well, I'll eat your food. The haggis looks rancid. Doubtless the cook is a relative of yours." With a flourish, she drew up the stool and sat down.

Devon found it was an exquisite pleasure to sit down. It had been well over two days since he had last slept, and his body ached with fatigue. Not that he paid any attention to his exhaustion; all his life, he'd had to ignore his own needs, to push himself beyond the limits of his endurance.

There'd been no other choice. His father had died when Devon was sixteen, leaving Devon as laird to five hundred people. Five hundred people, all of them relying upon him for leadership and land, and even, in emergencies, food and clothing. Devon had shouldered the responsibility honorably, and had never misused it. He was now head of the most powerful clan in the Highlands, a friend to the king, and his influence ranged even to England.

But the duties had been so great that it sometimes seemed as if his heart and mind were always elsewhere, with goals he'd set, with plans that needed making. Just for a moment, tired and all too aware of his wife's vivid presence, that struck him as unsatisfying. As if, somehow, even with all the battles he'd fought in, his life had been too cerebral, too involved in the future and with nebulous accomplishments.

Devon's fingers slid down to the gold medallion he wore about his neck. His thumb traced over the engraved nettle on it, the symbol of Scotland. The medallion had been a gift from his father. It was a reminder of the one truly crucial goal Devon had set for himself. It was that goal which had forced him into the capture of Catherine.

The medallion suddenly felt cold and lifeless. His fingers fell away.

He wondered if he would feel any more satisfied if he'd been able to share his thoughts more with another person. He knew he was a quiet person, inward and intense. He didn't give his faith lightly or trust easily. Indeed, the more famous he had become, and the more well-known his actions, the fewer the people who shared his private thoughts.

Now it crossed his mind that most men talked to their wives about their feelings. He looked up at Catherine, noting that she had skin the color of fresh cream, the fairness of it complemented by the dark shadow of her hair. What would he and Catherine have been like had events not ended their marriage before it truly began? What would it be like to share trust and love with a woman? Devon felt close to only a small handful of people. Just a few, but those who were his friends, he cared for fiercely.

Into the silence that had fallen between them, Catherine said, "You came a long way to find me. It must have been very important to abduct me."

"Perhaps I wanted a wife."

She sniffed disbelievingly. "And how many wives could you have bought with the price you paid for this vessel alone, not even counting the wages for your men? Hundreds, or thousands?"

"Bought women are never the same. Besides, rumors of your beauty had driven me mad with desire." He stretched out his long legs comfortably. It had been a long time since he'd had a conversation with someone for no other purpose than enjoyment.

"According to your reputation, you've never been driven mad in your life," she pointed out. "I watched you with your soldiers this morning. Every word you spoke, every action you performed, seemed measured and thought out. You're a very careful man. Aye, and very likely, a lonely one."

He raised his brows, aware of a deep sense of surprise. "Lonely? Surrounded by five hundred of my clansmen night and day?"

"Yes." She leaned forward and said impetuously, "You remind me of a portrait I saw once. The man in the portrait had eyes that were wary, as if he needed to watch the draperies behind the painter lest an assassin catch him unawares. As if he knew the times were treacherous."

"And so they are." It occurred to him that she was trying to feel him out, to discover who he was. Well, they would naturally be curious about one another. They were bound together, after all. He found himself speculating, too, wondering what it would be like to have her in his arms again, and this time, to give way to his desire and kiss her, richly and deeply. He stirred in his chair, aware that, even through his fatigue, she excited him.

He asked abruptly, "We have been apart for a long time. During that time, have you fallen in love with some other man?"

She raised her eyebrows. "I am married."

"At least on paper. But surely, given the unusual circumstances and the fact that you never expected to see me again, didn't you—"

Catherine swept an invisible crumb from the table with a decisive movement of her hand, looking angered at his question. "It has been fourteen years since you have deigned to notice my existence."

Devon's gaze wandered from her face to the bed in the corner and then back again. His voice was laced with a dangerous undertone when he replied, "An oversight. But one that has been remedied."

Her hand had stopped. "Very amusing."

"You still haven't answered my question," he reminded her gently. "Have you ever been in love? Has any man—"

"What do you really want to know? If I am a virgin?"

"Among other things."

"I am not," she informed him grandly, tossing her head so that the dark tendrils of hair bounced about her neck. "I have been seduced by dozens of men. Knights, bakers, blacksmiths—oh, a wide and interesting variety."

"Don't joke about it." When she remained mulishly silent, refusing to take back her statement, he said in a silky tone, "If you've slept with as many men as that, another will mean nothing to you. I daresay you're as aware as I am of the attraction between us, and the bed in the corner looks comfortable." He nodded at the straw pallet. "Clean linens, too, since I ordered them. What do you say? We could find out for ourselves what we have been doing all these years apart." He stood up from his chair, the supple body menacing in its power and grace.

She held out a protesting hand, looking thoroughly alarmed at the quagmire that had opened at her feet. "Don't come another step!" she cried. "You know perfectly well I was lying. Of course there were no other men. Even if I had wanted them, I've been at a nunnery. As doubtless you would have deduced, had you thought the matter through."

Devon didn't answer her. He sat down again, feeling a little surprised at his own persistence. Yet he'd had a burning desire to know whether she had ever loved another man. There was no reason for his curiosity, any more than there was a good reason for the relief sweeping through him now that she had no lover.

In truth, it was madness to have sat down here with her. The less he had to do with Catherine, the better. He was only supposed to escort her to her destination. Then, once this business was finished, he'd never see her again. Knowing that, he should stay away from her, avoid becoming friends—or more than that—with his wife.

Yet he was drawn to her. He'd met other women who were more beautiful, but beauty alone he found uninteresting. There were qualities of the mind and soul that were more important.

Because he was a man who always asked himself for answers, Devon hunted for the reasons for his strong attraction to his wife. She was what the Highlanders called canny and fendy. That meant she was nimble-witted, as she had proved in almost escaping from him, and resourceful. She had the sort of courage he admired. She'd done the best she could last night, bluffed when she could, ran when she could, and then tried to hide the fact that she was terrified.

One thing he knew for certain. There existed a disturbing sexual pull between them, stronger than any he'd felt before. Catherine might be too innocent to understand the current that flowed between them, but he knew exactly what it was. He watched her glance up at him, her lips parted in question, and felt his reaction speeding through his veins. Aye, he thought, nearly smiling. The pull between them was very, very strong.

Catherine asked, "What did you bring me here to talk about?"

He drawled slowly, "What made you assume talking was the only thing I was interested in?"

She tried to turn the matter into a joke. "I know," she said with a sad shake of her head. "You planned to poison me instead. I realized that the minute I tasted the haggis."

He laughed, and pushed his pewter plate away. "It does smell about as pleasant as a stable."

Catherine watched Devon slide out of his chair. Doubtless he'd leave now that he had eaten. She was relieved, for she didn't care to be alone with him. His teasing remarks about her being his wife, and about the pallet in the corner, had alarmed her. Just how much of it did he mean? And how could she tell?

Devon made no attempt to leave. Instead, he pulled off his doublet. Underneath he wore a lace trimmed voile shirt, of so fine a material that it was sheer. He tossed the doublet onto his chair, and said, "It's warm in here. Would you like to remove your oversleeves?"

"No." The clear outline of his chest flustered her. She could even see, faintly, the dark triangle of hair that flared between his nipples. Catherine moved her gaze up to his eyes.

He leaned his back against the wainscotted wall next to the brazier. "Tell me everything that has happened to you since our marriage."

"Everything?" she wondered. "Including fleeing from Scotland because you attacked our castle?"

A shadow from the oak beam near his head slanted across Devon's face, hiding his expression. "Your father made the mistake of plotting against the king, and then, to cap his folly, he raided my castle when I was at peace with him. Before heaven, your father had every reason to know how furious the king was over the ceaseless fighting in the Highlands. Weren't the two of us forced into marriage because of it? And yet, your father stormed my castle. Six people were killed during that raid. The king wasn't willing to tolerate such behavior any longer. He ordered me to raze your castle and scatter your clan."

"The king may have ordered you to do it, but I'd wager you were willing enough to obey him. Our lands marched next to yours and your clan has coveted those lands for centuries. Mayhap greed, not duty, spurred you on."

His eyes, blue as the sky, fathomless, unreadable, stared down at her. "I told you. The king put your father to the fire and sword. He ordered your castle fired and then torn down. He banished your father. I agreed with the king's decision, but I had nothing to do with it. And the land means nothing to me."

She bit her lip. The way Devon explained it, he made his actions sound reasonable. Worse, he even made it sound as if her father had been in the wrong. A memory of that terrible night floated into her consciousness, a memory of being dragged from her bed. Soldiers ran through their castle, and fire sheeted the galleries and the stables. She and her father and brother and their closest followers fled for their lives. It had been the most terrifying event of her life.

She told Devon stiffly, "I love my father. I don't want to hear you blame him for the destruction of our castle. Perhaps it would be best not to discuss it."

"Very well." He waited for a moment, and then said, "Doubtless that is one subject we will never agree upon. I suppose I just wanted you to know I was not quite the monster your father told you about. But let's leave the topic." He smiled. "Shall we call a truce, at least for this morning?"

"I don't think we can have a truce. It would be best if you just left."

"Not yet. I want to hear what happened to you after

you left Scotland. I always wondered about you, and felt responsible for you. In fact, I sent off a letter to you about a year after you left Scotland. A few months later, I received a scathing epistle from your father, Sheamus. He threatened me with dismemberment or other unpleasant tortures should I ever try to contact you again. I was never able to reach you and, at any rate, I naturally assumed you would be less than pleased to hear from me."

"You were right." She hadn't heard about the letter before, but her father's reply sounded likely enough.

Catherine couldn't understand why Devon felt she was his responsibility, even if they were married. In the Highlands, one's clan was everything. Wives even retained their own last names. No one, for example, would ever call her Catherine Macgowan. She was born Catherine Craig, and that is what she would be until the day she died. As her father would say, the family was the most central thing in life, the core of one's loyalty, pride, and honor.

He said, "Would you tell me what happened afterwards?"

Thinking that perhaps after she had told Devon what he wanted to know he might leave, she said, "I'm afraid it's not a very exciting story. After my family left Scotland, we traveled to Ireland. My father's cousin is the Earl of Bachoch, and he'd agreed to take in my brother and train him as a knight."

"How did you end up at the convent? I know that your mother died just before we were married. Is it because you had no woman to stay with you that you had to go to the nunnery?"

The compassion in his voice, for some reason, made her throat feel tight. She brushed a hand over her face. "That . . . yes. In a way. I was older, and my father had to be off, to . . . to France. I would have been a burden traveling with him, and he couldn't leave me with my brother at the castle, not, as you pointed out, without a woman companion."

Had she said that naturally enough so that he would accept it? For, although her father did leave soon after he left her brother in Ireland, he went to Scotland, not France. That had been perilous, since the king had threatened her father with death if he returned to Scotland. Yet her father didn't have any other choice. Somehow, he had to regain his lands. That meant returning to Scotland and trying to win support for his cause.

Catherine pushed out her joint stool and stood up. She walked away from Devon to the other side of the small cabin, her green skirt swaying in tempo to the rocking of the ship. "That's the end of my story. Why were you so curious about me?"

"I suppose I just wanted to learn who you are. You are my wife. Tell me, is it much of a shock to look at me and think that I am your husband?"

She glanced up at him. He was smiling, and, for the first time, she saw that his blue eyes were disarmingly frank. He looked as bemused by the circumstances as she was. He was right that this was a strange situation. And it was very, very odd to think of this man as her husband.

He asked, "Could you tell me something, truthfully? If we had no past, if you were meeting me for the first time today, would I be a disappointment to you as a husband?"

Catherine clasped her hands together. Across the small cabin, Devon stood with his back against the wall. Even relaxing, as he was now, he disturbed her. His body was lean and hard, utterly male. He exuded

36

power, cleverness, and a barely repressed sensuality. He had wit and could no doubt be an enjoyable companion. In fact, if she had only just met him she might have found him fascinating. Yet she was hardly going to admit that to him. "I don't know what I would have thought."

"Do I repel you? Would you run in fright if I came closer?" He took a step in her direction.

Her heart missed a beat. "Don't come any closer!" When he stopped, she added, with a relieved sigh, "No, you don't repel me. Or at least you wouldn't if I didn't know what you have done to my family."

"If you had just been introduced to me as my future wife, I would have been most glad."

"I suppose you are going to tell me why," she said, half knowing what he would say, but wanting for no sensible reason she could think of to hear him say it.

"Because I find you attractive. Fendy and canny and charmingly honest and very lovely. Because you have lips that I would like to kiss and breasts that I would like to—"

"No more!" She put her hands to her cheeks as if that could cool the heat that had sprung there.

But he went on, his deep voice sending chills down her. "Because I would like to see that lovely body unclothed. Because I would like to make love to you." He paused, and added in a different voice, "Tell me, in all those years you spent at the convent, didn't you long for a husband to say such things to you?"

"I don't know."

"You must."

"I never thought of such things."

"You didn't want love, and children?"

"I—yes, of course I did! But I was already married."

He interjected, "Yes, to me."

She dropped her hands to her sides again, and her eyes came up to meet with his. Very well, he was her husband. For the first time, that information truly meant something to her. They had spoken vows together, and now he had certain rights over her, just as she held certain rights over him. If he wanted her, by all the dictates of society and religion, she was supposed to give in. Of course that would not happen. And yet simply knowing that they had every legal, moral right to make love to one another made her edgy. So did his remarks. Especially his remarks.

"If we had just met," Devon went on, "what would you have wanted from a husband? Wealth, companionship, someone who could take you to visit the court often?"

"Just love. I would have wanted someone who loved me, only me." She asked rashly, "And you?"

"Love isn't usually a prerequisite for marriage, not to people in our position. It's usually the last thing we could expect. But perhaps that is what I, too, would have wanted. Did you ever wonder about me when you were in the convent?"

The conversation had gone too far. She was certain of it. Everything about Devon alarmed her. "Never. Except to hope that someone had razed your castle, too!"

Devon said, "I'd have wondered about where you were constantly if anyone had bothered to send me a portrait of you, once you had grown. In truth, I might have been induced to come calling much, much earlier."

It was the perfect opportunity to pose the question she had ached to ask all morning. "And what are you going to do with me, now that you have me?"

There was a pause. She waited for him to show a

reaction, any reaction, but he remained perfectly still, the tall body arrow straight, his eyes hidden in the shadowed bars of yellow and grey that fell through the shuttered window. Only the gold buttons on his shirt were any indication of some hidden, deep emotion, for they flashed with movement at his breathing, which had suddenly become deeper.

At last he answered, in a tone slightly huskier than any he had used before, "What am I going to do with you? That's just what I've been wondering myself. I've never really had a wife before, just a name on a signed contract."

"You could let me go."

"Ah, but then I would never know what it was like to live with a wife."

"Buy another."

"But I would rather know what it was like to be married to you. I like you."

The small room appeared to have taken on a charged aura. It crackled with tension. Catherine felt the vibrations all around her, threatening at every moment to draw her inside them too, to swallow her whole. His eyes caressed her, held her, forced her to consider the thing that was going on between them. She saw him stir slightly, take one step in her direction. Blindly, she held out a hand, trying to make him halt.

He did not. He came towards her, a look on his face that was somehow beyond her understanding and yet absolutely alarming. A small, warm glow had started in her abdomen, and her blood seemed to be moving thickly through her veins. How had he managed to make her react while still so far away from her? Was he going to come closer to kiss her? What should she do?

With a jolt, she realized what she had just asked herself. He was Devon Macgowan! It would be a betrayal of her father to so much as like him. Catherine tried to shake the confusing feelings from her body, to force herself back to normal.

He stood only a foot away from her, dappled in whimsical, cavorting shadows from the brazier. She asked, "Why are you doing this? Is it part of some plan of yours?"

"I don't know what you mean. This has nothing to do with your being taken prisoner. And as to why I am doing it, why do you think? Because I want you. Hasn't anyone ever told you how lovely you are? And that your lips are red and beg to be kissed? Or that you are a likable young woman?"

She shook her head. The very walls of the cabin seemed to be closing in and smothering her. She wished she had never let their conversation become so intimate. Somehow, skillfully, he had drawn her out, made her reveal things about herself. She had no skill at controlling the pace and the force of their conversation. He was the manipulator; he, the one who had done the charming. The most frightening thing was that he had done it so effortlessly, as if he had to put no thought to it, just as when he had captured her last night, the wild dash from the convent seemed not to tax him at all.

She looked about for a way of escape, but there was none. On the other side of the cabin door stood Devon's guard, and the cabin itself was tiny. The sole furnishings it could boast of were the pallet in the corner and the table and two chairs.

There was nothing to do but to try to bluff her way out. Forcing conviction into her voice, she said, "I don't want you to touch me. Not ever."

He had not moved closer, nor were his hands reaching for her. Yet she felt the full force of his personality come to bear upon her, casting the strangest spell upon her. Very quietly, he said, "I'm not suggesting we make love. Only that we attempt one small experiment."

"I have no interest in such things."

"Not even one kiss?"

Of all the possible experiments in the world, kissing Devon sounded like the most perilous. "Not even once. What will you do, force me?"

"No, never with force." He drew in a breath. "But, listen, Cat. We are not going on a long journey. We'll land sometime soon, and when we do, events will change things between us. We may never have a chance like this again. And yet we're husband and wife. Surely you must know how much I'd like to hold you in my arms once. Is that so wrong, so threatening? One kiss for what might have been?"

"What might have been ended the night you attacked our castle."

He went on as if he hadn't heard her. "We're man and wife. Why shouldn't we kiss one another? I want you."

"That makes no difference."

"You said you wanted a husband. I imagine you have always wondered what it would be like to be held by a man. I am giving you that chance now. Why shouldn't you take it?"

Beneath her feet, the vessel blundered and pitched as endless onslaughts of waves beat against the ship. She clutched at the wall, thinking that what alarmed her most was that his words had sounded reasonable to her. Somehow, dimly, she was sure he had to be wrong; there had to be harm in kissing him. But, as he'd said, she was his wife. Not that they would ever live together as man and wife. Yet the tie was there, curiously powerful.

And she did ache to know what a kiss would be like.

41

All those long years in the convent she'd wondered how it would feel to be held by a man. Devon was giving her the opportunity to find out. Perhaps after Devon had finished whatever business he had with her, she would go back to the convent again. This might be her last chance to know how it would feel. A yearning surged through her. Yes, just once, just this one time, she wanted to have a man's arms around her.

"I'm coming closer," he said. "If you're going to object, do it now."

Catherine stood silently. With one stride, he was next to her, and his hands came down upon the points of her shoulders. She raised her head to be kissed.

Chapter Three

SHE'D BEEN KISSED MANY TIMES. IT WAS THE CUSTOM TO greet both friends and relatives with a kiss. Yet, even before Devon touched her, she knew that none had ever been like this.

He stood only inches away from her. His fingers, which had clasped her by the shoulders, slid upwards, along her throat and onto her face. Delicately, he traced the line of her cheekbones and the curves of her brows. At last his fingers came to rest on her lips. He seemed motivated by curiosity, as if, like a blind man, he wanted to learn about her by the tips of his fingers.

"Do you know how gentle your lips are?" he murmured. He traced the outline of her mouth slowly, tickling her.

She didn't know what to say but Devon didn't appear to expect a reply. His hands soothed, carefully stroked away her doubts and fears. She could feel the intensity

43

of his interest, feel his slow gaze cherish her. All her mistrust of him was forgotten. For the moment, the only thing that existed was Devon. She wanted him to kiss her. What was there to fear, when she could always pull back? He made no effort to force himself on her.

His voice was low and husky. "Sweeting, I want to see you again with your hair down. Do you mind?"

His fingers worked their way under her cap and tugged it off. It dropped silently to the ground. Next he pulled out the pins, and waves of mahogany hair spilled over his hands, flowing like dark wine. Catherine stood with her arms resting at her sides, unresisting but not yet participating.

Devon gave a low moan, and thrust his hands within the mahogany tumble of curls. At last he tipped her head, raising it to his. Then he gently brought his lips down upon hers. Dozens of new sensations clamored within Catherine. She thought, how strange! A man's lips were soft. She had half expected Devon's lips to be hard, like the man himself.

This close, everything about him seemed strange. Brown-gold strands of his hair brushed against the side of her cheek, tickling her with its silky texture, while the sides of his jaw scratched her. The solid warmth of his body pressed against hers was much more real than any kiss she had ever imagined. She leaned against him, savoring each distinct new experience.

Beneath the voile shirt, his chest felt flat and strong, very masculine. She found the difference between them intriguing. Everything about him intrigued her—the heat of his body, the rough callouses on his palms, and the soft persuasion of his lips.

She realized that at some point she had let her eyelids drift shut. Dreamily, she raised her hand and wound it around his shoulders, delighting in the hardness of his back.

At that small response from her, Devon tensed, and the nature of the kiss changed and told her how much he had been holding back. Suddenly his lips grew demanding, clinging to hers with a passion that nearly shocked her. His hands moved down from her shoulders and began to roam over her arms and back.

The urgency of his mouth sent thrills coursing through her body. He aroused long dormant responses, scarcely dreamt of before. Everything, every part of her, seemed focused on him. Her nerves tingled and her breath began to come in strident onslaughts. Devon's large hands held her firmly against him, and then drew her even closer, flattening her breasts against his chest, imprinting his legs and hips upon her own.

She felt the tip of his tongue probing at her mouth. It was insistent, urging something from her she didn't understand. Catherine had no idea what he wanted, but then his tongue slipped inside her mouth, and she gave a little shudder. A stinging shock burst somewhere in her abdomen. Devon! she wanted to cry, at the warm, liquid taste of him plunging within her. His tongue set up a gentle movement that was so erotic she could scarcely bear it. The pressure of his lips increased, exhilerating her as the kiss grew deeper and stronger.

His hands roamed over her with increasing familiarity. He stroked the soft bend of her throat and the curve that led to her arm. His fingers slid over her face and then down, ever lower, until he had reached the moss-green material at her bodice.

She felt on fire, lost in a fever that destroyed all sense of time and place. All her senses seemed to have a brighter, sharper edge. She was aware of the smoky scent from the brazier, the tang of the ocean in the air, and the rocking of the ship beneath her. The swaying added to her intoxication.

She uttered no protest when his fingers busied themselves with the fastenings at her throat. Her collar came undone and fell away, and his hands grazed lightly over the smooth, creamy skin of her neck. Then she felt him caress her breast, stroking it through the heavy fabric of her gown, learning the shape of it. A sob escaped her at the keen, undeniable pleasure of his touch. One of his fingers found the raised point of her nipple and he teased at it, rubbing and massaging until the bud distended, and a throbbing pleasure radiated out from it.

He was murmuring words, strange and erotic, about his desire for her. "Catherine, sweet," he whispered, his words slurred, "I want to undo your laces. Let me. I want you, want to take off your gown and fondle you, explore you."

She had never known, never envisioned such wanton sensations. His mouth had left hers, and he bent his head to kiss the nape of her neck, and then lower, letting warm, voluptuous kisses rain on her face and throat and then to the fabric over her breasts. His hips were pressed to hers, and she could feel, even through the layers of clothing, the strength of his passion.

Catherine froze. The hard line of his manhood pushed against her hips shocked and frightened her. It was too real, too soon, too new. Her fingers and body went stiff from alarm, while Catherine tried to force away the red confusion in her mind, to force herself to think things through. She had never meant it to go this far, never! The only thing she had wanted was a small, chaste kiss. How had he managed to bring her to this state? She couldn't understand how she could have allowed him to hold her so close. And what did he expect of her now? Did he intend to end up with her in the straw pallet in the corner, making love?

The thought brought her to her senses like a slap. Never would she make love with him! What, before heaven, had she almost done? Catherine jerked out of his arms and stumbled back against the wall.

Devon was left standing alone. "Why?" he rasped, reaching for her again.

Catherine cried. "Please! Don't come nearer. I had no idea it would be like that. I'd never have let it happen if I'd known. And I don't want you to touch me again."

His voice was heavy with desire. "Why don't you want me to touch you?"

Her chest rose and fell in rapid gasps. "Because you're who you are. Because of everything that you have done to me and to my family. Because you're my enemy."

His arms had been extended. Slowly, Devon forced them to drop to his side even though a hot yearning continued to hammer within him. The keenness of his passion surprised him. He had never desired a woman so completely that it shattered his usual iron control. He'd never even guessed that a man could want a woman so. Even now, the need for her was so strong his entire body seemed to throb with it.

Yet he made no move toward her. Drawing on years of rigid self-control, he forced his hands to relax and to stay still. The cold air, bitter with the aroma of the coal fire, recalled him to the present and to their situation.

He reminded himself that whatever Catherine's reasons for stopping when she did, it was for the best. They had gone too fast; he had known that since the minute they walked into the cabin together. Had known it and yet insisted on sitting down to breakfast with her and then kissing her. Yet he needed to consider all the consequences before they went any further.

His glance swept over her, taking in the fact that her mouth looked swollen and well kissed, that her cheeks were flushed and pink, and her skin lustrous. Then his eyes fell to her white throat, where, the collar missing, her could see her pulse, beating in heated strokes. So, he had not been mistaken. She, too, had been aroused, perhaps as aroused as he had been.

Catherine knelt to pick up the pins for her hair. When she found them, she yanked her dark hair back from her face as if by fixing the damage there she could undo the past few minutes.

"It won't work," he pointed out.

"What?"

"Pretending it never happened."

Her fingers stopped in the act of picking up a pin for her hair. "I am most certainly going to try to forget. I have no idea why I ever let you kiss me. But one thing I do know. It was a mistake."

"It was a mistake not to have tried harder to locate you," he said silkily. "I can see that now. You are what? Twenty-six years old and still a virgin?"

She scooped up the pin with an angry jerk. "I daresay other women have lived happily enough as virgins until the age of eighty. Before heaven, if no one ever kissed me again I'd still manage to laugh and talk and enjoy my life to the utmost. I wouldn't even notice the loss of a kiss or two."

He had raised his eyebrows in disbelief. "How can you sound so positive, after only one experience? And don't bother to deny that mine was the only true kiss you've ever received. I could tell that no one has ever thoroughly kissed you before."

She clipped a lock of hair back, not looking up at him. "Why do you think so?"

"Certain clues convinced me."

Catherine found her collar lying on the roughened planks under the joint stool. She dusted it off with a tidy gesture and then wrapped it about her throat and tied the laces. "I don't know what you mean."

"I mean, no man had ever tasted you before. When my tongue entered your mouth, you were surprised."

Her lashes dropped to her cheeks; she refused to raise them and meet his gaze. Never, ever had she been so humiliated. First there was the humiliation of actually encouraging him to kiss her. Devon Macgowan! She had agreed, allowed, and then enjoyed kissing him. What had been wrong with her? The fact that it had even happened was enough to make her squirm with embarrassment for months to come. But now, to crown her misery, Devon was apparently going to discuss the embrace, step by step, in lurid detail.

She said through gritted teeth. "I believe I've given you a false impression. That embrace, I mean. I was not behaving properly—in a manner of which I approve." It sounded fair enough, but Catherine realized with a rising sense of panic that Devon was waiting for her to elucidate, and that she had nowhere to go from there. She scrambled for an explanation. Maddeningly, none came to her. Flailing about helplessly, she babbled, "That kiss had nothing to do with me, the real me. I've been taken prisoner by you, and it's shaken me. Besides, I have had no sleep." Her explanations sounded weak even to herself.

"And the stars were in the wrong positions and your

49

left shoe had a stain on it." He grinned. "In troth, you kissed me because you wanted to, and what is more, you enjoyed yourself."

She sighed. He acted as if he could read her mind. What was worse, he could. No wonder her father had been nearly driven to distraction by Devon. It was a source of deep amazement to her that her father had only raided Devon's castle on two occasions. "I don't know what you mean."

"The devil you don't."

She turned her back on him and walked over to the window. Outside, an ocean of frosted grey strode and surged against the vessel, breaking and foaming across the side. The agitation of the sea outside echoed her own inner turmoil. Her legs were heavy from lack of sleep, her body ached from her run through the meadow last night, and she felt half furious with Devon, and half intrigued by him. She wished she knew more about him. She said, "You speak a great deal about experience. It makes me wonder about the extent of your own experiences."

"Curious about my love life? I wonder why."

Catherine traced a finger over a plank in the wall. She did want to know about his relationships with other women. Surely he hadn't lived in chastity all these years apart from her. He had none of the somber look of a Puritan, and the merest glance at him would have been enough to convince anyone he was a man of driving passions.

So there must have been other females in his life. Mayhap, for all she knew, he was in love with some other woman, some heartbreakingly lovely mistress who presided over his castle and whom he adored. Or he could be one of those men who hungered for variety and frequented brothels. Either possibility made her feel almost queasy with jealousy, a jealousy she was amazed to discover in herself. Certainly she would never admit it to him.

Cautiously, she explained, "I was only casually interested. Of course, you do not have to tell me anything."

He stood absolutely still, with that awful smile still on his face.

She sputtered, "Well? Have you taken a vow of silence?"

He burst out laughing. With a fluid movement, Devon grabbed her hands and pulled her against him. The edge of the wide, moss green skirt fluttered about his leather boots. "No, I have not taken a vow of silence. Nor did I mean to withhold information from you. I merely wanted to find out just how interested you were."

She pushed at his hands. "I don't care what you've done, or mean to do."

"Catherine, how untruthful of you." His fingers held her still, while he stared down at her. "You should never attempt to lie. I've never met anyone before with such an easily read face."

She scowled. What did she care about her face? Catherine fastened a baleful look upon Devon's nose, thereby avoiding his eyes. Why wasn't he telling her about the subject she really wanted to hear about, his relationships with women? "I suppose you buy favors from hundreds of bawds every year."

"No, I'm nothing like that. Look up at me, Catherine." His fingers captured her chin and raised it so that she stared into his eyes. "For the last eight years there's been only one woman in my life."

"Oh." She made her features as composed as she could.

"Her name was Janet, and she was a widow. She was

51

small and pretty and she loved to laugh. We were good friends."

Catherine struggled to understand. The first thing she'd noticed was that Devon spoke as if his relationship with Janet was in the past. Beyond that, she latched onto the fact that he had claimed to like her, and that he called Janet a friend. Hardly terms of love. "You said you stayed with her for eight years?"

"Yes, until her son was old enough for the university. She was tired of the cold winters in the Highlands, and when her son went to Edinburgh, she followed him. She'd always longed for the excitement of the city. Just a month ago, she married again, this time to a wealthy English townsman."

"I'm sorry."

"Because I was bested by a Sassenach, of all the unlikely occurrences?" He shook his head. "Don't be. Janet and I parted the way we began, the best of friends. She was older than I was, and as the years passed, she wanted to marry and become respectable again. The comforts of town life attracted her, as well as the proximity to her son. Ours was a cheerful, pleasant arrangement, nothing more. It suited both of us, but it never involved our hearts. She could never have been a rival of yours, if that worries you."

Catherine tossed her head, shaking off his restraining hand. "I should not have been worried if you carried with you armies of painted women, all trained to perform indecencies whenever you so much as waved a hand. What is it to me?"

He stood quietly for a moment, and, far off, Catherine could hear the distant flat cries of sea gulls and the whirr of the wind against the boat's sails. At last he said, "It's not true. I've never been your enemy. Not now, or even before."

He sounded so sincere she might almost have believed he meant the words. Catherine struggled to remember that she had to hate him, that he had ruined her father and razed their castle. But it was hard to remember anything when she was so tired and when he was so close. "Will you please leave me? I wish to lie down," she announced.

"With me?"

He was deliberately teasing her. "Alone," she said with rigid composure.

Devon picked up a piece of the oatcake and took a bite from it. "Very well." He turned to go.

She blinked in confusion, for she hadn't expected Devon to accept the idea so quickly. "Then you'll go?"

"For now." Devon strode to the door. When he paused at the door, Catherine waited, with her heart thumping oddly. He turned to her. The white lace at his throat was askew, and Catherine recalled that she had stroked him there when they embraced. Above the froth of lace, his face seemed perfectly composed except for his blue eyes. Those stared at her with an intensity that made her throat go dry.

"For now," he reiterated, and left.

She raced to the door and bolted it with a satisfying slam of the latch. As soon as that was done, she took an angry turn about the room, kicking up her skirt with short, furious steps. At last, when her legs nearly buckled under her, Catherine realized that she was so tired even walking was beyond her.

She sank to the pallet. Her eyes closed, and, drowsily, she fell to recalling the first time she had met Devon.

She hadn't liked him. Not one whit. To her twelve-year-old eyes, Devon had seemed unbelievably tall and very old. A threatening, stern adult, whom she knew her father feared. She'd stood in the stiffened enclosure of her brand new gown with a smile that seemed frozen at both edges, terrified she was going to disgrace her family by crying.

But Devon had taken her hand in a kind, understanding way, and said he hoped he could make her happy. He seemed so nice she'd almost been tempted to plead with him to free her from their wedding. But begging anything from Devon would have embarrassed her father, so, of course, she had remained silent.

Her father. Catherine sighed, recalling how he'd come stamping into the great hall, his clansmen and henchmen clustered around him, his head thrown back in laughter at some jest. Her father had always been laughing. This time his face had seemed merry, until you were close enough to see just how angry his eyes looked. He was angry because he'd been forced to come to Devon Macgowan and give his only daughter in marriage to his enemy. She sighed at the memory of her father, who never spoke when he could shout, who always wore his heart on his face, who took ridiculously dangerous chances as a matter of course.

He had resented the fact that Devon, his junior by many years, was rising in the world, enriching his estates by becoming a favorite at court. Devon was one of the new men, educated, clever, and wealthy, and he heralded a new age for Scotland, a smoother, more elegant age. While her father was of the past.

Catherine's eyes squeezed shut, remembering the way her father had paced back and forth in their chamber once they were alone, vowing at the top of his voice that he'd pay Devon Macgowan back in coin for this marriage. She'd never seen her father so furious, and her father had been as quick to rage as he'd been to roar with enjoyment. Her father looked, and was, as straight and predictable as a sword thrust. No shadings for him, no hidden meanings or subtle searching for the truth. Nothing, as she saw now with her adult viewpoint, like Devon.

Bitter memories. For her father had raided the Macgowans, as soon as he'd thought it safe. And as the result of that raid, the king had stripped them of their lands and sent Devon against them.

Catherine shifted uncomfortably. She didn't want to remember any more of it. The last thought before sleep overcame her was that she wished she had some idea of where Devon was taking her.

The *Evening Star* found a fair wind near the Hebrides, and the captain took advantage of it, letting out the sails and allowing the sleek vessel to ride the high waves swiftly. It was December, so the ocean was clear and cold, with a brisk breeze to fill the canvas and ruffle the blue bed of the Atlantic.

The ship was headed for Aberdeen. That added days to their journey, since many ports in Scotland were closer to Ireland than Aberdeen. It also meant they'd be traveling through dangerous waters, for the area was infested with pirates. But Aberdeen was the most convenient city to Caldwell Castle, Devon's home, and it was also a city full of clan members who could be called upon in an emergency. Devon had therefore deemed it better and safer to travel to that city than make landfall in a place like Glasgow, from which they would have to travel across some of the wildest parts of the Highlands.

Having explained these facts to the captain, Devon spent the remainder of the journey alone, avoiding the others. He wore such a stony expression that his troops looked at him curiously. It was unusual for Devon to be so withdrawn, but no one dared say anything aloud.

They had nearly reached Aberdeen before Mouse decided to question Devon about his behavior. Mouse woke up to darkness, and then realized, uneasily, that Devon hadn't come to bed the night before. Devon's pallet was flat and unused. One of the men asked Mouse where Devon was, and jested that perhaps the Macgowan was sleeping in his wife's bed. Mouse shrugged without comment, and then went above deck to hunt for Devon.

He found the sailors already busy with cables and lanterns. They were preparing for the end of the journey, for the captain predicted that they would reach Aberdeen by morning. Already, the sky stood red at sunrise, with rivers of gold and yellow cutting into the blackness of the night.

Amidst the confusion on the deck, Devon stood quietly by the railing, his hands folded and still, his brown hair whipped back by the wind. Mouse walked over to him and said, "I dinna think I have ever seen you like this."

Devon pushed his hands from the railing. His face felt stiff with salt and cold, and he realized that the spray that showered the deck had drenched his doublet as well. How long had he been standing here, looking out at the ocean? He couldn't remember.

He glanced at Mouse, his cousin, who had been fostered with Devon's parents years ago. The two were close in age, and had grown up more as brothers than cousins. There was no one else in the world Devon trusted so much.

Yet there was little family resemblance between them. Even as boys, they'd always been different in temperament and looks. Devon pursued excellence in everything, even the least important game. He led the other children to victory with what had been, even then, a driving intelligence.

Mouse had been too reticent to excel at anything. Always shy and quiet, he had preferred to stand on the fringes of life, watching. In fact, it was his shyness that had earned him his nickname Mouse. It suited him until, sometime in his thirteenth year, he suddenly shot up in height. Yet, even when he had towered over other men, Mouse remained silently in the background until he met Alice, his wife. She'd been a merry young woman whom he had loved dearly. But Alice had died in childbirth only one year after their marriage. And since her death, Mouse had been more withdrawn than ever.

Mouse held out Devon's cloak. He said, with the affection born of their long relationship, "Man, ye look so grim no one else would dare to come close to ye. They had to flay me into it by vowing to push me overboard otherwise, and ye know how I am about cold water." When Devon didn't immediately reply, Mouse added proddingly, "Is it the lass? I know ye havenna seen her since that first day, but ye've seemed bothered ever since the two of ye spoke privately in her cabin."

Devon said shortly, "It is the lass, as you say." He added, with a slightly different emphasis, "My wife."

"How has she upset ye?"

Devon answered that question with another. "Would you forgive me if I mentioned Alice?" They had rarely spoken of Mouse's wife since her death. Devon knew how much she had meant to his cousin, and he had never wanted to hurt his friend by reminding him of the past. But when Mouse made no protest, Devon went on. "When you met her, did you feel—" He hunted for the words.

"What?" Grey shadows slanted across the deck and over Mouse's face, making it look more solemn than ever.

"Something I can't explain. An immediate shock. Passion, mayhap."

There was a pause, while the sea stammered around them, its troubled, restless waves moving in unceasing onslaughts against the bow. At length Mouse said, "I desired her from the first moment I saw her."

Devon waited. He knew Mouse well enough to understand that the slight hesitation at the end of his statement meant that he had additional information. "Well? You have something else to say?"

Mouse fixed his stare out at the fan of silvered stars which still held over the edge of the western horizon. "Perhaps ye should recall that it has been a long time since ye have last been with a woman."

Whatever Devon had been expecting, that was not it. He moved his hand restlessly over the railing. It had been a long time, and he was not a continent man. Mouse, as usual, was right. "Wisdom from the high mountain top. Yes, a very long time."

"In Aberdeen, before we left, the other men sought out the brothels but ye—"

Devon cut him short. "I've never had any desire to get the pox." He didn't add that he had always felt a vague distaste for buying favors from a woman, if for no other reason than that it was so joyless. He wanted more from sex than a business transaction. Even the friendly relationship he'd had with Janet had been curiously unsatisfying. "You're in no position to lecture me. I noticed you stayed away as well."

Mouse's reply was as stark as a tree in winter. "I am still in love with Alice."

Devon said nothing. It had been over six years since Alice's death in childbirth. Six years. Before heaven, could any love be so strong?

Mouse wondered, "Is your wife much like her father?"

"Sheamus? No. And yet she has some of her father's qualities." Devon conjured up the memory of Sheamus Craig, an impatient, hot-tempered fool who, in Devon's view, had begged for his own destruction. Yet Sheamus had, for all his faults, a gift for living. He could laugh uproariously even when one of his new, bright schemes had gone awry. And with Sheamus, there was always some scheme or other. He was crafty, passionate, and completely unreliable, yet he had such zest no one could dislike him. His very likability explained why Sheamus could always raise men to serve him.

Catherine had that same quality of likability. Even the first time Devon had met Catherine, when she was but a little girl, he'd recognized that.

He'd been furious at the marriage. Of course he knew he could never marry for love, not in his position. But he'd recoiled at the idea of being tied to a twelve-year-old, and the daughter of Sheamus Craig at that. He had been so angry he'd meant to treat Catherine coldly. But she'd looked so frightened his instinct had been to protect her, shield her from danger.

Mouse's voice cut into his thoughts, "Even if ye want her, what can be done about it?"

"She is my wife. If we like one another, why shouldn't we live together?"

"Man, think of the complications."

"Before heaven," Devon said wearily, "that is exactly what I have been doing for the last few days. I know I'm bound by a promise to the king to bring her back to Scotland."

Mouse pointed out quietly, "Ye have promised the king ye will deliver the lass to him. Once she's in his hands it's unlikely ye'll ever see her again. Have ye thought of that?"

"Yes." The word was harshly grated out.

"Then best to forget her."

Abruptly, Devon stated, "Will you leave me alone for a little while longer? Tell the others I'll be with them in a moment."

Mouse nodded. "I brought ye this," he explained, handing Devon his cloak. "I'll be below deck if ye need me."

Devon stripped off his wet doublet and shirt, shivering at the salty bite of the wind against his bare chest. The fur-lined cloak slipped over his shoulders like a comfort. Yet when he looked back to the wavering blue carpet of the ocean, his face was uneasy.

He had been trying for days, yet he couldn't seem to rid himself of his desire for Catherine. Mayhap Mouse had been right; he simply had gone without a woman so long he'd overreacted to Catherine's presence.

A soothing explanation, but he didn't believe it. All his instincts and past experience argued against it. Why had he wanted her so much? No other woman had ever disturbed him so profoundly. Mere attractiveness was not the answer. No, it was the woman herself, the qualities she had, that drew him to her.

He gripped the rail, his hands caressing the polished oak with an almost sensual gesture. Devon's body was finely muscled and lean, a well-honed instrument with a powerful sexuality. Yet he'd always been able to control his reactions before.

Not this time. When they kissed, he'd wanted Catherine to offer herself to him, to pull him down on that straw pallet and let him fuse their bodies together. He wanted it without questions about who they were or what the future could be. He wanted to feel her beneath him, eager and warm and desiring him, as well. He yearned to run his hands over the tips of her breasts, explore her, glide his hands down her abdomen, make her tremble in passion. Even now, days after their encounter, he could still feel the taste of her lips on his.

He couldn't rid himself of the insistent voice that kept saying Catherine was his wife and that they had every right to make love. Should have been doing so for years. By now he should know every curve of her body. Only the careless idiocy of her father had swept them apart.

Yet they'd been parted, and now, even if it were feasible for him to mend the arrangements he'd made with the king, he doubted Catherine would want him. She had every reason to mistrust him. And how could he explain the necessity of everything he had done? For her to understand that, she'd have to admit her father had been in the wrong. And she loved her father.

A dark cloud slid across the yellow horizon, and suddenly the deck was black. The wind drove a great wave against the prow of the *Evening Star,* washing the deck with midnight-blue, swirling water. Devon abruptly dropped his hands from the rail, meaning to go below deck. Then he spotted, before even the watch did, the city of Aberdeen. Against the half dusk of sunrise, the city lights sparkled like a piece of jewelry impacted with a hundred blazing gems.

Devon tied the cloak securely about his shoulders. He'd avoided seeing Catherine ever since their kiss. It had seemed best not to speak to her again until he knew if he meant to do anything more with her than take her to her destination. Now he would have to deal with her, even though he had still to come to a decision.

Chapter Four

"YE ARE TO COME WITH ME."

Catherine listened calmly to Mouse's announcement. She was already prepared to leave, for as soon as she had realized the *Evening Star* had docked, she had hurriedly put on her best gown and combed her hair in preparation. She had not been surprised when Mouse, dressed all in black like one of John Knox's reformers, knocked on her cabin door, and announced that they had landed.

"And my things?" she wondered, gesturing toward the leather box which held her clothing.

"They will be tended to, lass."

When Mouse held open the door for her, she swept past eagerly. She'd been cramped inside that awful cabin for days. It felt wonderful to run up the narrow, wooden stairway.

The sunlight fairly dazzled her when she rose out of

the dark stairs onto the deck. The day was bright and yellow and clear, without a single cloud to smudge the perfect azure sky. Even the sea lay flat as sculptured lapis lazuli.

Her head lifted, and she looked out at Aberdeen. Aberdeen! She hadn't been in the city since she was a child, and she couldn't help a pang of anticipation at traveling through it. She was unused to cities, so the town seemed huge, full of cheerful confusion and clamor and surprise. It rose in untidy lines of grey buildings up and down two low hills. Hundreds of people threaded their way through the narrow streets. The din of merchants calling out their wares and horses clattering on cobbled streets and children crying shrilly reached her even on the ship.

Then she felt the hairs rise on the back of her neck. The spot tickled with that odd sensation that told her someone was staring at her. She whirled about. Devon stood six feet away from her, his gaze unfathomable.

Catherine summoned up her courage, and made her hands rest composedly in the folds of her skirt. She'd wondered about this meeting ever since Devon left her cabin. Wondered, and feared it. She had no idea what he would say, or how she should react. What was he thinking and feeling? What would be the best way to convince him that that kiss had been an accident, something that had happened once and would never happen again? She clasped her hands together and waited to find out what his mood was.

He said, "You look lovely, my wife."

Devon, she noted, had dressed for display. His breeches, of fine batiste, fitted snugly over his narrow hips. The elegant Russian leather boots he wore were slashed and trimmed. A jewel-encrusted dirk hung from his belt, and in his velvet cap, instead of the long white plume of a courtier, he wore three eagle feathers, symbol that he was laird to a large clan.

She told him tartly, "Please do not refer to me as your wife."

"If you are not my wife, why do you wear my wedding ring?" he pointed out reasonably, nodding in the direction of her hand.

"Because I can no longer get it off."

Devon smiled at her response, that warm, slow smile of his that seemed to heat her. Catherine lowered her gaze, realizing with a vague stirring of her pulses that he still desired her. After their kiss, Devon had avoided her for the remainder of the journey. She'd hoped that the fact that he didn't come to see her meant he no longer wanted her, that, after consideration, he'd decided it would be best if they didn't have anything to do with one another. Apparently she'd been wrong. There was no denying the way he leaned toward her, the hard, lissome body alert to her in some unaccountable way, or the way his eyes touched over her figure.

Catherine changed the subject. "Surely now we've landed you can explain where we are going and why you had to take me prisoner."

His lids dropped, hiding his expression. "We'll be in Aberdeen for a few days. That's all you need to know." Devon knew he couldn't explain things to her now. She'd likely see some of her clan members in the city, and if she knew why the king needed her, she might be able to pass the information on to a friend. No, it would be best to keep it secret.

He walked toward her and proferred his hand. "Come. I'll take you to your room." When she only eyed his outstretched hand dubiously, he added, "I won't bite, and I swear I won't even try to kiss you again. At least not in front of everyone. Shall we declare a truce, at least for the moment?"

He looked so friendly she had to smile, also. "I'll agree to the truce and the lack of kissing. But I'd prefer to walk without your arm. Or why can't we ride?"

"On a horse, you might just escape."

Silently, since there seemed to be little other choice, she took his arm and allowed him to lead her out of the ship. Around them, the harbor was a forest of masts and trailing ropes, and below, on the wharf, stood a crowded fish market. Fishermen haggled over their goods, careful wives inspected the array, and burghers strolled through the throng. Next to the *Evening Star* was a merchant vessel which had just arrived that morning from France. Sailors moved up and down her gangplank carrying loads of wines, walnuts, and fine cloth.

Catherine's gaze, however, was not on the sailors but on the fascinating spectacle of the two women who stood at the base of the gangplank of the French ship. How brazen their clothes were! Only members of the gentry were allowed to wear silk. Yet these two, clearly not gentry, sported gaudy silk dresses which were cut so low over their powdered bosoms as to be scandalous. They called out in caressing voices to the sailors.

Catherine, who had been secluded from such sights both as a child and then in the convent, stared wide-eyed at the women. One of them called out to the sailors about the things she would be willing to do for adequate compensation, and Catherine strained to hear what those things might be. Half of the words she couldn't understand. To her disappointment, before any of the sailors could reply, Devon had pulled her away and led her down a street cobbled in flint stones.

There, houses with slate roofs marched one after another, each building having its own forestairs, and some possessing balconies and small gardens.

The city flowed about them, invigorating as strong wine, filled with a skywide confusion of spires and roofs and smoking chimneys. Aberdeen, she discovered, might have been carved from granite since all the buildings and streets were done in the same sad, silvered grey. The most brilliant splashes of color were in the shops. Such items as knitted hose, cloth, and shoes were displayed in inviting arrangements in front of them.

Catherine said, "Aberdeen seems enormous."

"This?" He shook his head. "There are only some nine thousand people here. Didn't your father and mother ever take you to Edinburgh when you were a child?"

She shook her head. "No, but I always longed to visit the capitol."

"I think you'll like it."

She blinked. The way Devon had phrased that sentence, it almost sounded as if he knew she'd visit Edinburgh soon. Had he meant he was taking her to the capitol? She leaned toward him and asked, "Where are you taking me?"

He answered her question literally. "Just up Castle Hill a bit. We'll be staying at a house of mine for the next few days. I think you will find the accommodations more comfortable than the ship's cabin."

A slight, anxious breeze caught the hem of her skirt and lifted it. "Will you be there, as well?"

"Yes." He had been walking with his hand holding her at his side. The fingers tightened about her waist.

Catherine knew he was clasping her firmly to prevent her from trying to escape down one of the narrow, dark streets they passed. Not that it mattered, she reflected. Behind Devon came the retinue of his soldiers who had been on the *Evening Star*. Everyone was there— seanachaidh, henchmen, bladaire, pipers and all. There were also numerous tall soldiers, carrying basket-hilted swords and matchlock pistols. The men followed Devon peacefully enough, but Catherine knew that if she tried running away from Devon, Mouse, who walked directly behind them, or one of the other men, would catch up with her.

She sighed. Being forced to walk this close to Devon meant she could feel the strength and the heat of his body beneath his doublet. He had leaned even closer to give his reply, and for a moment, the city street receded and all she could see was his hard, handsome face and the firm cut of his lips, so close to hers. She wondered what the bedroom arrangements would be in this house they were going to. "I suppose I shall be locked up?"

His blue eyes held hers. "Yes."

It was on the tip of her tongue to ask if she was going to be locked up with him or without him. If such an idea hadn't occurred to him, however, she certainly wasn't going to bring it to his attention. Instead she said, "You never came by to see me on the ship, after that first day."

"You were missing me, then?"

Hot color flooded her face. "By my troth, no!"

"Then why did you ask?"

"Only because—" She couldn't think of a reason. "Curiosity."

"Ah." He didn't seem to believe her.

Catherine said quickly, "You said you have a house in Aberdeen. I thought you only owned Caldwell Castle."

"I did, when we first met. Since then, I've acquired

three other castles, and houses in Aberdeen and Edinburgh."

An older man sauntered by Catherine, and his yelling drowned out any reply she might have been able to make. The man dragged a sled of fresh herring and shouted the praises of the fish to the houses nearby. One small boy who had come to purchase some fish from the man, stopped and stared at the great laird and his retinue.

Finally, when they had passed by most of the people, she got out, "There can't be many men in Scotland who own so much."

His mouth was close to hers, so close she could catch his whisper. "Yes. Only think, if you were to stay with me as my wife, you could live as a wealthy woman."

Her pulses took up the now familiar clamor at his nearness. "You're holding me too close. It hurts." That wasn't the truth, but she had to find some way to make him move away from her.

Instantly, his grip on her lessened.

Before she could add any further comment, a commotion on the street drew her gaze. It was caused by a woman in her late twenties. Due to a scuffle with the shopkeeper, the woman's coarse plaid skirt had been twisted up to reveal a crippled bare foot, and her red hair flew, unpinned, from her cap. She cried out hysterically, "I swear by all that is holy that I did not do it! I would never do such a thing, I vow it!"

The owner of the yarn shop was a small, tight root of a man. His sallow face matched the color of his stained saffron shirt. He shouted, "Woman, do not lie!" With knobby fingers he held her by her arm, his grip so ferocious it raised red weals on her flesh. "I shall bring the matter up before the magistrate and see how the law—"

"No!" She struggled hysterically, kicking at the man with her bare feet, her thin hands flaying against his chest. "Ye cannot do that! My bairn would have no place to go!" The woman's face, lined with streaming tears, jerked up. Suddenly her eyes locked with those of Catherine, who was walking only a few feet from her. "My lady," she breathed. The woman gave one last frantic push at the shopkeeper, and managed to slither out from under his arms and escape. Then she shot like an arrow in the direction of Catherine.

As soon as she had reached Catherine, she flung herself in front of her, falling into a kneeling position at her feet. "My lady, help me!" she begged. "I am Bess Macvail of the Clan Craig. You remember me, don't you? My mother helped in the kitchen. We used to be close friends."

The shopkeeper had followed after Bess, his breath coming in wheezing pants. He stopped short when he saw Devon and his retinue of soldiers. In recognition of the fact that Devon was a man of authority, the shopkeeper lowered his head and instead of shouting, muttered, "My lord, this woman gave me a false coin. 'tis a matter for the magistrates."

Devon frowned, and at that sign of his displeasure, the shopkeeper took a step back. When Devon asked sternly, "What happened?" the shopkeeper wiped his sweaty hands upon his apron in dismay.

Bess, from her position in front of Catherine, interjected, "I swear I did nothing! My lady, help me." She held onto Catherine's waist like a drowning victim clutching at a piece of wood.

"Quiet." Devon's voice cut into her crying. "You," he said, nodding at the man, "tell me what occurred."

Sullen now, his thin face mottled red from emotion,

the shopkeeper held out a coin. "She tried to pay me with a counterfeit lion. See for yourself, my lord."

Devon took the lion, turned it over twice, and handed it back. Then he asked Bess, "How did you come by this?"

"I swear I do not know." She didn't raise her head up from where she had fallen before Catherine. "I have naught to do with the coin, my lord, save that it must have been given to me. I make cloth. Someone must have paid me with it."

"So she claims," sneered the shopkeeper. "Twice this last fortnight I have been given these false coins. Since the first year they debased the currency, it has become a common occurrence. Mayhap the woman has a husband who is a goldsmith and makes them."

"I am a widow!" Bess pleaded to Catherine, "I know of no one who works at a trade such as goldsmithing. My lady, you must remember me. Have you ever known anyone in my family to be dishonest?" She raised a pale face to Catherine.

Catherine looked down at Bess, stricken by her tears and her unnatural thinness. The hollows about Bess's eyes and the pinched, white look of her wrists could only be due to starvation. Catherine, who had never been able to see anyone sad without wanting to help, could hardly bear the sight. What must Bess's life be like? She remembered Bess as a close friend, and she ached to do something for her.

Besides, the charge was ridiculous. Catherine remembered that Bess's mother had been an earnest, friendly woman who practiced the reformed religion with the devotion of a true believer. Bess had been much the same age as Catherine, but, perhaps because of her twisted foot, she'd been painfully shy as a child.

She, like her mother, had been quite devout. Catherine couldn't believe she could now be involved in anything illegal, at least not wittingly.

If only there was something she could do to help her. Poor Bess, to have only her as a savior! Her own position was little better than Bess's. Still, she could at least try. Catherine turned shining eyes to Devon. "I do know her," she told him softly. "And I trust her. She's of my clan, so I feel compelled to do something. Would you help?"

Devon had barely glanced at Bess. His eyes on Catherine, he drew out his purse, opened it, and threw the shopkeeper two heavy gold coins, both ten times the value of the lion. "Here, you may have these for your trouble. Now, let us be done with the matter."

But Bess wouldn't release her hold on Catherine. "Please!" she cried. "My husband died two years ago. I am alone with a small bairn. I can barely manage to feed my child, let alone myself. Will ye help me?"

Catherine held her hand tightly. The poor woman. She could feel Bess's frail hands shaking from fear. Catherine fought back tears. This was all Devon's doing. If he had left her family in peace, Bess would still be living in the Highlands with them at Cree Castle, and would never have come to such a state. "I wish there were something I could do," Catherine told Bess with a rueful smile.

Bess raised her head, her eyes shy. "I could come to work for ye. Do ye need a maid, perhaps, or a seamstress? I'm very quick with a needle, and I'm strong, much stronger than I look. I swear I'd work for ye until I dropped."

Catherine glanced over at Devon. Bess's words had given her an idea. If only she could talk Devon into letting Bess be her personal maid, as Bess had suggested! Then she'd have an ally amongst Devon and his soldiers. With someone to help her, anything was possible. Perhaps she could even escape.

"Devon," she said in a sweet voice, "I do need a maid, and she is of my clan. I can't leave her like this. Perhaps I could use some of the jewelry my father gave me to pay her."

Before Devon could reply, Mouse, who had been standing behind Devon, interjected, "Man, ye must not consider it!" Mouse strode a foot closer, and looked down at Bess. His face softened perceptively when he saw her white, hungry face and the twisted foot.

Into the silence that followed, Devon said quietly, "As you see, we cannot leave her like this."

Mouse frowned. "No. Give her money then, enough to let her live comfortably. Or mayhap she could be hired as a servant to your home here in the city. But she canna be taken into yer retinue, not when she owes loyalty to your wife. The risk would be too great." He cleared his throat, and added to Bess, "I'm sorry, lass. But we'll provide for ye somehow."

Catherine cried, "Please, Devon, I beg you."

Everyone had turned to look at Devon, who stood fully in the sunshine, his gold chain necklace glittering and the three eagle feathers in his hat swooped low over his forehead. Devon said to Catherine, "I am about to do something very foolish. I am going to give in to you. Tell me," he wondered, "what will you do for me in gratitude?"

Before Catherine could reply, Bess began to cry, a dry, wretched sound of relief. Through her tears she sobbed her thanks. Devon turned to her, and explained, "Go and get your child and your things. Come to the house at the top of Castle Hill when you're ready."

Catherine told Devon. "Thank you. That was kind of you. I shall not forget it."

Devon's face was as bland as a bishop's, but his reply held a deep undercurrent. "I hope you will repay me someday."

He began to walk with her again. They soon reached the house he had mentioned, which turned out to be an attractive place with more furnishings than Catherine was accustomed to, furniture being so expensive. The building itself was narrow, like most of those in Aberdeen, with a long flight of stairs that wound up through the house. The stairway opened out into small, well-heated rooms enriched by oak paneling. Woven mats rested on the floor, instead of the more common strewn rushes.

Devon led his wife up to a room on the top story. She took one glance at the clean, sunny chamber with its canopy bed and plaid bedhangings, and then turned to him. Too late. Devon had left, and the click from the door announced that she was locked in.

It was evening before Catherine had a visitor. There was a knock on the door, and then Bess entered, carrying a plate of food. "My lady?"

"Please don't call me that, Bess." Catherine was so relieved to see her she could have hugged her. "Use my first name."

Bess nodded timidly, and brought the plate to her. "I hope ye like venison pasty."

"Anything would be better than fish. That was all they gave me on the ship, fish and haggis." She pushed out an oak stool for Bess. "Please, would you sit with me while I eat this? It's been so long since we've seen one another. Or are you hungry? Mayhap we can share the meal."

Bess sank down upon the stool. Since the melee this afternoon, her red hair had been combed and tucked under a neat white cap, and she'd put on a fresh white apron over her blue plaid skirt. "I've already had my meal, but thank ye. They were very kind to me in the kitchen. They even insisted I feed my bairn before I brought this to ye." She asked in a shy voice, "Ye said ye were on a ship?"

Catherine nodded, and related the entire story. Bess was gratifyingly horrified. They traded stories about what had happened to them after the destruction of Cree Castle, Catherine's home. It turned out Bess and her mother had fled to Aberdeen. They had lost contact with the other members of their clan, ever since Bess's mother had found work from a merchant who traded cloth. It was at this house that Bess had eventually met her husband. "He was a good man. I was very happy to have known him," she explained.

"I'm sorry it didn't end happily, Bess. But at least you have his baby."

"Aye, Will. That's his name, just like his father. He's bonny. I know that all mothers's say that," she added, her face pink, "but Will is different. He's perfect."

"I'm sure he is. I hope you can bring him up here some time so that I can see him."

"I'll bring him up when I visit ye for breakfast."

"Good, then." Catherine smiled at Bess's enthusiasm. After taking a bite of the venison, she suggested, "By any chance did you happen to hear the men talking about where we were going, or why I had to be captured?"

Bess shook her head. "No. I'm sorry." At the lines of

concern that marred Catherine's face, she added hastily, "But I shall listen much more closely to their conversation, now I know the story."

"That would be kind of you." Catherine laid aside her plate, and stood up to pace anxiously about the room, her hands bunched into the folds of her skirt. Aye, it was kind of Bess, and mayhap it would even mean that she could find out what Devon intended for her, but that wasn't enough.

Catherine looked out the window. Far down the cobbled street, past the shops and homes and spires of the city, stood the wild Highlands. She cried, "Bess, I must escape."

"But even if ye could escape, where would ye go?"

Catherine stared at the window. She hadn't been in Scotland since she was young, yet she loved it passionately. Ireland had been a land of mist and bogs and mystery, a land of half-sunshine, half-shadow. Scotland had the scrubbed clarity of fine glass, and was a harsher, more brilliant place, as sharp and real as the spiny heather. Out in the Highlands, the mountains would be steep and well wooded, with hundreds of deep, icy lakes, their surfaces reflecting the jagged frieze of high mountains like mirrors. She ached to go there.

Perhaps that was the reason that she answered, "To the forests near our castle. Many of my father's tenants and even some members of the Clan Craig remain, don't they?"

"Aye, I suppose so. Only the closest clan members fled. Those that remained would never have agreed to stay and pay manrent to the Macgowan, but the old laird—yer father—told those who stayed to cooperate. Yer father insisted anyone who remained had to take up the Macgowan's offer of a truce. I don't know, but I would guess that many of them now pay manrent to yer husband."

"I thought so." Catherine ran her finger over the window sill, considering. "I'm bound to know someone there who will help shelter me until I can locate my father."

Bess rose from the stool, a hand clasped to her heart. "Yer father! But he canna come to Scotland. Perhaps it might be better to stay with yer husband."

"With Devon!" Catherine almost started to laugh at the idea. Flatly, she told Bess, "That is impossible."

Bess twisted at her apron. When she spoke, it was in a hesitant voice. "I saw the way yer husband looked at ye. I know that look. He likes ye, likes ye very well. I canna think it a good notion for ye to run away from him. Wouldn't it be better to stay with him, and see what happened?" In a rush, she added, " 'Tis a wonderful thing to fall in love with a man, to be his wife and bear his child."

Catherine couldn't speak, she felt so frustrated. Before heaven, Bess seemed to have no idea of how impossible it would be for her to ever live as a wife with Devon! The burning of Cree Castle must have receded in Bess's memory, receded so far it no longer mattered. Apparently once Bess had moved to Aberdeen, the ties with the other members of the clan had grown weak. All Bess knew was that Devon appeared nice.

Perhaps Bess no longer felt the pull of family and loyalty, but Catherine knew such things would always be important to her. With the clan scattered, and her mother dead, she and her father and her brother had only themselves to rely upon. Of course she had to side with them in such circumstances. And Devon was their enemy.

Bess claimed it was a wonderful thing to fall in love, to be some man's wife. Catherine shrugged the idea aside. Of course she'd had dreams. She'd lain awake at night in the convent and stared into the silent, lonely darkness and dreamt of some man holding her, kissing her in just the way Devon had on board the ship. She'd yearned for love.

Catherine dismissed the memories. Such fantasies were like smoke. They hung in the air for a few minutes, insubstantial, beautiful, and then vanished. They'd never had anything to do with her life, nor did it now seem as if they ever would.

Bess said coaxingly, "You can have no idea of how nice a man can make you feel."

Catherine burst out laughing. "I think I have. Shall we talk of other things? Look at that house with the flower pot on the balcony. Below it, do you see the gown that woman is wearing? Her farthingale is so wide! Is that usual?"

A deep, masculine voice behind her answered, "At court, ladies can barely manage to sit down." Devon added, "They look idiotic."

Catherine pretended to continue to study the view out her window. How long had Devon been behind her? Had he heard her say she knew how nice a man could make a woman feel? Praying that he'd only just entered the room, she said, "I think they look splendid. I wish I had a gown with a farthingale like that." She refused to turn around and meet Devon's gaze.

"You are about to get your wish," Devon replied.

"Bess, would you please leave us? I wish to speak to my wife."

"No! Stay here." Catherine left her place by the window to look and see if Bess had remained.

Bess, her pale face graced by a smile, was shutting the door to the chamber. Leaving Catherine and Devon, as he had wanted, alone.

Chapter Five

CATHERINE MOVED TO THE JOINT STOOL IN THE CORNER farthest from him and sat down. Her blood seemed to have quickened as soon as she saw Devon. The day seemed shinier; more alive. Yet she didn't want to be alone with him. "Well," she said, "are you going to enlighten me? Why will I have a farthingale?"

"Because I'm having a number of court dresses made for you. A clothier will arrive soon, bringing bolts of cloth for you to choose from, and there'll be a seamstress as well to start the fittings."

"But why do I need court gowns?"

He shrugged in answer to her question. The warm sunlight slanted in from the window, brightening his doublet of gold and blue braid. "You can choose whatever fabrics and designs you like," he said. "Pick anything you fancy, even if it is a satin covered in rubies and diamonds, or, even more expensive, pearls, and even if you want one of those ridiculous iron farthingales. The cost is inconsequential."

She looked at him from under her lashes. "The gowns imply there will be some reason for them in the future. I had hoped you would be done with me quickly."

Devon strolled over to the oak turner's chair, and pulled it near Catherine before sitting down. "It seems I am always disappointing you."

"So it does." She noted he'd placed himself inches away from her, his long, booted legs crossed negligently by her feet. He was so close she could see the blue braid on his doublet, and the knitted pattern of his blue hose. She wondered at his choosing that color. Blue symbolized fidelity and honor. Most courtiers despised it as insipid. They preferred instead to wear the subtler hues of russet or silver or wine. "Now that you've imparted the information, is there any reason to remain?"

He smiled. "Only for the pleasure of your company."

Her chair was as comfortable as a pine cone. She shifted against the stiff, flat seat, wishing she had a cushion, wishing, most of all, that she was out of this room. Devon was watching her closely, and it unnerved her. She said, "I have to thank you again for taking Bess in. Have you seen her child yet? I wondered how he was faring."

"The last time I saw Will he was wearing very wet smallclothes. He had attached himself to the kitchen staff and was attempting to convince anyone within range that he needed more table scraps to suck. Since he had an infectious grin and since he drooled his undying gratitude, he was having great success."

She giggled. "I like babies."

"So do I. I've always wanted one of my own. And you?" His tone was bland and friendly. Yet there was nothing bland about the expression on his face.

Her smiled faded. Of course she had always wanted a child of her own. Devon had taken that possibility away from her by marrying her and then forcing her to flee the country. "It would depend upon the identity of the father."

"Surely the father would be your husband."

Catherine had the baffled feeling of a hare caught in an unforeseen trap. "If I were really married." She hunted for something to say to change the topic of conversation. "I have been wondering how your mother reacted when you brought Janet to Caldwell." She remembered Devon's mother from their wedding, a tall, stately woman with a strict look about her mouth.

"Janet, my mistress?" Devon's eyes slid over Catherine. "We're back to her, are we? Interesting." He said, "My mother disliked Janet. She longed to see me properly and faithfully married. Indeed, my mother always left me with the impression that, since I was her only child, she expected me to grow up into a combination of the soldier Robert Bruce and the saint John Knox."

"Will I have a chance to meet your mother?"

"Not soon. She's off in England, visiting friends. She won't be back until the winter is over. In the meantime, we'll be going to my home soon. Will you need any other things? The Highlands are colder than Ireland. I thought perhaps you might require some additional clothing, especially underthings."

She didn't like the idea of Devon's mind dwelling on her underthings, one way or the other. However, she had a more important point to pursue. "Home, to Caldwell? But why would you be ordering court dresses for me if we are only going to your castle in the Highlands?"

He hesitated. "Later, I may take you to Edinburgh."

She widened her eyes. Ever since Devon had captured her in Ireland, Catherine had wondered about his motives. Now she had an excellent clue. "Court dresses would imply I am going to see the king. Why? Why did you take me hostage?"

"I can't tell you exactly, but it has to do with the king and your father."

"With my father?" She drew in a breath, feeling as stricken as if someone had slapped her. Of course. She should have seen it earlier. Why would Devon have traveled all the way to Ireland to find her? Why was she important? Not because he was going to ransom her— she had no relatives with money enough to make ransoming worthwhile. Instead, it was some matter that involved the king and her father.

She looked up at Devon and cried, "Please! What is going on? I must know."

Caution had returned to Devon's face. It held that wary, measuring look she had seen before. "I have already said too much."

She had never felt so frustrated or helpless. Ever since her capture, she'd worried why Devon had sought her out. If it had to do with the king and her father, surely the matter was very serious. Very likely it also meant the king knew that her father was back in Scotland. It had been well over a year since she had last heard from her father, letters being so difficult to deliver. His last message had told of trying to find ways to make the king return his lands. But what had her father been doing, and why would the king be interested in her?

Jumping to her feet, her hands clenched and her skirt swirling about her legs, Catherine exclaimed, "I have to know what this is about! Is my father in trouble? Is the king going to kill him?"

"Upon my honor, no one means to harm Sheamus."

"Your honor!" She shook her head. "You will have to swear on something better than that to make me believe you. Please leave." She swept to the door and flung it open.

Devon's face was tight and angry. He stood up from his chair in a quick movement and strode through the door without another word.

Catherine slammed the door shut. Then she put her hands to her cheeks. Before heaven, why hadn't she seen it earlier? The extravagant expense of the ocean voyage to take her prisoner, and the many soldiers Devon had to keep her must have meant she was important to someone. Devon and the king had planned it all. And to think that she had been starting to like her husband! All along he had some plan of his and the king's against her father. But why had they needed her?

Whatever their reasons, she would have to escape. For if they had some plan against her father, she had to stop it somehow. Her escape was imperative, no matter what the risk.

Pacing restlessly, she walked over to the window and stared down at the street below. Outside, there was a cloud-teased sky with gulls and rooks wheeling overhead, casting flying shadows on the sun-dappled city. Aberdeen was a delicate pattern of sun and shadow.

She pressed her forehead to the glazed glass. Light

and dark—that was how she thought of Devon. He seemed warm and friendly, honorable. But how could she justify that picture of him with the way her father described him?

One thing stuck in her mind. Devon had said they'd leave soon for his home. If they were at Caldwell, she'd be close to those members of her clan who hadn't flown with her father. If she could escape, there should be no difficulty in finding someone to help her.

She smiled in sudden excitement.

Devon spent the rest of the day checking with his spies for word of Sheamus and picking up any other stray information he could hear in the city docks and taverns. It was very late when he came home. All the lanterns had been extinguished in front of the shops, and the narrow, cobbled streets were dark. A cold December wind whipped back his cape and stung his face with bits of dead leaves and dust.

He walked without thinking, making low, desultory conversation with a few of his henchmen. Then he heard a lute song. It was against the law to make noise after ten o'clock at night, but someone, in one of the houses he passed, was playing anyway. The melody was sweet but far away, like a pleasant memory. For some reason, it put him in mind of Catherine. And once she was there, he found he couldn't get her out of his thoughts.

When he reached home, most of his men were already asleep. The fire in the kitchen had dwindled to a pile of dusty silver ashes, but the one in the front parlor still blazed. He stood by the hearth for a while, considering. He should head for his own room. Yet he felt wide awake, and filled with an unnamed impatience, a restlessness that wouldn't leave him alone. At last he found himself climbing the stairs to Catherine's bedchamber.

Even as he walked, he told himself that if he wanted to remain awake there were a dozen things that required his attention. No, a hundred things. There always were. Two days from now they'd be leaving Aberdeen. Sometime before then he had to decide what to buy while they were in the city. Of course Mouse and his steward would attend to many of the details, but Devon knew he'd need to give the final approval.

He could catalogue decisions that needed to be made with weary recall. There would be farm implements to pick out that they couldn't make at the castle; and weapons too. And there were other things that would be needed at Caldwell Castle, imported cloths, for instance. Flemish lace and silks from China for Catherine. Wire and tin. For entertaining and special occasions, they'd need to buy dried fruits—oranges, raisins, and lemons. Nuts, too, and spices, as well as paper and books from England. And all of that was just the beginning.

Well, he would attend to all of it. The lifetime habits of discipline were too hard to break. But just this once, he wouldn't worry about them.

Devon walked up the stairs quietly, so as not to wake Catherine. When he unlocked the door to look at her, he could hear the evenness of her breathing. Plaid bedhangings hid her from his eyes, so he moved silently to her bed and pushed them aside.

The yellow glow from the fireplace fell softly over her still figure. Against the white linens, her hair looked black as pitch, and her lips were a dusky rose. He leaned forward and brushed away some strands of hair that had caught in her eyelashes.

She was the problem that had been nagging at him for days. What was he going to do with her? He had sworn to release Catherine to the king. And so he would.

But afterwards? Doubtless, after the business with the king was finished, Catherine would end up back in that convent in Ireland. Devon frowned at the idea of her returning to that life. A stray memory teased at him, of walking into her room this afternoon. She'd been leaning out her window and looking down at the busy street below, fascinated by sights she had never seen before. She'd bent toward the crowd like a flower to the sun, her face alight with laughter and longing.

Then he recalled when she'd pleaded with him to help Bess. He'd been struck by Catherine's anguish over Bess's plight. Catherine could care deeply, and would care, at some time and with true passion, for a man. He looked down at her in bed and felt arousal curling through him. Truly, she deserved better than the paper marriage they had.

And better than to be sent back to Ireland, back to endless fear of the king and the peaceful emptiness of life in a convent. But what other choice did she have? Even if he and Catherine could dissolve their sham of a marriage, she'd never be able to wed a man of money or importance, not with her family under the law of fire and sword. And he couldn't bear the thought of her married to a poor man, one who would have to work her as hard as the man himself worked. For that matter, Devon thought, his mouth firming into a harsh line, he couldn't bear the thought of any other man having her. Ever.

Therefore he was not going to let her go back to the convent when this was all over. He couldn't. Instead she would remain with him as his wife. They were married, after all. Why shouldn't they live together? And he wanted her, desired her, and liked her more than any woman he had ever known. It was almost as if . . . he shrugged the thought aside.

But having at last admitted to himself that he meant to keep her as his wife, it felt as if a band around his chest had come undone, allowing him to breath freely once more.

He couldn't bear for her to be sent off again, away from him. All his life he had done things for other people, for his country, for a set of beliefs. For once, he had set a goal for himself that was entirely personal. He wanted Catherine, and, before heaven, he meant to have her. Damn the risks and the fury of the king and the difficulties. Damn all of it.

And as for her . . . The thought was troubling. He watched her hand move drowsily against the covers. Perhaps she wouldn't want to live with him. There was all of their past history to overcome, and the enmity of her father. But he'd do his best to convince her. Then, if she truly didn't want him—but he'd consider that later.

A slight rustling noise behind him caused Devon to turn his head. Mouse stood at the top of the stairs. Devon frowned, and allowed the hangings to slide out of his hand and back into place. So as not to disturb Catherine's sleep, Devon paced quietly out of the room and down to his own chamber. Then, since Mouse had followed him, he turned, closed the door on the two of them, and said in a rougher tone than he usually used, "Yes?"

Mouse held out a flagon of heated wine for him. "'tis a hard, cold night. I thought ye might be needing this."

Devon took the cup silently.

Mouse leaned against the wall, looking so tall that the bed nearby, in comparison, seemed made for dwarfs. "Ye left before making the final arrangements for the horses. The matter of the horses canna be settled until ye have told us when they will be required."

"I plan to start for Caldwell two days hence."

"Good, then." Mouse made no attempt to leave.

Devon stifled a groan. "Very well, what is it that you want to tell me that you know I don't want to hear?"

There was a pause. Finally Mouse said, "They are saying belowstairs that ye visited your wife this morning, and that ye were with her a fair time. And I found ye with her again tonight."

"Ah." Devon took a long pull from his flagon. "Of course." He said amiably, "I have often wondered what it would be like to live without having your smallest action, your slightest word, picked over, commented upon, and worried about. Aye, I've wondered, but I daresay it is something I shall never know. In truth, I cannot even conceive of so much privacy."

Another man might have, after apologies, left the room. Mouse stood his ground, like a mountain unmoved by storm clouds.

Devon said at length, with a suggestion of wry laughter underlining his words, "I daresay you're not going to go until I tell you?"

Mouse didn't answer his question directly. "I thought ye were only to escort her to the king."

"Leave it be," Devon said in a tone as sharp and as definite as a knife thrust.

"No. How can I? Ye are my friend. I have some care for ye. The fact that ye canna leave the lass alone worries me."

A draft of wind must have hit the fireplace, for the fire suddenly grew larger, leaping and hissing against the blackened bricks. Like some emotion flaring up in wild heat, a shower of golden sparks exploded behind the iron grating. Devon watched it for a second, lost in thought, and then said quietly, "I am already in far too deep to pull back. And no lectures from you. What would you have said if anyone tried to stop you from marrying Alice?"

"I dinna know. Nothing. Just knocked them down."

"Admirably direct. Then at least you understand my position."

"Is it like that, then? Ah, well." Mouse lowered his eyes. "In that case, there's nothing more to be said, except that I pray ye will forgive me for my persistence, and that I hope it turns out well. She's a likely lass."

Devon raised his cup. "Very likely."

The door closed, fluttering the fire, when Mouse left. Devon finally slid between the covers of his bed. Yet even then he continued to stare sightlessly into space, his thoughts on his wife.

Yet it wasn't for two days that he saw her again. It was only at dawn of the morning that they were to start off for the Highlands that Devon once again climbed the stairs to her room.

Chapter Six

HE STRODE INTO HER BEDCHAMBER AND FLUNG OPEN THE shutters. Outside it was a dirty, damp grey, with the stars still glittering in a dull sky. Nevertheless, he pulled her hangings aside. "Wake up, sweeting," he announced in a bracing tone.

Catherine peeped open one eye, took one look at Devon's grinning face, and shut it quickly. He had looked happy, wide awake, and in the mood for fun. She wriggled into a ball and arranged the blankets over her head. "It's still dark," she complained in a voice that was muffled by her pillow.

"It only seems that way under the blankets. You present a pleasantly rounded lump underneath them, and I could go on watching you forever, but we have to leave." Devon flung back her covers. "Up," he commanded.

Cold air struck her into total wakefulness. "Devon! Beast!" she moaned, wrapping her arms around her

91

chest, and pulling her feet in under her nightsmock. "Haven't you noticed yet that it's pitch black? The town crier must still be cozily asleep in his bed."

"Aberdeen wakes up to the sound of a German whistle, not a town crier. I'm amazed you haven't noticed that already."

"Are you always this unpleasantly cheerful and alert at this time of the morning? If so, it's a good thing we never tried to live together as man and wife. I could never have survived the hours you keep."

"I have ways of making a wife happy, no matter what the time," he said silkily. "But to return to the original point, although the whistle hasn't sounded, it is most certainly time for us to get up and leave. We need to get to Caldwell today. To avoid having to camp out, we have no choice but to leave now."

He didn't need to explain further. Catherine knew why they couldn't stop anywhere along the road. There was scarcely an inn anywhere in the Highlands, and sleeping outside without protection was nothing short of madness. There was some danger from wild animals such as wolves, but there was greater danger from other clans. Most travelers either limited their journeys to one day, or made arrangements to stay with friends or relatives along the way.

"Very well," she said with a sigh, "I'll get up." When he didn't leave at that sign of her compliance, she pointed out, "If it's urgent that we leave quickly, I must get dressed."

"I thought you might like some help taking off your nightsmock."

"I can manage by myself," she grated out through chattering teeth.

"Pity." He shook his head sadly. "Of course I could just stay and watch."

She threw a pillow at his head, which, just as she'd expected, he dodged neatly before he vanished out of her room. Pushing the covers from her, she hopped gingerly onto the cold floor and headed for her shoes and stockings, thinking that not even her leather shoes with the painted cork heels would be enough to ward off the iciness of the floor. It was so cold she picked out all three of her petticoats to wear. By the time she was trying to lace her bodice, there was a knock on the door.

Bess poked her head in. "May I help ye?" she asked.

Catherine yanked at the fastening at her front. "There's no need to worry about me. You should be taking care of your baby."

Bess entered the chamber, smiling shyly. She wore a neat cap with her red hair knotted underneath it. "Will is fine. In fact, I had to fight off the others in order to feed him this morning." She moved forward into the room, and added, "Here, I can finish the lacing on your gown."

"Please, Bess, sit down."

Bess shook her head and walked closer to Catherine. For such a timid woman, she could look very firm when she wanted to. Taking Catherine's laces in her hand, she began to fasten the points of the false sleeve to the armscye. "Have ye seen yer present?" she wondered, nodding in the direction of the joint stool.

Catherine glanced down. Upon the stool rested a rich, fur-lined cape of deep blue velvet. Only the very wealthy could afford such a piece. And attached to it, she marveled, was a jeweled mirror on a long velvet ribbon, a real mirror, too, not polished bronze. Catherine knew instantly that Devon had brought it.

Bess said enthusiastically, "Isn't it lovely? Yer husband is a fine man to give ye such a thing. A fine, bonny, generous man."

"Did the fine, bonny, generous man say why he gave me this?"

"Aye." Her lashes tumbled to her cheek. "Perhaps I shouldna say. He told me in secret, like."

"Please."

"Well, then. He was laughing and said he hoped ye'd be grateful to him, aye, grateful enough to kiss him."

Catherine flushed. He'd been trying to bribe her, and he'd actually talked about it to other people. It was very embarrassing. "He paid for it with money gotten from the land and the manrent he stole from my father. Bess, how could you have forgotten that?"

Bess repeated with stubborn insistence, "He is a good man. Ye should try to be kinder to him."

Catherine's jaw dropped. "Kinder to him! I am his prisoner!"

"He looks worried. I feel sorry for him."

"The wealthy, powerful Devon Macgowan, friend of the king? There's no need. Even if he did have a problem one of his adoring lackeys would attend to it forthwith. Or haven't you noticed how they all stare at him worshipfully and obey his slightest whim?"

"Only because he is so nice to everyone," Bess pointed out reasonably. "I tell ye, he is upset."

Catherine rolled her eyes heavenward. "Even if he had a problem or an enemy, someone would see to it for him. Mouse alone, I daresay, could take care of a dozen enemies simply by rolling down a hill at them. You forget I'm his hostage. I'm the one who deserves some sympathy." Catherine adjusted the stomacher of her gown with a fretful gesture. Of all the absurd situations! A member of Clan Craig feeling sorry for Devon Macgowan. Did everyone in the world like him?

Nevertheless, when she tried on the cape, Catherine had to admit it was pretty, the loveliest thing she'd ever owned, in fact. There was even a blue satin mask. Catherine touched it gently. Elegant ladies wore masks whenever they went out during the day to protect their complexions. Nothing was considered more vulgar than a tan. Besides aging a woman and giving her freckles, tanned skin carried the dreadful implication that the woman was a peasant who worked outdoors.

Once the mask had been fastened on Catherine, Bess pronounced, "Now ye look perfect. Ye arena angry with me for talking about ye husband, are ye? I wish to be yer friend," she explained, her color high.

Catherine's soft heart immediately melted. "I should be honored to be your friend. And of course I don't mind anything you've said." She hugged Bess close, smiling, and she was still smiling when Mouse came to her door to lead her downstairs.

Catherine was grateful for the cape as soon as she went outdoors. The day was bitterly cold. A wet grey fog shrouded the line of shops and clung sullenly to the cobbled streets. Wind dragged up through the city, billowing skirts and piercing even the heaviest plaid.

Devon stood by a long-legged black stallion. Around him were a hundred men, all on horses and carrying weapons. In addition, there were carts, donkeys, and a banner bearing Devon's family crest.

Devon must have noted the way she had tightened her cape around her because he said, "It will be warmer later on."

"Aye, once the sun is up," she agreed with the acid satisfaction of one who is in the right. "Am I to have a horse to ride?"

He nodded at the cart. "I'm sorry, but I think it would be better if you travelled in the cart."

She took one glance at the crude vehicle and thought that not even the cape would make up for the humiliation of riding in such a thing. Devon's stallion blew air out its nose at her as she climbed into it.

They started their journey with a flourish. The piper played a bronchial tune, and the long line of Devon's troops started to move, the horses' hoofs on the cobbles clattering like a thousand pistols exploding. At the racket, heads popped out of windows in the houses nearby.

Catherine hissed to Devon, "Someone is going to throw a basin of slops at us. We're waking all the good burghers and their wives up even before the German whistle, whatever that is."

"Nonsense."

But even as he spoke, a woman in a house a little ways in front of them stamped out onto her balcony and tossed a bowl of water—or something—onto the flint stones of the street. The liquid splashed onto the middens and steamed ominously for a second, giving off a smoke that mingled with the swirling fog.

Catherine glanced triumphantly at Devon.

They crossed the Brig O'Dee and started to follow the road by the river. Or, Catherine reflected, the cow path by the river Dee, for the road turned out to be a deeply rutted, meandering, badly-kept-up trail. Every other year the king passed another law insisting that each laird keep up any roads through his lands. Catherine grinned at the thought. Laws made in faraway Edinburgh rarely had any effect in the Highlands.

By the time they were away from the river and riding up into the high country, the sun was out, surrounded by grey clouds. They met only a few other travelers: packmen with their strings of donkeys, a family off to sell their chickens in town, and a lone old man, walking, his grey hair in long strings about his face and a ragged, ancient blanket wrapped around his shoulders.

They passed by the castles of other clans and the small farms that surrounded the castles, with their fields of oats and barley that were fallow now. The rigs between the fields were ferociously high, for each tenant jealously guarded his soil from anyone else. Beyond the farms lay clusters of what were called black cottages, some so poor that they were windowless and had roofs of simple heather. When it was rainy, as it was today, the sheep and cattle would be kept inside along with the families, a single peat fire smokily keeping them all warm.

Soon, they had travelled into the wild Highlands, and the scenery changed dramatically. The air became the winey air of late autumn, as clear and sparkling as Venetian glass. Darkly shadowed crags were interspersed with barren meadows carpeted in rough grass, broom, and low, clumped bracken. Waterfalls fell in delicate blizzards of silver. And then there were the mountains.

Catherine loved the mountains, with their forests of birch and oak and pine. They filled her with a sense of wonder and freedom. Water sprouted everywhere—in the mist that threaded through the forests, in the occasional salting of rain. Each leaf seemed dappled with dew. Water ran in rich green ribbons down from the mountains and into lakes of measureless depths.

Even though she enjoyed the traveling, by the time it was late afternoon, Catherine's back and leg muscles ached from having sat cramped inside the cart all day. When Devon ordered another rest stop for the horses, she told him, "Aye, and for us, too."

"Tired, sweeting? At least it shouldn't be much

longer now." Devon stood by the cart. He put his hands around her waist and swung her back to the dark, loamy ground. His fingers should have slid away once she was down, but they didn't.

"I don't need your help anymore," she pointed out.

Reluctantly, his hands dropped to his sides. "Please alert me if you should again." Water ran off the brim of his hat. Underneath, his lips were smiling.

Catherine dragged her eyes from his face. Instead she glanced around at the pine forest they were in. "How long is it before we reach Caldwell? I've been away from the Highlands for so long, I'm lost."

"We should be there in a little over two hours. This is the last time we'll stop."

Catherine bit down on the inside of her lower lip, considering. Their last stop, he had said. And mayhap the last chance she would have to escape, then. Once she was within the high grey walls of Caldwell Castle, it would be nigh impossible to escape. Nor could she escape from the cart.

Yet her own clansmen must be close by. If they were within a two or three hour ride to Caldwell, the ruins of her home and many of her clansmen must be within easy walking distance, even though she didn't recognize this spot.

Catherine allowed her gaze to roam with a feigned indifference over the scene before her. Devon's troops were busy. Some men sat with their backs against trees, their eyes closed in rest, some were eating oatcakes from flat tin plates, and some were hunched by the fires trying to keep warm. Only Devon and Mouse were watching her.

Somehow, she had to figure out a way to get away from Devon. Then she spotted Bess, walking towards her. "Bess!" she cried. "It's been so wet, I've been worried about you and Will."

"Will is damp but happy. He's playing in the cart. And ye?"

Catherine was aware that Devon was watching her tolerantly as she stepped away from him to get closer to Bess. She wondered how far he'd let her go with Bess. "Come," she announced loudly to her friend, once she was only a few feet from her. "I need a few moments of privacy. Would you accompany me and watch to see no one gets too near?"

Bess glanced up at Devon, who made no comment. "As ye wish."

They strode over to a large bush. Catherine's bones had turned to rope and her heart had started to beat in rapid thrums. She knew exactly what she wanted to do. If only it would work!

While they were walking to the bush, Catherine whispered to Bess, "No matter what you say, I am worried about your child. Would you let me do something for you? I want to exchange my cloak for your blankets. Yours are soaked but, as you can see, I am quite dry. And it won't bother me to get a little damp, not when this is the last stop and there is only a few more hours of riding."

Bess hesitated. "Ye're kind, but I canna accept such a gift, even for a short while."

"For Will's sake. You can cover him with it. He'd like the feel of the fur," Catherine urged, her voice low enough so that Devon, even if he strained, wouldn't be able to hear.

Catherine hated using Bess like this, but she had little choice. Not that she would try it if she imagined it would get Bess in any trouble. But Devon would know

99

both her and Bess well enough to realize Bess had played only an unwitting role.

"Ah, for Will." Bess bit on her lip. "Very well, then."

They'd reached the bush by the stream. Catherine clasped Bess's hand and drew her behind the thick foliage. The exchange had to be over quickly, for otherwise Devon would come to check. Dragging off her mask and cape with hands that shook a little, Catherine thrust them into Bess' hands. Once Bess had pulled the hood well over her face, Catherine said, "Please, I'm so hungry. Could you go and get me an oatcake?"

Bess slid a hand over the soft lining of the cloak. "Aye." She started off towards the fires.

Catherine watched her go, holding her breath in excitement. There! Just as she had hoped, Devon was watching Bess walk toward the fire. He thought it was her. Now she could escape.

Catherine turned. In front of her stood a peat-colored stream. It cascaded over layers of broken rock in a tumult of flashing water. Wild bracken and stones festooned its sides. Beyond the stream lay a dark, dense forest.

She took one step forward and froze. It would be dangerous out there, alone in the forest. She could be hurt. Or worse. What if she couldn't find anyone of her clan? What then? Catherine swallowed. She didn't want to escape, but she had to. It might be her only chance to save her father.

Feeling frightened and sick, she plunged across the icy stream. The water burned, it was so cold. Catherine stumbled on the mossy rocks lining the bottom and almost fell. Somehow she managed to right herself and go on, the water splashing about her, flying in bright, glittering furls, drenching petticoats and dress hem and blankets all the way up to her knees.

Then she was across it and running wildly into the forest. Behind her, carried on the swooping wind, she could hear shouting. It must be Devon discovering her ruse. She didn't dare take the time to look behind her. Instead she shoved frantically into the densest part of the forest, where the foliage was so thick that the layered branches of birch and pine obscured light like a roof.

She pushed into the forest with her hands and shoulders, her head bent down against the clawing, spikey branches. Her blood pounded through her in quick hammer strokes. Just go on, she told herself. Go on, no matter what. A sharp limb gashed her on the arm. Blood oozed from the cut, and it stung painfully, but she ignored it. Nothing mattered but to get away. She heard that phrase, over and over again, in her mind, like a repetitious melody. Nothing mattered but to get away.

Then, behind her, she heard the crash of brush and birds flying out from trees, their shrieking breaking over her head like glass. Someone was nearby, and coming closer. Whoever it was, they would soon be upon her.

She had to hide! But where? She had no time to search for the perfect place. It would have to be close. The thick, round bush over by the small clearing, perhaps. If she crouched down within it, it might hide her completely.

There wasn't any time to consider. She plunged into the thick green of the bush, crashing into it with splinters and leaves flying about. She fell onto the hard ground inside with a force that bruised her body. Then, fighting for air from her exertions, she settled herself back and tried to assess her situation. Could anyone see her?

She arranged the branches and leaves around her, making certain they covered her completely. Her back was to the trunk and dense greenery sprouted around her, thick as a blanket. It didn't seem to her that any part of her showed. Then she waited, forcing her breath to come so faintly it couldn't be heard.

Somewhere close by there was a noise. A pounding noise of someone running through the forest. Goose-bumps shivered over her and the hairs raised on the back of her neck. Let them not see me, she prayed silently. Let them pass by and not notice me.

A long legged spider crawled slowly down a twig next to her face. It had a large, horrible brown body. She didn't like spiders. She'd always had a dread of them. Every sense in her itched to swat it away, but she didn't dare move. The spider hesitated, and then put a leg on her cheek.

A scream built in her throat. She couldn't utter it. The pounding noise was nearer.

Mouse stepped out into the glen. She could see him, dimly, through the green lace of the leaves. He paused, the mist curling about his legs in white ribbons, his head turning this way and that as he looked around for signs of her. Had he heard her hide herself in the bush? Would he spot her?

The spider crawled wholly on top of her cheek, its thin legs tickling her. It moved delicately over to her mouth. Waves of horror beat in her ears like a drum. She hated it. This was a nightmare, worse than any her imagination had ever conjured up. She was terrified, afraid to breathe lest Mouse hear her. The spider walked over her lips exploringly. She gritted her teeth together to stop them from chattering, to stop the scream of sheer fright that was lodged in her throat.

Mouse moved on. He disappeared from view, his tall body melting into the forest like a rock disappearing in a stream. She could hear his feet thundering across the muddied ground and plushy pine needle carpet, hear his breathing fade to a barely discernible sound as he ran away from her.

And then faded away entirely. She batted at the spider with a slamming swipe of her hand and watched it drop to the ground nearby and scurry away. At last. It was off her.

And she had managed to escape.

Catherine closed her eyes in relief. With any luck, the men wouldn't find her now. The forest went on for miles, and even if they assumed that she had hidden herself somewhere close by, it would take days to search through every bush, every possible place where she could hide. Nor did they have any hounds, or time to get them. It was late. They could only look for a little while longer before having to seek shelter. And now, what was she going to do? Catherine gave a giddy, nervous trill of laughter. Aye, that was a difficult question. It looked as if she'd have to spend the night out here in the forest. Tomorrow she'd look for one of her clansmen.

She didn't much like the idea of sleeping in the open. Still, one night wouldn't be too bad. Catherine slid off her shoes and stockings and set them out to dry on the ground. She unwrapped the blankets from her shoulders, and hung them from branches over her head. They wouldn't dry quickly, and maybe not at all, but at least she'd be warmer with the wet things off. Thankfully, her dress wasn't in too bad a condition. Only around the hem, where it was still soggy from the stream, was it uncomfortable. She spread out the brown material so that the wet part didn't touch her legs.

Then she waited patiently for another hour, planning what she should do and pulling the needles and bits of twigs from her hair and dress. No one but a badger disturbed her peace, and it vanished into the forest without noticing her. When she didn't hear anyone searching close by during any of that time, she judged it might be safe to start to look for a cave.

As quietly as possible, she slid out of the bush. She stood for a moment in the clearing, waiting for something to happen, prepared to jump back into the bush if she heard anything strange. But there was nothing. Just the eerie cry of the peesweep far above her head and the whirr of the wind through the trees.

She looked about, assessing her situation. Surrounding her, a dozen mountains rose with strong shoulders. On their tops, clouds clustered like ghosts haunting ancient monuments. From the clouds, she guessed it would rain tonight. Catherine sighed, and started out in the direction of the tallest mountain, hoping to come across a crofter's cottage, one of the ones used for summer grazing. They stood empty during the winter.

Yet, after she had walked for an hour, she had seen nothing that would offer her secure shelter. Worse, she began to fear that she might even have gone in circles. The cold bit into her skin and her entire body ached. She knew a moment of despair. Why had she ever tried to escape? She should have waited, and tried to contact some of her clansmen when she was at Caldwell.

Wearily, she pushed aside yet one more tree branch. In front of her stood a fern-rusted glen, heavy with the scent of resinous fir needles and bog myrtle. A low granite hill stood on one side; on the other, separated from the clearing by a deep, jagged ravine, stood a mountain. She could see a stream weave a giddy silver trail as it fell down the fissured hillside.

And, far above, a veil of pink-shot mist. It was sunset.

This clearing would have to do. Bone tired and sore and cold, she trudged to the base of the hill and sat down. At least the hill provided some protection from the elements. And she could pick up leaves and needles to cover herself.

But before anything else, she would have to rest. Catherine made a low groan as she sank to the ground. She'd never felt so awful, or been so hungry. Her eyelids closed. Why hadn't she thought to take one of the oatcakes with her? She let her mind float aimlessly, dreaming of finding a cottage with a fire already lit inside.

Then something roused her, she had no idea what. But all of a sudden, every one of her senses came alert. Just as she snapped her eyes open, she heard it—a hoarse, deadly growling.

Surrounding her stood a circle of wolves, their heads lowered, their teeth bared in menacing grins. She stared at them helplessly, at the sharp white teeth and gem bright eyes.

Without question, they were going to attack her.

Chapter Seven

RAW TERROR SHIVERED THROUGH HER. SHE BACKED UP AN inch and felt the sharp scrape of the hill behind her. There was no way to escape, not when she was caught between the hill and the wolves. If only she had a gun—something, anything to frighten them away. But she was helpless.

Catherine did the only thing she could. She threw back her head and screamed, a wild, hysterical scream that went on and on. She could only hope desperately that it would bring help.

One of the wolves moved closer, his growl deadly with menace. Frantic, she cast about for a weapon. But there was nothing, not even any rocks lying on the ground. One of the wolves nipped at her skirt and then ran back to the others.

Her shriek, high-pitched and shaking, only made the wolf braver. It prowled closer to her again, snarling roughly. She started to cry. It was going to attack her! Before heaven, it was going to attack her!

Then a clattering noise jerked her gaze toward the ravine. It was Devon riding the black stallion. He must have heard her cry out, for he galloped toward her with his long cloak swooping around him, his head held low and tense against the wind.

For a second, relief left her so limp Catherine thought she'd faint. Then she realized just how wide the gorge was that separated them. Wide, very wide. Surely it was too far for any horse to jump without falling in. She watched Devon take in her situation in one glance, watched him dig his heels fiercely against the side of his mount to urge him across the ravine.

He was going to be killed! "Devon, no!" she cried.

Too late. He had already spurred his horse to jump. She watched, too terrified to scream, her mouth open with horror, as the black stallion leaped gracefully past the clustering gorse bushes and off the cliff, his hoofs cleaving into the air, the rocks showering and clattering around. And then the animal came down, with a thunder that shook the earth, on Catherine's side of the gorge.

At the same moment, the wolf sprang at her. His teeth reached savagely for her throat. She jumped aside. Just in time. But the animal had gotten hold of her dress and was shaking it brutally, pulling her into a cloud of stinging dust, loud, furious noise, and dizzy movement. She could hear Devon's horse hurtling toward her but she was too desperate to look up. She hit at the wolf with her hand, slamming her tight fist against his head, and praying she could keep her fingers away from the snapping, raging jaws. She hit and hit until her palm went numb from the vibration of the blows.

A second, smaller wolf sprang, and she screamed. Before it could reach her, Devon had shot it. The animal dropped to the ground. Then Devon appeared at her side, and the large wolf that had been attacking her leaped at him in an explosion of fury. Devon raised his dirk like a scythe and brought it down in a precise, skilled sweep. There was a yelp, and a flow of bright blood, and the wolf slid down to the dirt and lay still.

Catherine whirled about, the breath still shaking in her ribs and looked out at the glen. The clearing was empty. The other animals had fled. A tremor ran through her as she realized it was truly over. She sagged against the hill, crying with relief.

Devon flung his dirk aside and grabbed her into his arms. He held her possessively, his head buried in her dark tangle of hair. "Sh, sweeting," he murmured against her hair, "don't. Don't. They're gone now, and I'm here. You're safe. And I will never let you go again. I swear it."

"I was so frightened," she whispered, and didn't know whether she meant she'd been afraid for herself or for him.

"It's over now." He sank his face in the curve between her throat and her shoulder and said in a muffled, strange voice, "I thought I had lost you. Cat, sweet Cat."

She couldn't speak. She could only cry and lean against him, feeling his arms holding her close.

He asked anxiously, "Were you hurt?" His hands slid over her body looking for injuries. But she shook her head.

Devon pulled her back against him. When he discovered Catherine had managed to escape, he'd been filled with a blind, desperate rage. He knew just how dangerous the forest could be. Never before had he been so

108

frightened for another human being. Images of her injured or dead tortured him.

He'd been so scared for her that when he finally spotted her he'd made the jump across the ravine without thinking. Looking at it now, he had no idea how he'd survived. Perhaps just by the sheer determination to save her.

Needing physical contact to reassure him of her presence, he pulled her closer and rested his cheek against the top of her head. He stroked her like a child while she cried, soothing her, murmuring comforting things against her ear. Around them, the wind teased and tugged at their clothing, and the gold sunlight of late afternoon tinseled the leaf-strewn glen.

Gradually, as he held her, Devon grew aware of the softness of her breasts pressed against his chest. She nuzzled her face against his neck, and the dark curls of her hair tickled his chin. She was only holding him close because she'd been frightened. He knew it. But now, the sweet scent of her teasing his nostrils, and the pleasant weight of her leaning against him, unbidden, his body began to react to her nearness. His stroking hands slid lower to brace her hips against his. She had pleasantly feminine hips, and they fitted into his as if they were meant to rest there.

Passion stirred in him. He struggled to ignore it, knowing how near hysteria she was, yet he couldn't help himself. She'd come close to death and he'd been shaken by fear for her. It taught him just how much he wanted her as wife, wanted the sweetness of her, the warmth of her, wanted her to love him and stay with him.

His hands moved across her hips, enjoying the sensation of touching her firm flesh. Desire for her heated him like a fever. He found himself raining light, sweet kisses over her brow and nose and cheeks. She tasted like heaven. He slid his fingers up the slope of her breast. Devon gave a shaky groan, and raised his hand so that he was cupping the breast, feeling its soft swelling, and stroking the small nipple beneath the layers of her clothing.

At first, Catherine noticed nothing wrong about his kissing her. The drift of his mouth was as weightless as a shadow. Caressing, soothing. Then his lips sought, and found, the red warmth of her mouth, and she realized at last what he was doing. She tried to yank herself away, but he held her too tightly.

His mouth became wanton and coaxing and she couldn't seem to conjure up the will to push him away. Not when she wanted to kiss him back and when the pressure of his mouth against hers was so exquisite. So bitterly honeyed, and so sweet; she ached with the knowledge that this was forbidden. She pressed her lips harder against his, a faint moan rising from her throat.

Had she claimed that she didn't want him? If so, she'd lied. The truth was this, with her body shivering with desire, a desire as ardent and persuasive as his own.

She brought her hand up to the base of his neck, touching the edge of his hair, and then let her fingers graze downward to stroke the flat plane of his back. She breathed in the scent of him, the aroma of wood and resinous pine. His lips held something of the sharp tang of the forest in them.

When Devon's tongue sought access, she parted her lips for him, tasting him, feeling his body enclose her own even more tightly. His mouth and tongue claimed hers in a kiss that made itself the ruler of each of her senses, a kiss that made time and the past things of no

110

meaning. There was only Devon, and the heady, erotic pleasure of this moment.

He stroked his hands over the material at her breasts, fondling, lingering, sending all her thoughts flying. Devon's hands were busy with her dress. The fastenings came undone. She barely noticed, for her head pounded dizzily and an exhilaration raced through her veins.

He undid the front of her bodice and pushed aside her shift, freeing the two soft breasts from the civilized confinement of clothing. For a moment, the chilly air smote her naked flesh. But then his hands closed over her bare breasts. Her eyes flew open and she nearly protested.

But he was kissing her again, and his fingers traced delicate, entrancing patterns over the swelling of her breasts. She had never felt anything like it. Never guessed anything could be so delightful. Shocks of pleasure bolted down to her abdomen as his finger trailed over her nipple, and then trailed over it again, stroking, lingering, until she could hardly bear it. His head bent down, and he took the rosy nipple into his mouth. His tongue was deliciously wanton, rousing the tip, hardening it, drugging her with his passion and the feel of his lips upon her breast. She shuddered. A wave of passion swept over her, nearly swamping her with its intensity.

Abruptly, Devon jerked away from her. He strode into the glen and didn't stop walking until they were separated by a dozen feet. His hands were clenched and his face was hard with desire. Catherine didn't understand, and, blindly, she took a step toward him.

"Stay away!" he grated out. "Before heaven, if you come closer, I swear I won't be able to stop myself from

111

taking you here, on the ground." He brushed a hand over his face. Devon was furious with himself for kissing her. She'd never forgive him if he took advantage of her now, when she hardly knew what she was doing. He didn't want Catherine like that. When the time came, he hoped she'd come to him without reservations or regrets.

Slowly, the pounding in his senses stilled. He walked back to her when he was calm, and explained, "We have to set out for the castle now. It will be dark soon and it's best not to be out in the forest past nightfall."

He unfastened the wet plaids that clung stickily to her shoulders. They dropped to the ground with a heavy noise. Without a word, he grabbed her fur-lined cape from where it was tied to the pillion of his saddle, and fastened the cape about her shoulders. Then he swung her up onto his stallion, and, with a lithe movement, jumped up behind her.

Before he picked up the reins, Devon blew on his horn, letting the sound alert those of his men who were out searching for Catherine that she had been found. He urged his mount to the right and they began to canter through tall pines and purple, glistening shadows.

They soon reached the road, and one of Devon's men appeared, and then two others. Devon longed to speak to Catherine about their embrace, but once they had company, he regretfully postponed it. Perhaps tonight, after they were at Caldwell. Yet he found his thoughts wandering back to that moment when he'd kissed her bare breasts. He could feel the warmth of her body in front of him, moving in motion to the horse's hoofs, and he nearly groaned aloud in frustration.

Desperately, he tried to think of other things. He

began a list of what needed to be done tomorrow. The first thing, he vowed with a frown, was to see to the wolves. It was rare for wolves to attack people, but there had been famine this year due to the drought. There were always accounts of wolf attacks during a famine, because the animals became reckless from hunger. The drought had been especially bad these last few months. Indeed, only the unusual weather had enabled them to make it from Aberdeen to Caldwell in one day. By late December, snows usually make the Highland mountain roads impassable.

He was considering the possible effects upon the next year's crops when he first spotted Caldwell. Catherine must have seen the castle too, for she said, "I never thought I'd be glad to see it."

"Tired, my sweeting? It's only another minute."

Before them was a deep lake, very still and sheened with glassy red from the last flare of the sunset. Caldwell Castle stood on a green hill next to the lake, wreaths of blue smoke curling out of its chimneys.

Everything about the vast stone castle had been built with an eye for defense. It rested close enough to the loch so that those inside could escape by water if they had to. The hill the castle stood on had been stripped of vegetation so no enemy could ride up without being seen, and only out by the loch was the forest allowed to grow freely again. Nor were there any huge windows, as in the new English manors, to let in light and warmth. Each window was a narrow slit, just wide enough for an archer to shoot from. Four high round towers, one for each side, looked attractive, but had been built as looking posts. Within, the stairway that led to the bedchambers was so narrow only one person could climb it at a time, making it simple to protect the upper rooms. The fact that all this was necessary was attested to by the blackened stones at the base, which showed that the castle had been put to fire at least once.

Once she and Devon were inside, Devon noted how tired Catherine looked as she walked through the great hall. He picked her up in his arms, ignoring her feeble protests, and carried her to a large bedchamber.

The room proved to be as finely furnished as the great manors of the English were said to be. White candles burned in silver candlesticks, their light glowing over the vast canopied bed. There were carpets splashed extravagantly on the floor, and rich tapestries hung on the walls to keep the dampness out.

Devon carried her to the bed and laid her gently down. She smiled drowsily up at him, feeling limp from spent emotion and the exertions of the day. "Thank you," she said before sinking back upon the pillow.

"Before you go to sleep, we'd best take off your wet things." His hands came down upon her, and he undid the tie at her cape, pulled it from her, and let it drop in a slither of blue to the carpet. Then he knelt before her to remove her wet shoes and hose.

When Devon drew off the last stocking and reached up to untie the points at her armscye, Catherine said, "I'd prefer to have a woman help me with the rest. Mayhap Bess—"

He continued busily at her points. "I'll do it."

She fell silent. How could she protest when Devon had just saved her life? Indeed she was very grateful to him, very grateful. Yet it made her nervous to have him removing her clothing, even for so reasonable a purpose as to take off wet clothes. As his fingers continued untying her clothing, she couldn't help but recall the moment when he had caressed her breasts. She looked away from him, a warmth flooding through her.

Drawing off her sleeves, Devon said, "You told me

you weren't hurt." His hand slid over her upper arm, where there was a long, jagged scrape. "I'll wash it with soap."

She blinked. "Why?"

"Once my father had a Moorish physician here. All the cuts the doctor soaped out healed so miraculously we now wash off even the smallest cut." Devon had picked up the round soap that stood beside the wash basin, dipped it into the water, and reached up to her arm.

The wet soap gleamed like a pearl while Devon's hands moved over her. He acted quite businesslike, but Catherine was all too aware of his rough, calloused palms against her skin and the nearness of his body. His touch was gentle, but it sent vibrations fluttering to her abdomen.

She blurted out, "Please let me do it. I find it embarrasses me to have a man wash me." Devon's gaze locked with hers, and in his eyes she could read his reaction to her words. As soon as Devon opened his mouth to reply, she muttered, "Past experience tells me that you're now going to make vulgar remarks about how I desire you."

A corner of his mouth curved in amusement. "Experience serves you well. You're not embarrassed because a man is washing you. If Old Archy, the pig master, were helping you, I daresay you'd scarcely notice. What bothers you is that it's me, and that my fingers are touching your bare skin. And what's most bothersome is that you like it. What was that?"

"Nothing. I moaned."

"I like that reaction of yours. You moaned when I kissed your breast this afternoon, too." He finished with her arm, and announced, "You must be hungry. I'll go downstairs and bring up some supper for us while you change into your nightgown." Without giving her a chance to protest, he vanished into the next chamber.

Catherine stood for a moment, staring at the door, and then began to remove her remaining clothing. She found a thick white nightsmock laid out on the trestle table and put it on. Now that she was warm and dry, Catherine felt much better.

Better, except that she now had nothing to do but think of Devon, and the fact that he'd soon return. She shouldn't be alone with him, especially after what had happened this afternoon between them. And yet she enjoyed his company.

Nor could she forget that he'd risked his life to save hers. The jump he'd made today had been terrifying. No reasonable man would have risked it. So why had he? Surely not just because he needed her as his prisoner. It wasn't reasonable to risk death to save a prisoner.

Restless, afraid of what the answers to her questions might be, she picked up the mirror Devon had given her and used it while she combed out her hair. She pulled the comb through her hair with long, snapping strokes.

What she'd avoided considering was their kiss. Granted, her rescue from the wolves had left her shaken. But that hadn't been the only reason Devon had made her feel so exalted. She had only to close her eyes for a second, and imagine the sensation of having his mouth on her breast to send a jolt of pleasure running through her.

Their relationship was becoming ever more complicated. She'd expected Devon to be the man her father had told her about; he was not. He was warmer, more amusing than she would have expected from his austere face. Aye, certainly he was warmer. She put a hand to her cheek, realizing she was blushing. Yet to learn to like him would be wrong. He was her father's enemy. The best thing to do would be to stay away from him.

Devon knocked. She met him at the door and said, "I hope you brought plenty of food."

He held up a tray laden with goblets and heavy pewter plates. "As you see." The plates held chicken, crusty venison pies, spiced cake, and fresh barley bread thick with butter.

He laid them down on the trestle table, and Catherine joined him at the table. For a while, they ate in comfortable silence, the only noise the crackle of the fire in the hearth. Catherine was aware of Devon's gaze on her. Whereas she ate heartily, Devon barely touched his food. He seemed deep in thought.

At last she wondered aloud, "What is it? Why have you been staring at me?"

"Have I?" Devon pushed out his chair and stood up. Restlessly, he walked to the fireplace and tapped on the great tiled mantle. "There's something I have to tell you. Have you finished with dinner yet?"

"Yes, of course." She put down the piece of bread.

"Perhaps we could finish our drinks by the fire."

Slowly, she nodded, and rose from her place at the table. She sank to the carpet in front of the fireplace as he did, the white hem of her nightsmock forming a wide, graceful circle on the brilliant colors of the rug. Then she waited for Devon to sit down next to her.

Devon handed her her goblet. "Drink up," he said.

Obediently, she took another sip. The cider had not been cut by water, and it was strong, heady stuff. "What was it you wanted to tell me?" Before he said anything else, she asked quickly, "It's about my father, isn't it? You are finally going to tell me why you had to capture me."

"I'm afraid that was not—"

"I must know. Please. Why did you take me prisoner? Am I to be used as bait to lure my father out of hiding?"

There was a pause, while the fire sent waves of light running over his face. At last Devon shrugged, and said, "I suppose there isn't any reason to keep it from you any longer. What happened is this. Your father has been busy the last few years, doing things that caused the king a great deal of trouble. One of the things he did was to waylay some messengers of the king's, messengers who were carrying letters from the king to England. The king sends hundreds of letters to England each year—to the English Queen, to his spies, to friends. Most wouldn't matter. In this case, your father captured messengers who carried letters to the Duke of Essex."

"And the letters are what? Compromising to the king?"

Devon gave a short laugh. "Compromising? Aye, you would say they are that. Essex was involved in an uprising against the Queen. Our king sent Essex letters of encouragement. The letters, if they should fall into the wrong hands, might well end the king's hopes for succeeding to the throne of England."

"The king must have been mad to send them, then!"

A log flared, turning Devon's hair a brighter gold. He scooped up his own goblet and took a drink from it before replying. "I agree. But James has always peppered Europe with his letters, promising anything to any person who would listen, to anyone who could help him get the throne of England. And Essex wrote saying that he supported James's claim—or at least he would, if the king would support him in the rebellion. Of course the king never expected the letters he sent to Essex to be seen by anyone unless Essex's rebellion succeeded. The king told his messengers to dawdle in Scotland until they'd heard how the rebellion went. In fact, that was how your father happened to come upon them."

"And in the meantime, the rebellion against the English Queen failed, and she tried and beheaded Essex." Everyone in Ireland had been very interested in the fate of Essex, since he had led an expedition against them.

"Now Queen Elizabeth is close to death, they say, and, although her closest relative is James, our king, she has yet to announce the successor to her throne. If she learned of James's involvement with the traitor Essex, she might be furious enough to name one of her other relatives her heir."

Catherine stared at the tiled hearth. In the convent, she'd nearly forgotten how treacherous life outside could be. Her father had always said that the men who went to court could never be true to any one master. Each one lied, sought power, supported first one nobleman and then another. She looked up at Devon at last and wondered, "What has any of this to do with me?"

"Your father is trying to force the king to give him back his lands. Sheamus Craig has said he'll send the letters to the English Queen if the king doesn't agree to give him back his land." Devon swirled the cider in his goblet idly, watching the amber liquid move to one side of the cup and then the other. "But the king won't be blackmailed. He has no intention of allowing your father into a position of power again."

She went pale as her gown. "So the king ordered you to capture me in order that the king can force my father to return the letters in exchange for me. What if my father refused the exchange? What would happen to me? Am I to be thrown into one of the king's prisons?"

Devon was silent.

Catherine drew in a sharp breath of air. "I can see why you didn't want to tell me at first why you'd taken me prisoner. I'd have been frantic to escape if I'd realized how important this is to my father and to my clan. With those letters, my father could actually have won back our estates." She sighed. Her one real attempt at escape had ended in failure. She ached for her father. There didn't seem to be any way to help him. Curiously, she felt no anger at Devon for his part in it. The entire plan had really been the doing of the king. Devon had only followed his orders.

Devon's deep, masculine voice cut into her thoughts. "Can we forget about all of this, at least for tonight? I'm tired of politics."

She looked at him from under her lashes. "You? I can scarcely believe it. You first went to court when you were, what? Seventeen?"

"Don't you think I can be tired from a long ride, and I can want to relax in front of a fire with my wife?"

"Devon Macgowan?"

"Aye."

She shook her head mockingly, and at her response, he smiled, a lazy, slow smile that seemed to alter the severe contours of his face. "Do you know, we'd present a cozy picture if someone came and saw us like this."

Catherine nodded. They would present a cozy picture. She sat by the hearth in her white nightgown, her dark hair hanging loose about her shoulders; and Devon sat next to her, with his boots propped negligently on the tiled edge of the fireplace. Anyone just coming in and knowing nothing of their past history would guess they were a happily married couple relaxing by the fire before going to bed.

She said, "Yes, but we're not really man and wife."

"Ah." His white shirt was stirred by a draft from the window. The lace about his wrist swirled uneasily. "That, exactly, was what I wanted to speak to you about."

Catherine put down her goblet, aware that her heart had started to thrum a little more rapidly. What could he mean? "You said there was something else you wanted to tell me. What is it? About my father?"

"No."

Impatiently, she dug her hand into the soft texture of the carpet. Why was he dragging this out? It was almost as if Devon were reluctant to talk to her about it. "Please, just tell me."

"I have to explain something about this room."

She gaped at him. His words seemed to have no connection to the expression on his face. "This room? You claimed you wanted to discuss something important, and now you want to talk to me about this bedchamber?"

"It's my room."

Catherine glanced about, and realized that she should have known it from the moment they came in here. The heavy, blue velvet hangings, the rich carpet on the floor, the exquisitely carved oak chair with the brocade cushions, all could only mean one thing. This was the bedchamber of a very rich man. It was Devon's room. "Very well, it is yours," she conceded. "And your point?"

"As soon as you have recovered from your run into the forest, as soon as you are no longer sore and tired, we are going to discuss the arrangements for this room." He shook his head, and the light picked out the glitter of his gold chain and highlighted his face, which had tightened abruptly. "I'm doing this badly. What I mean is that as soon as you are feeling better, I want to discuss sleeping with you."

There was a moment of thick, heavy silence. Catherine stared at him with wide eyes. All at once everything about this evening became revoltingly clear. Devon had known what he was going to say ever since he carried her up here, and knowing it, had delayed until just the right moment to tell her. Clever, careful Devon. He'd waited until she was tired from the long and terrible day, waited until she had reason to be in a good mood with him because he had saved her life. Then he'd put her before a fire and made her drink cider until her head swam and talked with her until she was soft and pliable.

She announced, "There is nothing to discuss. I do not wish to sleep with you."

"I told you, we will speak of this later."

She ignored him. "I want to clear this matter up now. I will not accept having you in this room with me."

"No? And how are you going to enforce that? Cat, just as soon as you are better, I am indeed going to start sharing this room with you."

Catherine cried, "The only way you'll ever have me is by rape!"

His brows snapped together. "I'd never harm you."

"Then the only thing we'll be doing on that bed is sleeping?"

"I am not in the habit of raping women. The reason we'll sleep together is that you are my prisoner, and I need to keep a watch over you. After all, you did escape once."

She picked up a poker and jabbed it at the logs in the

hearth. "Your prisoner, yes! But most prisoners are kept safely locked in one of the lower cellars of a castle. You want me in here with you because you desire me and you hope that one night, in a moment of weakness, I'll make love with you."

He regarded her blandly. "Of course."

"Devon!" she fumed. "No prisoner should be treated in such a—"

"Cat, you are my wife! No one, not even the strictest member of the Kirk, is going to object to our sleeping together." When she glared at him, he added, "Yes, I do want you in my bed. Yes, I desire you. And yes, I will have you."

He'd spoken to her in a husky, rough voice, with a passion that was so raw it made a shiver run down her back. She could feel the tension in the air, as palpable and hot as the fire in front of them.

"Do you hear me?" he repeated, "I will have you."

"That—" She swallowed. His words, and the look on his face, had turned her legs to wax. She struggled to recall that he was her enemy. No, it was impossible to believe that. Not when he had saved her life today. "That is impossible."

"Is it?" he drawled, and, although he was not touching her in any way, she could sense the desire in him, running through his body in the same, warm way it was running through hers.

Catherine could see the bed out of the corner of her eye, huge and imposing, covered in blue damask and velvet. To go to sleep every night, next to a man who desired her and who was trying to seduce her! "I suppose you expect me to fall into your arms," she said, trying, as ever, to brazen her way out. "Nonsense. If you won't rape me, nothing will happen on that bed."

The fire hissed, and yellow flames shot out against

the dark tiles. Devon, all golden elegance and certainty, put the flagon up to his lips and finished his cider. "How long do you think this attitude of your will last, Cat?"

She sputtered, "Until the day I die."

"I think not. I think we will refrain from making love only as long as you can tell me you don't want me. Only until then, and not a second after." His voice was as thick as honey. "My own guess is that it will take one or two nights before you give in."

Chapter Eight

"GOOD MORROW, MY WIFE," DEVON SAID CHEERFULLY.

The basket of weeds Catherine had been holding crashed to the ground. Just seconds earlier, she'd been peacefully helping the other women in the castle herb garden. Then Devon appeared from nowhere, and boomed out an unhappy arrangement of words like "my wife." She turned to look at him. It was a warm day. Sunlight yellowed his hair and illuminated his clothing, reddening the high polished boots and narrow plaid trews clinging to his hips.

"I'm sorry," he went on, as if she had spoken, "did I startle you?"

The women who had clustered around her had melted away like ice in a fire. She and Devon had been left alone. Catherine said, "You not only startled me, you seemed to have had an odd effect on all the serving girls. They vanished as soon as you approached."

He strolled past the knotted hedges toward her. "They were being tactful and giving us a chance to speak in private. Doubtless they secretly longed to stay. Everyone at Caldwell is in a froth of curiosity to find out what is going on between us."

"Don't they know about the letters?"

"Only Mouse knows. It seemed safest. The secrecy of the letters is, after all, vital to the king and to Scotland." He added, "But as a result of my reticence, my clansmen are delirious with curiosity. They've been dreaming up all sorts of lurid possibilities for my capture of you, and have been bombarding me with questions all morning."

The sun warmed her back as she bent over and tugged a weed away from the row of sweet potatoes. "What kind of questions?"

"About our bedroom arrangements."

Her fingers stilled. The last thing Catherine wanted to discuss right now was their bedroom arrangements. She'd been more or less hoping the subject would evaporate.

Devon continued smoothly, "They've decided I needed you for breeding purposes."

"Oh." No wonder all the women had been so nice to her. She was expected to produce their next laird. Catherine let her gaze roam idly over the yarrow, dog fennel, and medicinal lily.

A pity, she thought, she was so tired from her escape yesterday. When dealing with her husband, all of her faculties needed to be razor sharp. At the moment, Devon glowed as cheerfully as a lit candle. The long and exhausting ride yesterday had apparently only served to invigorate him. He must have the hearty, unwithering constitution of a work ox.

Whereas she ached in every bone and muscle of her

body. All the places that had been merely sore yesterday, now throbbed with pain. It was not fair.

It was especially unfair if she was forced to deal with the subject of sleeping with Devon. Last night, after he'd left, she'd lain awake for hours wondering what would happen. What could she do? Not escape, not once they were inside the castle. After her one attempt, Devon would be twice as cautious about her. And if she couldn't run away from him, she was going to have to face the prospect of sleeping with him.

She glanced up at Devon, at the tall, lissome body. He looked like a man who knew exactly what he wanted and how to obtain it. Catherine tried to sift through her emotions about him, and came up with a confused tangle. He infuriated her. He wanted her, and she found that frightening. But he also made her laugh, and she enjoyed his company. And he was kind.

Kind. She winced. What would her father say if he could hear her describe Devon Macgowan as kind? And yet Devon was. His clansmen were glad to follow him. He was generous and patient with those under him, never asking the impossible, and frequently taking on unpleasant tasks himself rather than giving them to someone else. Even though it had been risky he'd agreed to bring Bess with them. Devon must have realized that Bess, as an old friend of hers and a member of her clan, might well try to help her. Catherine doubted that even her own father, glad-handed as he was, would have taken in Bess under similiar circumstances.

She said, "Don't any of your clan members care that I'm the daughter of Sheamus Craig? I'd have thought they'd dislike having me as the lady of the castle."

He shrugged. "No one remembers your father with any fondness, but they have no reason to hate you.

Doubtless they've been worried about my lack of children for years. They're ready to greet any wife of mine with joy."

"It's nice to be wanted," she muttered, dragging out an especially ugly weed. "At least now I understand why I was pulled out to the herb garden and told mournfully how untended it has been. They listened to my suggestions breathlessly."

"They wanted to show you how much a lady of the castle is needed. Hardly subtle." Devon looked at his wife. Dusty shafts of light dappled her like golden ornaments, and her dress was attractively mussed from her work. The morning air was heady with the musky scent of herbs and flowers and damp earth.

Last night, he'd blurted out that he meant to sleep with her. As, indeed, he had every intention of doing. He should have waited to make his announcement. He should have realized she was too exhausted to deal with such an issue then. He'd simply have to go slower. Court her. Then, when she was ready, and when she understood that she had nothing to fear from him, he could explain that he wanted her as his wife.

Devon said, "I came to tell you that I don't want you to escape. I never want you to risk your life the way you did yesterday. Not that you don't have the free run of the castle. Within the walls, you can rearrange things as you please, dig up every plant in my herb garden, do anything and go anywhere you like."

She turned, and noted four huge soldiers standing by the dovecote. "But I'm to have company everywhere I go."

"Aye."

"If you are this kind to all your visitors, I wonder that you ever have guests."

He laughed. He took one step toward her and for

one edgy second Catherine thought he was going to touch her. Instead he merely picked up the basket she'd held and handed it to her. "I must spend today hunting. As I'm sure you'll remember, there's a wolf pack close to the castle. Besides hunting down the wolves, I also need to bring in some game for the festivities later."

"Festivities?" She had nearly forgotten, but it had been close to Christmas when Devon took her prisoner. "You must mean Christmas. I've lost track of the days. When is it?"

"I'm afraid I wasn't referring to Christmas. We can't celebrate that holiday. The Kirk doesn't approve of any kind of display on religious days, so I could hardly give a feast and expect any of my more religious clansmen to participate."

Since Catherine had been in Ireland, she'd almost forgotten how strict the reformers could be. "What festivities, then?"

"New Year's eve. Surely no one could accuse us of being Papists for celebrating New Year's eve. I suspect that holiday must hail from some pagan ritual, not a Christian one." He shrugged.

"It sounds as if you'll be very busy."

"Yes. Because I have been away so long, first at court, and then off to find you, I am deluged with work that's been put off until I was home to oversee it. But what you're really asking is when will I be free to start sleeping with you."

She tilted her head to one side and studied him with her breathing a little quickened.

"You can sleep alone until I am finished with my duties and until you are recovered from your escape. In the meantime, you can do as you please, so long as you don't try to leave the castle. Then, afterwards—"

She knelt down in the soft, red dirt. Around her, rows of plants, many of them brown and dead now, due to the winter, spread out in neat lines. "Yes? What about afterwards? I suppose you are going to make more threats, and in the early morning, too, when you know I am too feeble to combat them?"

"Afterwards, sweeting, I hope you are feeling far from feeble. And I make no threats. As I have said, I will merely be sleeping next to you. If you find that disturbing, I suggest you ask yourself why."

He turned, and left her.

As it turned out, Devon was so busy that he was away from her for days. Catherine only caught glimpses of him. She saw him once in the thick of an argument between two tenants. Both men were walking in the courtyard, shouting at the top of their lungs, with geese and chickens scattering from their path like raindrops. She saw him again as he went out hunting. His hounds grouped around the legs of his stallion in a rollicking, yipping army. Once she spied him discussing his accounts with a clerk.

It wasn't until the fifth day that she had an opportunity to speak to him. Devon was leaving the castle, apparently, for he nearly crashed into her as he descended the narrow stairs.

His blue eyes swept over her. "Poor Catherine," he said as he took in her expression, "you must be bored, with nothing to do but watch other people. I'm sorry I've had to neglect you."

For the first time in days, she felt truly alive again. She smiled at him dazzlingly and said, "I'm not. Even being bored is preferable to your company."

"Which is, by inference, not boring but unpleasant? We'll see." Devon turned, and said to the men who had

130

followed him down the stairs, "Before we leave, I'm taking my wife for a ride."

"A ride?" Catherine repeated, feeling a quickening of excitement.

"Aye, if you don't mind doing it astride while wearing all those petticoats. I daresay not more than a few inches of your legs would show, and I swear not to look. At least not much. My men wouldn't dare so much as cast a glance in your direction." He raised his tone so that the other soldiers behind him could hear. "Since they know how handy I am with a sword."

She grinned at him. "I don't care about the petticoats. Not one whit!" Cooped up inside the solid grey walls of the castle, she could think of nothing better than a chance at some riding. Even being with Devon would be worth it.

Catherine followed him outside. It was a curious, pristine day. Winter should already have smothered the mountains in layers of white snow. Or, if not snow by this time, then at least rain should be running in rivers, should be hanging down the mountains in silvery dragon's claws to the lake.

Instead it was clear and cold. The pine trees shivered under an icy wind, a wind that flounced the edges of the lake and sent the horses' manes flying.

Devon had ordered a small, sturdy Scots horse for her. He asked, as soon as she was seated, "Shall we gallop?"

"Aye," she said, not caring that it would mean riding next to Devon, with a tail of his soldiers following them in hot trod.

"So be it," he said, and spurred his black stallion in the direction of the lake.

She followed him. They rode with the wind lunging

at them, their clothing tossed and whirled, the fast pace whipping the words from their mouths. Catherine let her hair tangle freely behind her, and pushed her mount to his limit, pressing her legs hard against the churning muscles of the horse, and urging him to use every ounce of strength.

He was no match for Devon's huge stallion, of course, but by the end of the ride, she thought she had given him at least some interesting competition. When they reached Caldwell again, she told Devon, through breathless pants, "Thank you! It felt wonderful."

"I'm glad you like to ride," he said. "So do I."

"Can we do it again?"

"Often," he said, and nosed his mount in a different direction, leaving Mouse and several other men as her guards.

She watched Devon for a long time after that, until he and his men were only dark motes moving on the rim of the horizon. It had been kind of him to take her out. And she rather thought he had done it only out of kindness, not from any attempt to soften her response to him.

What would it have been like if she had met Devon for the first time only a few weeks ago, and if there were no bitter past lying between them?

But there was no point to asking herself such questions. Nothing would change the past, or alter the fact that they were enemies. Nor was it likely that the future would bring anything to change them into something other than enemies, she thought.

Certainly they would never make love, as Devon wanted. She loved her brother and her father. How could she then make love with the man who had chased them from their home? The man who would take her to Edinburgh and exchange her for a pack of letters?

She scowled blackly in Devon's direction. Aye, that was another thing. How dare Devon imagine he could sleep with her and then send her merrily back to her father as if nothing had happened, like some trollop he could easily forget? Didn't he think she had some pride? No Craig could tolerate such a thing.

He would soon find out just how idiotic his idea was. She'd spent the time apart from him forming an argument against his sleeping with her that was so excellent, so logical, she knew it would sway him, when and if he ever found time for her again. Catherine told herself she felt happy about being left alone for so long.

Happiness ended one night later, when Devon entered their bedroom.

Catherine had been busy with preparations for the New Year's festivities. Although it was late in the evening, Catherine and a dozen other women continued their work of tying bells onto ribbons and making tinsel crowns. Strewn over chairs and tables and ladies' feet were odd bits of scarves, paper, fluted nut shells, and mock badges. The air was fragrant with the aroma of nuts roasting in the fireplace.

One young woman leaned toward Catherine and asked, "Do ye know what the laird intends by you? Forgive me for asking, but we have all been burning with curiosity. 'Tis common knowledge he hasna been sleeping in his bedchamber with ye."

Catherine slunk lower in her chair just as Devon stepped into the room. Moving like an arrow to its target, his eyes sought out Catherine. There was a moment of silence while the women gawked at the laird, and then back at Catherine. Finally Devon turned to the women and announced, a little lamely, "It's late."

The women all glanced slyly over at Catherine, who

was trying to muster an ordinary looking smile. None of the women said anything aloud. Giggling, whispering to themselves, they edged their way from the chamber.

"That," Catherine told Devon, when the other women were gone, "was most embarrassing."

"My coming into my own bedchamber?" he asked innocently, and walked over to the fireplace to warm his hands. "What on earth are you making?"

She held up an admittedly lopsided tinsel crown. "This is the coronet for the Lord of Misrule tomorrow night. Don't you dare criticize it. I've just spent the last hour creating it."

He narrowed his eyes at it. "Now that I take the time to examine it carefully, I can see that it is the most dazzling crown ever made. James himself has never had a better one."

She smiled at his gallantry. "Everyone was wondering whom you would name to be the Lord of Misrule this year." Catherine's father had never named a Lord of Misrule, that particular custom not being generally followed in Scotland. It was mostly an English practice. But she had heard of it and was delighted to have a chance to see it. The laird was supposed to name a mock ruler who would try to lead everyone astray—or at least into silly play and loud dancing and an orgy of overeating.

"I haven't given it a thought. I'm afraid I need a wife to remind me of such things."

She made her face carefully expressionless. Wife, again. He seemed to use that word with alarming regularity. The beeswax candles, heavily scented with herbs and perfume, suddenly seemed cloying, even stifling. "Why did you seek me out? Has whatever it is

134

that has kept you occupied for so long been completed?"

"Aye. Now I intend to devote myself to you." With a graceful carelessness, he took off his belt and tossed it onto the table, where it hung at a rakish angle. Then he started to undo the fastenings at his blue doublet.

The needle she had been using to sew with jabbed into her thumb, and she dropped it. "Just to me?" she asked faintly.

"Yes." Off came the doublet.

Catherine picked up the needle slowly. The last few days, she had been preparing herself for this moment. She'd outlined a fine speech to give Devon that would convince him to leave her alone. If he was going to take his clothes off—no doubt with the intention of going to bed with her—it was imperative that she change his mind immediately.

"Devon." Catherine folded her hands together. Keeping her eyes averted from the sight of him pulling off his linen shirt, she asked baldly, "Why do you want to seduce me?"

The shirt dropped to the floor. "What?"

"Why do you want to seduce me? 'Tis a simple enough question. Is it only because you find me desirable?"

"I am not in the habit of seducing women I find undesirable." He frowned, and then said, "I regret the way I told you about our sleeping together. It was clumsy. I should have been clearer. I—"

"Please listen, Devon." She brushed aside his remarks brusquely, since they didn't fit in with her argument. "Of course you only want to seduce me because you desire me. But you can't have thought out all the implications of our making love."

"The devil I haven't."

Catherine felt tempted to stamp her foot in irritation. These interruptions of his were ruining her fine speech. "No, you have not," she informed him curtly. "We can't stay married, not when the king is going to exchange me for some letters. I'll go back to live with my father, and we won't meet again. But surely you want a wife, and children. Yet we are tied. The only way out of that tie would be divorce or annulment. Divorce is nigh impossible to obtain without a powerful bribe to the Kirk. But surely an annulment wouldn't be so impossible for us to get. We could do it—could break the tie, so long as we never make love."

He gave a hoot of laughter.

"Well, we could! And how else will you ever have a marriage unless the two of us get an annulment? So, if sleeping together would rule out annulment, obviously, we should—"

"Catherine, are you ever going to let me get a word in?"

"That depends on what you want to say." But she fell silent.

Devon sat on the bed to remove his boots. He was naked from the waist up, and she could see the long, flat expanse of his chest, lightly dusted with brown-gold hair. His arms were leanly muscled, hard looking.

Devon said, "The possibility of losing an annulment with you doesn't bother me, for a simple reason. I want you as my wife. My wife, Cat. Not my mistress, if that is what you were imagining." He stared straight at her, his eyes a midnight color in the stark light. "I have no intention of ending this marriage. On the contrary. I want to see it begun. That was what I meant the night I told you I was going to start sleeping with you."

The earth seemed to shake beneath her. All her

nicely set up arguments crumbled like sand hit by a wave. She repeated numbly, "I see." But she didn't.

"Before you collect yourself enough to sling more arguments at me, let me assure you that I know we'll make a good marriage. We like one another."

"But what will you do when I go back to my father?" she cried. "Find another wife, or two? All you really want is a mistress. You know perfectly well you mean to exchange me for those letters. And if we make love before then, all we will do is destroy the possibility of our getting an annulment."

He had little left on but a pair of hose and his breeches. "Nonsense. I have no intention of ever letting you leave me."

She clasped onto the solid side arms of her chair. It was not solid enough. She seemed to be swimming weightlessly through a river, surprised and gasping. One after the other, Devon had pulled out all of her arguments from beneath her feet. And now, what did he mean? If she wasn't going to leave him, how could the king send her back to her father? Would Devon consider helping her father because of her? "Let me understand you. Will you let my father do as he pleases with the letters?"

There was a pause while the fire threw lazy waves of shadowed surf across his face and the wind whispered under the blue draperies. "No," Devon said at last. "No, I can't do that. I am committed to Scotland and to the king, and your father stands against us. I've pledged myself to recover the letters. But I still mean to keep you by my side."

She nodded, though her neck felt stiff. She should have known. He merely wanted everything. "I'm sorry, then, but I could never consider being your wife. In truth, there's no point in discussing it. I seem fated to go back to my father, and from there, to the nunnery again."

"A life that sounds dull as ditchwater. Certainly I mean to keep you from the convent, something you seem especially unsuited for. And when are you going to get into your nightclothes?"

"What?" She rolled her eyes up at him. "Do you mean in front of you?" Her voice had risen to a high-pitched squeak.

In reply, he began to undo the fastenings at his breeches. Her jaw dropped. She flung herself from the chair and strode over to the window. The wind must have leaked in behind the velvet draperies, for they billowed excitedly. She could feel the edges of the draperies shudder against her legs.

She glanced anxiously in the direction of her nightgown. It rested on top of the trestle table. How was she going to get into it without letting Devon see her? Careful not to turn around so she could see him, Catherine said, "I'm not yet sleepy. If you are, please go to bed. I shall stay up and finish the crown."

"No. It's late, and I want you in bed with me. Are you going to come by yourself, or do I get the thrill of undressing you myself and then carrying you to bed?"

Catherine scowled. She asked with considerable asperity, "Have you finished undressing yet?"

"Yes."

"Are you sensibly gowned in your nightshift?"

"No."

She all but ground her teeth. "What are you wearing?"

"Nothing. I never wear clothes to bed."

Catherine rolled her eyes at the ceiling. Worse and worse. A veritable sinkhole of awfulness. To be in bed next to him, with him naked! To mayhap roll over during the night and touch him! She asked, "Are you in bed yet?"

"Not yet."

"Well, go there! Please. Climb in and stay put for a second." She listened carefully to the sounds of someone rustling the bed linen and then the soft shush of a body weighting down the mattress.

Devon said, "Very well, I have complied. Now, do I get to watch you undress? I must tell you that I have been looking forward to this all day."

She went back to the chair and sat down to remove her shoes and hose. Once those were settled under the chair, she stalked over to the trestle table which held the silver candlestick. She snuffed out each candle, sending white feathers of smoke curling into the air. That effectively darkened the room, but it was still light enough for Devon to see her due to the fire from the hearth.

Picking up her nightgown, she drew it on over her head, and then, wearing it dangling around her like a blanket, she undressed under it. She could hear Devon sigh, heavily.

Once she had finished, Catherine walked toward him with feet that took each step with dragging reluctance. Devon rested smack in the middle of the bed. She noted accusingly, "You have not left me enough room to sleep."

"It's warmer if we sleep closer together," he explained with silky persuasiveness.

"I am quite warm enough," she said, refusing to allow her teeth to chatter in the chilly air. She drew the hangings and then slid beneath the sheets. The night had a crisp, bright hardness to it, and the fireplace smoked and flickered gold light into the darkness. Her heart skipped crazily.

For a moment, there was silence. Catherine had arranged herself on the far edge of the bed, as far away from Devon as possible. Devon, hovering between a desire to laugh and the desire in his loins, was considering what he should do. He didn't want to push her. She would have to come to him slowly, of her own accord.

Which was going to be painfully difficult for him. He could smell the delicate scent she wore, and feel the curve she made in the mattress. How, before heaven, was he going to stop himself from taking her? Already, he was hard with passion.

He slithered closer to her. "Catherine."

"Um."

"It might be pleasant to kiss one another before we go to sleep. If you want to go to sleep."

"I do not want to kiss you! Stay away from me, Devon!"

"If there were a minister or priest here, you realize, you would be getting a scolding for refusing your wifely duties."

She stared stonily ahead.

"Cat, answer me this." His voice in the dark sounded like black velvet. "Do you really not want to be my wife? If there were no other problems, if your father didn't exist, or the letters, or what happened before, what would you say?"

She swallowed. "That isn't fair. All those things do stand in our way."

"And if they didn't? Answer me."

Catherine squirmed uncomfortably beneath the linens. He wanted an answer to the very question she was afraid to think about! If none of those other problems existed, would she want to be his wife?

He had grace and humor and intelligence. He was kind. She liked him. No, more than liked. Was attracted to him. Then she discarded that phrase too. None of them were right. The only other thing she could imagine was that she loved him—and that, of course, was not true.

And yet every time he was near, everything speeded up, became brighter. Her pulse leaped. She enjoyed their verbal sparrings as much as she feared them. If, perhaps, they had met recently, and had no earlier relationship, what would she think? That he was the most interesting man she had ever met? That she would like to be married to him?

None of which she could admit to Devon. "I don't want to discuss what could have been," she told him.

"So you don't want me?"

"No!"

"Shall we prove it?" he asked. "Prove it to me now. Let me kiss you. If you can call a halt, mayhap I will start to believe you."

"I don't need to prove anything." She pounded a hand into her pillow. "Now, if you would be quiet, I think I shall go to sleep."

"Catherine, I am only asking for one small kiss."

She said nothing.

"I'll stop as soon as you tell me to."

She felt his fingers slide up to her ears and tilt her face up to his. Her body seemed to have turned to stone. It wouldn't move. Yet she could feel the blood pounding through her in hammer strokes.

He urged, "Tell me you want me to kiss you."

"No."

"If you don't tell me, I'll be forced to leave you alone. And only think of how frustrated you're going to be, lying uncomfortably on the bed and wishing you had been more accommodating."

"I am not going to be accommodating!"

"Too bad." There was a pause. His hand slid down from her chin, trailing down her breasts and then even lower, until he had reached her abdomen. He spread his fingers out, so that he could touch the widest arc of her, and said, "I'm going to give you pleasure, Cat, pleasure that will make you shudder. Can you feel the desire that is between us, feel, at least a little, of the way it will be?"

She had gone very still, her eyes staring into the blue night. His fingers seemed to be curiously filled with warmth, a heat that spread down her legs and up to her breasts. Under her nightsmock, her nipples tightened deliciously, pleasurably. He moved his hand, caressing, over her abdomen, and she nearly sighed aloud at the altogether alarming and altogether wonderful sensations he aroused. What would happen next? And what should she do?

But Devon did nothing but drop his hand away, and slide to the other end of the bed. There was a moment of silence, and then he said, "Sleep well, wife."

She pulled the covers up to her chin. Sleep well, indeed! Doubtless she wouldn't sleep a wink all night.

Into the quiet, Devon dropped one word. "Tomorrow."

Not a single wink.

Chapter Nine

THE GREAT HALL WAS A RIOT OF COLOR AND NOISE AND people when Devon was informed that a messenger awaited him in the solar.

Devon left the New Year's eve festivities with a set, grim face. He had already guessed what the messenger brought, and he was already angry about it. Once he had reached the sun room, Devon shut the door behind him quietly, and then turned to look at the messenger. He was a young man with a thin, sallow face, his doublet and breeches mud-spattered and his dark hair ruffled by hard riding.

Devon said, "I daresay you are from the king."

"Yes. I bring you this." He held out a letter with the royal seal on it.

Devon took the letter and dismissed the man with a curt nod. Once he was alone, Devon flipped the letter over between his fingers, unwilling to read it just yet.

He walked to the window and stared out at the lake below.

They were setting up the wood for the bonfires later tonight. Laughing and calling out, a dozen of his clansmen busied themselves with the task. It looked as if it would be a clear evening, although a fine haze hung over the water, drifting restively over the lake like white smoke. Far beyond stood the strong Highland mountains, their outlines spiky with clustered pine trees. And over everything, flooding everything, was the tender, burnished gold of the setting sun. Which, all too soon, night would extinguish.

Someone outside wanted to know the time. He didn't hear the reply, but the words recalled Devon to the present, and the fact that he had crumpled the letter in his hand. He stared down sightlessly at it for a second, and then, impatient at last, he tore it open and read. Just as he had expected. The king had arranged for a meeting with Catherine's father. The king ordered Devon to bring Catherine to Edinburgh as soon as possible for the meeting. Where, presumably, Catherine would be given to her father in return for the documents.

Devon had never allowed himself the luxury of displays of temper. Yet now he tore the letter into shreds, and then threw the pieces into the fire. He watched until it was reduced to ashes.

That done, he strode out of the solar in a cold and anxious fury. Fury with himself and with the situation. He knew he should never have become interested in Catherine, should never have grown close to her or held her in his arms. He'd seen all the dangers ahead. He'd known exactly what was to come. And yet he had gone on, like some daft moth drawn to the flame.

Everything about her seduced him. The long drift of

mahogany hair, the red mouth, the full curves of her breasts. He had only to look at her to feel the need for her aching within him. He had never wanted another woman with such yearning. The other night, when he had held her, it had taken every ounce of self-control to stop.

But more than his passion for her, there was another quality about her, hard to define, and yet . . . She had something of her father in her, in the vividness of her presence. But she stood head and shoulders above Sheamus in everything else. There was something about her soul, the loving spirit that was in her and the gritty courage that made her try running out into the forest when she was frightened near to death of doing it.

He could not let her go. Could not bear the thought of never seeing her again.

But by all that was holy, what was he to do now? The king expected him to give Catherine back to her father. Back to Sheamus. Where she would be lost to him.

Devon uttered a low and violent curse and swung up the stairs with his boots slamming onto the steps. He had no intention of giving her up, if for no other reason than he couldn't send her back to constant danger and flight, not even back to that poor convent, to a life of silence and prayer and contemplation.

He had counted on making love with Catherine before they left for Edinburgh. No, more than that. He had counted on her learning to care for him. Once they were truly married and had come to trust one another, even if Catherine did return to Sheamus, she'd come back to him. At least he had hoped so. Hoped with a kind of fevered desperation.

But it all had happened too fast. Although he'd sent off a messenger to the king as soon as he arrived in

Aberdeen, he hadn't thought the king would be able to arrange matters with Sheamus so quickly. He'd expected to have at least another week with Catherine.

There was only one thing he could do. He could try to seduce Catherine tonight, try to bind her to him before they left.

Devon pushed open the oak door to the great hall. The first person he spied, standing near the dais, was his wife. She was talking to Mouse. She stood straight as a fawn, her head tilted to one side, her dark hair drawn into two mahogany wings from her face.

"Catherine." He realized she couldn't hear him over the cacaphony of noise from the crowd, so he walked closer.

As soon as he was within earshot of her, he could see that the excitement of the night had captured her, for her face was bright as a new coin. "What have you and Bess been doing?" he asked.

"Bess? Nothing. She thinks all of this is heathenish. She was so upset she volunteered to watch some of the babies for the other women rather than attend. Never mind that." Catherine cried to him, "You still haven't crowned anyone the Lord of Misrule! Everyone's been waiting for you. We all want to eat, and how can we have dinner without a Lord of Misrule?"

"Ah, yes." She held a tin crown in her hands, sparkling as if it were real in the blaze of lights. He took it from her and placed it on his head. "This year, I will be the one. And you shall be my lady."

She gave a giggle, and batted ineffectually at his hand when he picked up the second tin crown to put on her head. "Devon! That isn't right! You're supposed to choose someone raucous and silly, someone to lead us all to folly."

"To lead us to folly? Tonight, there is no one better

for that than me." He noted that she wore a plain blue dress, with a plaid bodice that fitted tightly against the full curves of her breasts.

Hot images filled his mind of what he wanted, of removing her clothing, piece by piece, until she was naked. Of their bodies entwined, of his lips roving over her body. He wanted her to cry out to him to take her, to merge their bodies until they were truly man and wife. He wanted, more than anything else, her acceptance. Her caring. Her arms holding him. Tonight . . .

She had her hands on her hips. "How are you going to lead us astray?"

He kissed the tip of her nose, in plain view of hundreds of his clan, and didn't care that everyone was gaping at them. "Wait and see," he told her.

He led her to the dais. Down from the wide trestle table where they would be seated, the long lines of other tables stretched, reaching all the way to the end of the hall. Nearly every member of his clan, every tenant and friend, was already in the hall. They had all worked hard during the last year, and now, for once, everyone was ready to play at childish games, laugh at silly jokes, and dance and eat until they dropped.

Light glowed and flickered and sparkled over everything, for all the oil lamps and candles and rush lights had been lit. There was a smoky warmth, thrown off by the hundreds of people jammed into the vast room, by hot food and the smudgy heat cast from the cavernous fireplace. The benches were jostled by people trying to find a space to sit down and eat from the enormous feast. On every table, there were wooden bowls tied with ribbon, bowls which were swimming with wassail.

The noise, ringing back from the ancient rafters, was almost deafening. Hundreds of men, women, and children, all speaking at once, created a babbling roar.

"Pass the jug."

"Is that brawn? Ah, now. I hope to have some."

"Hoo! I have never seen so much food."

"'tis a long drought. I'm glad the laird declared the feast."

As laird, Devon had to share his wealth with his entire clan. Tonight he did it beautifully. The thirsty could choose from hot spiced ale, imported sweet wine, and home brewed aqua vitae. The hungry could choose from bowls of new sowens, smoked and fresh salmon, roasted fowl in sauce, oatcakes, brawn, venison, tarts, a huge meat pie carried in on its own cart, pears cooled in a candy sauce, bowls of frumenty, puddings thick with sugar and cinnamon, grouse, boar, cheese, fruit jellies, haggis, toasted apples, and cakes glazed with raisins and walnuts and honey.

Just as Devon was about to seat Catherine next to him, a young woman jumped up from her place at the table to shout to Catherine, "If ye're to be the Lady for tonight, ye canna sit down! They're waiting to bring in the peacock."

Catherine looked at Devon, who only laughed, remembering the enormous bird he'd brought up from Aberdeen. "Go," he told her, and watched as she vanished in the direction of the kitchens.

A few minutes later, she reappeared. Catherine pushed a low wooden cart. On top of it sat a large, roasted peacock. Once the bird had been cooked a glossy dark brown, the tail feathers had been stuck back in, and now they bobbled at Catherine's face as she wheeled the cart toward the dais.

As soon as she had reached him, Devon slid gracefully from his chair, and plucked out one of the peacock's feathers. Then he knelt in front of Catherine. She

148

gaped at him, astonished, so he hissed at her, "This is what I am required to do, wife—stop looking at me like that! I'm supposed to pledge myself to you."

Her eyebrows rose. "Indeed? Verily, your proper place is at my feet, and if you wish to know what to pledge me," she airily informed him, "I rather think I'd most appreciate all your money and your lands."

He smiled, and then, in a much louder voice, so that everyone could hear him, he pronounced, "I pledge, to this my lady, not one of my worldly goods." Catherine exploded into laughter, and he went on, ignoring her, "Unless she accepts my heart, too—"

"On a platter, mayhap," Catherine said.

By now the hall was filled with people shouting and hooting suggestions for more pledges. Devon continued doggedly, "And unless I can have her body."

There was a wild clamor of hilarity behind them, made all the more riotous because everyone had heard the rumors that the laird had spent last night with his wife. Speculation about what had occurred had been so overwhelming that Catherine had heard people talking about it in the halls. She went red, and then scowled down at Devon. He rose to his feet and made an exaggerated bow at her before they sat down again.

The meal went on for hours. While the storyteller droned on in the background, telling the history of the clan, Devon was kept busy naming various people to be the members of the court, with the most important members being the Fool and Sir Prankster. Everyone he named had to don lime-green blankets. The blankets were thrown over shoulders as livery, with mock, paper badges of the lord stuck to them. There were tinsel rings to put on fingers and ribbons with bells tied to them to wrap about legs.

Then, at last, the festivities moved outside. Boisterous young men shoved open the thick doors of the castle, and the crowd of people spilled out onto the hills, with the wind lifting their ale-stained clothes and freshening their faces. There was the tinkle of bells, coarse jokes, and shouts of, "To your health, then!" as the men continued to drink from bowls and flagons.

Devon took Catherine's hands and pulled her against him to walk outside. Her cheeks were flushed from the spiced ale she had drunk, and she leaned against him without trying to pull away, her hair soft against his chin.

He whispered in her ear, "What shall we do to misbehave?"

"Devon." She shook her head, but she was smiling.

"What folly shall we commit?" His hand tightened its grip about her waist, drew her so close that the soft swelling of her breast pushed against his chest. They moved out of the great hall and into the open meadows, where the air flew at them, cold and heavy with the scent of pine, and the starlight dazzled in a cup of black. The loch had a skirt of lush moonlight. "I know what folly I plan on doing. Shall we go upstairs? I can tell you about it there."

She tilted her head, and her long lashes cast feathered shadows on her cheek. "Just how wicked do you mean to be?"

"Don't you know?" His voice was husky, laced with a strong yearning. "I want to make love to you. Tonight."

In front of them, the torches were put to the piles of wood, and the bonfires sent out a roar of red flames. There were shouts and a few of the children began to jig around the fires. Some parents must have ignored the reformer's disapproval of Christmas gifts, for one young girl held a new wooden doll and an older boy tooted on a shiny horn. Above all the other thunderous noise was the hilarious discord of the bagpipes, the pipers booming their hearty music into the thin, streaming night air.

Catherine said, "Do you really expect to make love to me tonight? The wine hasn't made me that fuzzy."

"I don't want you fuzzy. Only willing." But all the hot ale and the cups of wine had loosened his own tongue. "I want you . . . want to take off your clothes and kiss you and touch you until you tremble with desire."

"No." But the word was spoken faintly, and snatched away by raucous music and the hissing of the fire.

"Nothing that you can say will dissuade me." He bent his head to breathe in the sweet scent of her hair.

"Not tonight." She leaned a little against him, and let him slide his hand around her waist, her petticoats and hem fluttering against his legs.

Just then his tacksman came up to them, and asked to know what the Lord of Misrule ordered for the evening's entertainment.

"Let's have at dancing," Devon announced, his arm possessively around his wife, "and then let's have at games with the lasses."

The lutes began, their pretty, high-pitched notes in colorful contrast to the bellow of the pipes, and people began to play the horns and beat the drums as well. The music made the vast, star-dazzled night seem friendlier and closer.

Someone brought out a cowhide, and a rowdy young man was chosen to wear it. It was an old custom, so old that no one knew the meaning of it. But every New Year's eve, a young man was chosen to wear the cowhide, and then he was chased around the castle with everyone following after him carrying straw whips to flail the mock beast with.

And there was dancing, as Devon had said. Devon grabbed Catherine and began to pull her around and around, his hands too strong for her to fall even though she told him she was afraid she might. The dress whirled, and her laughter, breathless, joined his. Next to them, the bonfire was a rickety city of blackened spires, sending out dazzling bits of fire and ash which were taken up by the wind in giddy waves.

Devon said they should play shoe-the-mare. He chose Catherine to be the mare, and everyone chased her to try and shoe her. She ran among the pines and then back to the bonfire, shrieking, with Devon always inches away. He caught her, and yanked her against his hard chest.

And, then, although he was supposed to take off her shoe and tickle her, he grabbed her close to him, so close he could see the wind-pinked length of her nose. He bent down and kissed her. It was no swift brush of the lips, but a full, fair kiss that lasted until Catherine thrust her arms between them.

"Devon," she wailed, "everyone is staring at us!"

"Everyone," he lied, "is far too busy singing and dancing to care about us." He kissed her again and said, "It's time for bed."

Catherine let him lead her back inside and up the stairs to their bedroom. Since most of the others were still outside, they climbed the stairway alone, the oil lamps throwing violet shadows on the stone walls. Once they were inside the bedchamber, Devon shut the door and the noise from below vanished. They stood alone in a silent, dusky room, with only the wavery light from the hearth to see by.

She walked to the side of the bed she had slept on last night and began to unpin her hair. The dark, glossy curls fell to her shoulders. Her hand reached for the fastenings at her sleeves, and then stopped.

"Catherine?"

She closed her eyes at the sound of Devon's voice. What was she going to do? She'd been careful to avoid drinking much ale, yet, abstemious as she had been, something had possessed her making her head swim. Her legs felt as though they might buckle beneath her.

She wanted to blame it on the ale. She knew she could not.

All the last week, he'd been trying to talk her into sleeping with him. She'd countered every one of his arguments, but that hadn't meant that some of his statements hadn't sounded reasonable to her. In truth, as Devon kept insisting, they were man and wife. And if Devon could find a way to keep her with him, they might make a life together. It might even be the best thing she could do for her family and clan. As his wife, she could help her father, certainly more than she could at a convent.

But she had no time to consider. None at all. Devon intended to seduce her in just a few minutes. Without understanding why, she realized that tonight, he would make no attempt to leash the passion that was in him. All evening he had charmed her, made her laugh, teased her, touched her, until she could see only him, until her entire being seemed centered on him and only him. When he had kissed her during the bonfire, she'd felt an ache to kiss him back.

"Catherine?" He spoke softly.

"Yes?" Her heart seemed to be beating too quickly.

"I'd like to undress you."

She whirled about, and discovered that Devon was naked.

He said mildly, "You look shocked. Haven't you ever seen a naked man before?"

Catherine had taken one appalled glance at Devon and then jerked her eyes in the direction of the ceiling. Of course she had seen naked men before. But never in a circumstance like this.

Devon gave a low laugh. "Sweeting, tonight won't be so terrible. I promise. Nothing I will do tonight will be terrible."

She continued to study the ceiling. "Truly, I don't want you to touch me, tonight or any other night."

"No?" He sounded disbelieving. "Do you hate this, then?" His fingers grazed over the curve of her cheekbones, and down to her chin, tickling her a little. Moving with a leisurely thoroughness, his hand glided downwards until he had stroked both of her breasts. His touch was light, but Catherine could feel the response singing in her from head to toe.

"I'm going to make love to you," he told her with a calm, seductive determination, "because I want you and because you want me. Tell me the truth, Cat. What do you want me to do?" He cupped her chin and brought it down so that she was looking at him.

She didn't try to pull away from his clasping hands even though she had no idea what she should say. He wanted the truth, and she didn't know what it was. Unless it was that she did desire him, but that she was too afraid of the consequences to allow him to make love to her.

At last she said, "I don't think we should." That sounded weak, almost a confession of her yearning for him.

"Never mind what we should be doing. Let's explore what we want." He bent down, and kissed the middle of her brow. "What do you want?"

She made no response. Silently, he reached for the fastenings of her sleeves. He untied them and placed the sleeves on the table. Next came the plaid bodice with its pointed waist, and the overdress of linen, and the petticoats.

Catherine stood so close to him she could feel the heat from his body. At last, not able to stop her curiosity, she let her gaze drift over him. His body had a clean strength, a fine, leanly muscled hardness, with long legs and arms. There was a dusting of gold-shot brown hair on his flat chest. The hair trailed, in a long line down to his navel, and then beyond. Her eyes followed the line, unable to stop, until she had seen that he was already hard with desire. For her.

She took a step back. "Devon, no."

If he had noticed her glance, he made no comment. He only told her, "There is still your shift." He reached down to pull it off, and, with a throat-stopping slowness, drew it past her hips, her chest, and then over her head.

She stood naked in the flickering light of the fire, red highlights dancing over her pale skin. She watched Devon's eyes roam over her, moving from the fair shoulders down to her breasts, which were round and tipped with rosy crests. Her waist curved in before the flare of her hips. Then Devon's gaze dropped past the fresh skin of her abdomen to view the dark, downy curls between her legs.

"Cat." The word was muffled. He swung his arms around her and carried her to the bed, where the moonlight poured like seafoam over the glossy brocade and velvet. He laid her down upon the blue covers. The blankets were cold, and she gave a little gasp, but Devon had lain down next to her, and pulled her against his body, so that they touched chest to chest, and leg to leg, and suddenly she no longer felt cold.

Instead, a heat flushed her. Every part of her grew warm. It was strange to be this close to a man. It was a shock to feel him against her, to feel the hair-roughened chest against her smoother one, to feel the strength in his body, to put her hand on his hip and realize how silky his skin was there, and even, through the hammering of her heart, to feel his manhood against her. It pressed insistently against her abdomen, hard, urgent, and wanting. Her breath came in quicker draws, betraying, she was afraid, her reaction to him.

He kissed her lingeringly, his lips moving from her cheeks to the lobes of her ears and then down the line of her chin until he reached her lips. Nibbling gently on the lower edge of her softened mouth, he moved against her, his hips pushing into tighter proximity to hers. He outlined her lips in small kisses, as if he wanted to learn their shape through touch, until, with the utmost patience, he claimed her mouth. It was a tentative, searching kiss, light and caressing, with Devon waiting for a response from her.

Catherine tilted her head back to help him meet her mouth. Her body was already languid and rich with desire, a slow, melting desire that made her yearn to give in. Her body tingled. She wanted him, wanted to feel him, just once, to know what it was like to make love to him. She could no longer deny that desire to herself.

Yet she knew she wouldn't let him make love to her. She could not give in to him. More than any other reason, she feared making love with him because she knew that, if she did, she would be lost forever. The attraction between them was so deep and powerful she would be caught up in it, would fly up like a bit of ash from the bonfire, consumed by him. She was afraid if she let herself love him, it would be with a love so strong she'd never be able to leave him. He'd be part of her forever.

Yet she kept kissing him, telling herself that surely she could enjoy herself for just a little longer without harm. She had every intention of stopping before long. In a few minutes. She knew that if she really objected, Devon would release her.

He kissed her again, his mouth assertive now, possessing her with a thoroughness that left her gasping. His tongue probed, and she parted her lips for him, and let him enter. The kiss grew longer and deeper, as they tasted one another, as his tongue moved rhythmically within, and his hand curved to the base of her back to draw her closer to him.

His body had half covered hers, but now he shifted so that he could trail kisses over her shoulders and throat, and then lower, on the upper curves of her breasts. He pressed heated, erotic kisses there, and she clutched helplessly at the bedlinens, lost and dizzy with passion.

Devon raised his head so that he could look at her. "Sweet," he muttered. "You are like wine."

Catherine inhaled raggedly and turned her face away from him.

Devon could sense her withdrawal before she said anything. He knew that she was not ready for this. She didn't trust him yet. Although he never meant any harm to come to her, she doubted him. Nor was she certain that he meant to keep her with him as his wife.

157

He almost wished he didn't have to push her. He would have preferred to court her slowly, until she understood and accepted him.

But there was only this night for them, no more. And by now he was past the point of return. He wanted her with a passion that amazed him, it was so strong. A hot, demanding passion that made every inch of his flesh aware of her. The taste of her mouth, the heady scent of roses that clung to her, the dark halo of her hair, the softness of her body, all were driving him to a need of her that was so raw, so urgent, he doubted he could pull back from her no matter what the reason.

She put her hands between their bodies, apparently to stop him.

Without thinking, he said, "I love you."

Catherine stared at him. Devon guessed she was as surprised as he was. Where had the words come from? He'd never spoken them to any other woman, and hadn't asked himself before this if he loved Catherine.

But it was true.

The realization struck him, like the hitting of just the right chord, as absolutely correct. The truth is narrow, and hard, and when it fits, it fits with an exactness that leaves no doubt. He loved her, loved all the strange mixture that she was, the ready, giving warmth, the way she held her head when she talked to him, her needle-sharp conversation, the sweetness and the strength of her, her courage and her fears.

And if he should ever lose her—but he never would. He'd never give her up now, no matter what the cost. Aye, never. She was his wife, in the most primitive and absolute of senses, and he wanted all of her, not only her body. He wanted her to love him back, to accept the fact that she was his wife, and would be, forever.

His finger brushed back one dark curl from her cheek, feeling the silkiness of it, and of her. He couldn't see the color of her eyes in the dim light, but her mouth was a dusky rose, parted, ready for him.

She didn't know it now, but she would love him. He vowed it. Once, she'd told him he was lonely. Perhaps she had been right. Perhaps, in all the busy, endless circles of his life, he had needed one center, one person to fashion his life around.

"Cat, sweet, sweet, Cat, I love you." He buried his head in the tangle of her mahogany hair upon the pillow, and felt her body relaxing against his. Her arm came up around him to draw him closer. That small signal of acceptance on her part stimulated him as nothing else could.

He pushed her hands away from his chest, and turned his head to kiss her again. He kissed her as he had never kissed anyone before in his life, with a fierce and blinding wonder, with all his love for her and his passion for her in his hands and mouth. Her lips moved against his, and then opened, and he thrust his tongue within. The taste of her was as warming as wine.

Drifting, his hands fell across her body. He learned the pattern of her throat and the sleek length of her legs, the slight rise of her abdomen. His fingers explored each bend and curve of her, bringing desire and delight. Moaning, she tossed her head. His hands and mouth caressed her until he was certain that her need for him matched his.

His hands slid down to cup her breasts. He ran his fingers over them, marvelling at their velvet texture, at their softness, at the stiffness of the dark centers. The nipples pouted with desire. He grazed his thumb across one small tip, and it firmed deliciously at his touch. He tickled at it with his fingers and felt it grow swollen and tight. At the realization of how he was arousing her, he began to rain kisses over her bare skin.

Enticingly, he brought his mouth down upon the nipple. He took it between his lips and licked at it with an erotic slowness, easing the ache that he knew was in her, and strengthening it. He drew it into his mouth and sucked on it until she trembled beneath him. Then, his hands moved in revolving circles down her hips, grazing even lower, until he had reached the womanly junction between her thighs. When he attempted to slide his fingers within, she stiffened, momentarily frightened by the strangeness of having someone touch her there.

He whispered huskily, "Don't be afraid. There are no secrets between us any longer, and what I am going to do will only give you pleasure."

This time when he brought his hand, caressingly, to her soft inner curls, she parted her legs a little and let him enter. He was kissing her again, kissing her breathless.

He explored the moist warmth between her thighs tenderly until his fingers settled upon a spot so sensitive that the lightest touch made her tremble. His fingers played there, and Catherine cried out in pleasure. A tightness built in her. A tight, tingling knot that contracted and contracted, sending waves of aching pleasure through every vein in her body. It built until she could hardly bear it, and then the knot came undone, and a jolt shook her, in waves.

Now, with her body throbbing and open, Devon positioned himself over her, his manhood probing at the soft inner flesh. He found he could wait no longer. "I love you," he told her again and moved inside her.

He met the resistance of her virginity, and thrust within. She flinched in sudden pain, and he held himself still, not moving, until he thought the ache had sub-sided for her. He wanted her so badly that it strained every ounce of his self-control to remain patient.

When, finally, he felt that she was ready, he drew his hands under her hips, and began to move within her. She had no idea of the rhythm, but his hands guided her. Soon she clasped hard at his back, and began to arch in response to his thrusts. He was saying some-thing to her, he had no idea what. Broken, thick words of desire and love. They moved faster, and he lost all sense of place, of time, of anything but her and the wonder of moving within her. Pleasure throbbed in him, mounting and mounting. Then she cried out his name, and he, too, reached his peak even as he felt the shuddery aftershocks of hers.

Afterwards, his hands roaming tenderly over her damp body, he told her, "Now we're truly man and wife."

She looked at him, but although he strained, he couldn't read her expression.

Chapter Ten

CATHERINE ENJOYED WAKING UP AS MUCH AS SHE EN-
joyed plague, famine, and other natural calamities. Yet
this morning she found herself wide awake at the first
hint of dawn. Perhaps it was the unaccustomed weight
lying on top of her that had aroused her, for she
discovered Devon still asleep and sprawled across her,
his head nesting on her breasts, one tanned, hard leg
thrown over her body.

Memories of last night rushed in upon her, making
her smile shyly. She'd had fantasies of what it would be
like to be married. Vague, romantic fantasies about
bodiless people kissing and swooning with delight.
Reality had proved it to be noisier, warmer, heavier,
damper, and far more satisfying. She'd really had no
idea of how utterly physical it could be.

Devon claimed to love her. She'd wanted to believe
him last night. It had been easy to believe him with the
excitement of the celebration and the wine making her

dizzy. Now, in the clear, chilly light of morning, she remembered how her father had always said Devon would lie to get what he wanted.

Had Devon been telling the truth? She longed to believe it. Before heaven, she'd never ached for something so badly in her life. All along, ever since they'd met, she'd been fighting an attraction to him. But nothing could stop that attraction from growing and building. Not that she loved him, Catherine assured herself quickly. Given their circumstances, it would be idiocy to fall in love with him. Yet she felt something for him, an attraction that came so close—no, it couldn't be love. She refused to be in love with him.

Yet they had consummated their marriage, and Devon had once told her he wanted her to live here as his wife. Catherine stared at the white shafts of light that poured in through the windows. If she and Devon lived together, she might be able to help her father and her clan. She glanced down at Devon's brown-gold head, picturing herself as the lady of Caldwell, settling here, making friends, overseeing duties, tending to their children.

A nervous, happy anticipation filled her at the possibilities for the future. To live in the Highlands again, and to have Devon love her. A shiver ran through her, not entirely caused by the chilly morning air.

Her slight movement must have awakened Devon, for he stirred suddenly, and his eyes opened. "Catherine," he said.

"Mm?" Now that he was awake, she hardly knew how to act or where to look. She'd given in to him completely last night, had behaved, she was afraid, like a wanton. What would he think of her?

Devon shifted so he could see her better. He propped his head upon his hand. There was a pause, while they both stared at one another in the dim, pearly light. She couldn't read anything in his expression. Finally, when he spoke, all he said was, "Good morning, wife. You were heaven last night." The blue eyes, roving knowledgably over her body, left no doubt as to what he meant. "Much more delicious than the feast."

"Mm." No intelligent response to his words occurred to her. And was he really going to discuss what they had done last night? She wasn't up to it. Not now, not ever.

"I've never slept with a woman who excited me so much, or who pleasured me so greatly." He paused, to wait for her reply.

Once again, she couldn't think of any. How was a woman supposed to respond to a compliment about her lovemaking? If there was a way, she hadn't learned what it was, not at the convent. Staring at the draperies with great interest, she said in a small voice, "Oh."

Devon went on, his words husky with remembrance, "It's rare for two people to be so compatible as lovers the first time. And we were certainly more than compatible. I was delighted you enjoyed yourself so much."

Mortified, Catherine dragged her gaze from the draperies to look at him. That was when she realized that Devon's brown eyebrows were raised in amusement. He was smiling. He knew perfectly well he was embarrassing her. "I'd like to change the topic of conversation," she announced regally, although her grand manner was hindered by the fact that she was naked, and lying beneath him.

"Very well, no more talk about lovemaking. You have the most beautiful breasts I have ever seen." He brushed aside the covers to look at them again.

"That is not changing the topic of conversation!" she said, slithering a little lower beneath the sheets. She

164

pushed futilely at his hands, but he held them firmly cupped underneath her breasts. "I want to talk about something else. Something other than lovemaking, breasts, or anything—anything even remotely connected to them."

"What topic could be more interesting than this?" He nibbled on the soft flesh of her throat.

She opened her mouth to reply and realized she didn't have an answer for him. What, indeed, could be more interesting? A tingling began where his lips caressed her.

His fingers drifted over her throat lightly. He told her, "You're beautiful in the morning."

"Thank you." She recognized the thickness of his tone and knew he was becoming aroused.

"In truth, I find you lovely all of the time."

She smiled. "I'm beginning to get suspicious."

"You have reason to be. I was being charming for a reason." He reached his arm around her and drew her on her side, so that they were lying face to face, their bodies touching. He tightened his grip on her.

"But we just made love last night."

"Is that supposed to be an impediment? We've finally had our wedding night, and I enjoyed it so much, I'd like to try it again." He touched her cheek with his finger. "Don't flush. There's no need for embarrassment between us, not any longer."

"I am not embarrassed," she said untruthfully.

"No? Then I daresay you won't mind when I do this." He was looking at her, with his blue eyes intent upon her every gesture as he drew down the covers. The linens glided down from her body. Devon began to caress her. Catherine closed her eyes as he did so, yearning to ask him if he still loved her, or if he'd only said that to make her willing.

"Catherine," he said, and this time the word was muffled because he was kissing her breast. "My love, my sweet love."

Then he had no more words for her, for he reached up with his mouth to claim her lips. His hands stroked lightly, teasingly over her body. Catherine thought vaguely that she should protest, but all too soon, she didn't care about anything but what they were doing. Passion overwhelmed her, and she flung an arm around him to bring him closer.

Later, languid and warm, she lay curled up next to Devon. Her lids felt heavy, and she nearly fell asleep. Before she did, Devon nipped her on her shoulder. "Now you are truly mine, and nothing can ever be done to alter it."

"Do you think so?" she asked vaguely, thinking of the letters and her father.

Devon raised his head to look at her. The lines around the side of his mouth deepened. "Never," he said curtly, "imagine that you'll be able to leave me."

"You mean to keep me here forever, as your wife?"

"Yes." Then he brushed a hand over his face. "Wife," he told her, "I'm sorry, but we can't while away the entire day in bed."

"Why not?" She pulled up the covers, wanting nothing more than another hour of sleep.

"You like bed more than any other person I have ever met." He smiled at her, and added, "I daresay it bodes well for our marriage. Nevertheless, we must get up now." Devon sat up and pushed away the covers. He explained as he strode across the room to his clothing, "I'm needed downstairs. Besides, if we stay abed one more minute, we'll only feed the rumors that are flying about Caldwell as to the nature of our relationship."

She found it a pleasure to look at him. He thrust his arms into the overshirt and tied the points with quick, bold movements. It seemed strange to think that she would watch him like this, every day for the rest of her life. "Shall we never tell them?"

He glanced over at her. "They'll discover the truth sooner or later." Devon straightened the medallion about his neck, his thoughts on the day ahead. It would be a long, hard day of traveling, and they'd have to leave soon.

He'd avoided telling Catherine about the messenger who had arrived last night. He couldn't avoid it any longer. Fastening his dirk into his belt, Devon wondered about the best way to explain matters to his wife. He was reluctant to hear her reaction. Last night, he'd made sure that they became man and wife. He'd thought it would bind her to him permanently, and that, at the least, it would end his body's aching need for her.

Neither goal had been accomplished. As for the first, although he'd admitted to her that he loved her, Catherine had hardly reciprocated with a vow of undying love.

His fingers tightened on the wooden handle of the dirk. What did she feel? He couldn't understand why he wasn't able to read some clue in her words, or the way she held herself. Usually, he found it easy to read people's expressions. Understanding the people he dealt with was an art he'd had to learn early on. The difficulty was not that Catherine was a hard person to read; she was as straightforward as a schoolgirl. It was just that today he couldn't even guess at what she was thinking. Perhaps the very fact that it mattered so much to him made it impossible for him to fathom her thoughts anymore.

Why had she made love with him? Only because she desired him? Her pleasure had been real enough, not feigned, and she'd been willing enough again this morning. Yet, maddeningly, she hadn't given him any clue as to what her reaction had been when he told her he loved her. Certainly she hadn't responded in kind. Had she made love with him last night because she thought it would mean he wouldn't want to exchange the letters for her? Had she been using her body as a bribe? The thought jolted him. She hadn't said anything when he told her he loved her. Did it matter to her? Why hadn't she told him anything about her feelings and why had she questioned their staying together this morning?

He frowned. He couldn't bear to have her leave him, not now. Devon raised his head to stare at Catherine. She rested snugly under the covers. Above the softly curved lips and the frank, lucent eyes, her dark hair spilled in shining waves over her shoulders.

He remained perfectly still. Yet it felt as if there were a band of iron constricting him, pulling his chest tighter until he could scarcely breathe. Every ounce of him ached to love her and to have her love him back. He couldn't bear to lose her. Could not bear the thought of his life without her. What else would ever have meaning if she wasn't with him?

Making love to her hadn't solved anything. It didn't appear to have tied her to him, and it hadn't even managed to satisfy his desire for her. On the contrary. Now he knew exactly what he wanted, and what he had been missing before. He'd explored every curve and hollow of her body, felt her shudder in passion beneath him, and it had only increased his need for her. If they didn't have to leave immediately, he'd be ready to take her again right now.

But there was no more time for seduction, or to convince her to stay. He kept his face impassive when he said, "You had best climb from bed, Cat. We're leaving in an hour for Edinburgh."

She sat up, and the covers fell away, exposing one white shoulder. "Why? Has some message come about my father?"

"A messenger did arrive, but from the king. James has arranged to meet with your father in Edinburgh. The exchange will take place there."

She bit down hard on her lower lip. How dare Devon stand before her and speak to her so calmly of an exchange, when it meant they'd have to part! Pride added a sharp edge to her voice. "Indeed? I thought we were going to live as man and wife. Only a few minutes ago, you warned me that I'd never be able to leave you. Now you say we're not only going to be separated, but that you're taking me to Edinburgh, where I am to be given to my father. Afterwards we may never see one another again. What am I to think? If you mean for us to remain married, how can you go ahead with the exchange?"

Devon walked over to her slowly and sat down on the side of the bed. "I thought you understood. I've no choice in this matter. Those letters are far too important to Scotland. I can't do anything that might hinder the king from getting them back. But we are married. I hope you'll come back to me after the exchange for the letters. Of your own free will."

She tore her gaze from his face and looked at the fire. It seethed and sighed at her from the hearth. So, Devon had known, throughout their night together, that this separation was coming. There could be only one conclusion. He'd known it was their last evening in bed together, and, since he'd wanted her, he'd told her he loved her. That way, poor, addled fool that she was, she'd let him make love to her.

Catherine felt sick. The wine and food she had partaken of last night, as well as the early morning exercise with Devon, combined to send a wave of nausea to her throat. She lay back down against the pillow to quiet it. That made her head swim less, but nothing would quiet her troubled thoughts.

Had Devon lied about loving her? Did he really want to be married to her? She didn't know, and had no idea of how she could prove it, one way or the other.

The fact remained, he'd had every intention of sending her back to her father. Whatever reasons he gave her, allowing her to be sent away from him hardly sounded like the action of a lover. And the only consolation he offered her was that she was supposed to come find him after the exchange had taken place. She was to come back! She, a Craig, to come creeping back to him, hoping he'd feel like taking her in.

She said doggedly, determined to try and talk the problem through, "You claim you want me to return to you."

Devon stared down at her with a hard, set face. "Was that what I said? I meant that you'll return to me, no matter what. If you don't, I'll come and find you. There is nowhere on this earth that you can hide from me. Remember that, Catherine. You are my wife now. Nothing will change that. And I won't let you go. Not ever."

He sounded so fierce she nearly believed him. Before heaven, she wanted to. But all the early, fresh anticipation of the day was gone. She was anxious again, and the future was once more an unknown blank. Mayhap he did love her, and maybe he would come to find her,

no matter what. She hoped it was true. But he might
well be lying.

Catherine turned for one last glance at Holyrood.
Holyrood was the king's castle, and it was lovelier than
any building she'd ever seen. She and Devon had
arrived in Holyrood just over an hour ago. But there
was no time for a long look, for Devon had grabbed her
by the hand and was leading her into the city of
Edinburgh.

She asked her husband, "Why did you want to take
me out on this walk?"

He shrugged, "I probably shouldn't be taking you
out into the city, not even with all the men we're
bringing. But after the long journey to Edinburgh, I
thought you might enjoy a chance to see the city. In
addition, there was something important I needed to
show you."

Devon strode along High Street, looking thoroughly
in his element. The doublet of gold braid and embroidery on velvet suited him, as did the silk stockings. He
seemed every inch the famous, wealthy courtier.

Catherine felt miserably out of place. Although
Devon had presented her with an elegant court dress,
she'd insisted on pinning to it a huge crystal brooch
given to her by her father. To her dismay, it looked
crude against the gown.

She became even more conscious of how little she fit
in when she saw some of the court ladies walking past
them. They had powdered their faces and bosoms a
snowy white, and on top of the powder they had
painted false blue veins to make their skin look translu-
cently fair. They looked as worldly and mean as swans.

She didn't like the city, either. Edinburgh seemed

incredibly large and different. With its towered, spired, and multi-storied buildings of grey granite, the city flowed out on all sides around her, larger by far than Aberdeen. Tunnelled wynds and tall houses encroached against the sides of the second wall that had been built to enclose it. Far beyond the city stood the Firth, a wide, wind-whipped, white-capped expanse, with gulls and terns swooping overhead, and a spray rising from it, filling the air with a salty, tangy sea taste.

Catherine clung to Devon's arm as they walked. This was the first time they'd been together since they left Caldwell. They hadn't had any privacy while on the journey to Edinburgh. On the trip, when they stopped overnight, it was at a single-towered castle of Devon's. The tower had been crowded with the soldiers who had ridden with them. Catherine had to sleep in a tiny chamber on a pallet, with Bess and a few other women in the room and Mouse at the door, tirelessly keeping watch.

After they had walked for a while, Devon came to a stop. He gazed at her for a moment, and then said, "Look up the street."

Obediently, Catherine turned to look in the direction he had pointed. They stood on High Street, which Scots boasted was the widest street in the world, and which was paved in perfectly cut square stones. The street slashed through the city, reaching all the way up to the old castle. Between them and the castle was a clamorous confusion of people, store signs flapping in the wind, chimneys smoking vaporously, horses, vendors hawking their wares, and washerwomen. She couldn't decide what he wanted her to notice.

"I'm sorry," she told him, "but I don't see anything odd."

"Look at the two castles. At one end of High Street

stands Holyrood, where the king lives and where we're staying. Holyrood looks like an English castle. It has rows of large windows, decorations, and it is surrounded by gardens and a forest kept for hunting. Holyrood could never be defended against an enemy, nor was it ever intended to be. It was built only for comfort, elegance, and display. Now look at the old castle of Edinburgh, at the other end of the street."

She stared in the direction of the old castle. It was centuries older than Holyrood, a grim and battle-scarred veteran of a dozen wars, serious and dour and fierce as any Highland keep. No one could have said the old castle looked English. It was, in every way, impeccably Scots, even to the fact that it rested on a volcanic plug of earth, a plug with sides so steep it would be child's play to defend it against invaders.

Devon explained, "Take this street as a symbol of Scotland herself. Part of the country lies in the past, like the old castle. Especially in the Highlands, people live the way they did centuries earlier."

She shrugged. "And?"

He stared at her with a hard, earnest face, with the medallion he wore flashing in the sunlight. "And those constant clan wars and endless bickerings keep the entire country poor, divided, and unable to move ahead, as the English have done."

She protested, "Surely not. Why—"

"Cat! Listen. Just listen for a moment to the sounds around you."

All around them, people chattered away in English. It grated against Catherine's ears, even though, as a member of the gentry, she had been taught the language. But in the Highlands everyone spoke Gaelic, just as the Irish did. English sounded strange, as strange as some of the ways people here cut their hair

173

and wore their clothes. In truth, the entire city felt odd to her—unlike Aberdeen, which had been a Highland city. Here there were alien ways with clothing and manners and food, dialects with which she had no familiarity, and a difference which made her feel out of place.

Devon continued. "Did you hear it? Even in the way we talk we are divided. Can't you understand it's got to change, Cat? England is growing stronger and richer every day. The English have already invaded Ireland. Many times they have invaded Scotland as well. We've always driven them back; I don't think we'd be able to again."

She stared at his medallion, with its engraved nettle. "Do you truly think the English could overwhelm us?"

"Aye." He sounded grim. "When I was young, my father sent me abroad to the university. Later, after my father's death, I traveled to England. I know what I say is true, because I have seen it with my own eyes. The English are strong, much stronger than we are, because they aren't divided. If Scotland is ever to become a true country, to be able to feed and care for every person, we have to change."

"How?"

He made a small gesture with his hands, and the light caught and shimmered on his wedding ring. "Our king stands next in line to inherit the English throne. If he does, it will save Scotland from an invasion. We will have time to catch up with the English, time to change. That's what I am bound to, what I have been fighting for all my life. That's why James must succeed to Elizabeth's throne. Otherwise, we'll be a conquered people."

She shook her head, not wanting to admit any good

174

of having the hated English connected with Scotland. "Why did you want to explain this to me?"

He drew in a breath, and told her flatly, "I'm trying to explain to you why I won't allow anything to impede the succession. If it were anything else, Cat—if it involved money or my position, I would help you."

Now she did understand why he'd brought her here, and understood all too clearly. "If my father used the letters by sending them on to Queen Elizabeth, he could impede the succession." Her fingers tightened over Devon's. Her father had always called Devon an ambitious and unscrupulous man, and Catherine was now ready to acknowledge how wrong her father had been. Devon had supported the king out of duty to his country and to his people. She could understand that, even honor him for it, although she disagreed with his beliefs. And yet . . .

And yet it meant that he was going to send her away from him.

Devon slid his arm under her cloak to pull her tightly against him. "Now, I thought we'd spend a little while shopping. What would you like? Silk hose? An embroidered cap?"

They moved on, walking past hawkers calling out to them to buy their wares. Soon they were at the High Kirk of St. Giles, where the street was thronged with shoppers, children and vendors. The reek of food and animals hung in the air, and the area was a jumble of people and booths with blistered paint and bright ribbons jerking in the wind.

"Beef pasty!" One gnarled old woman thrust a pie close to Catherine's nose, filling her nostrils with the stinging scent of beef.

"Would the lass like a gold chain?" called out

another. "She'd be grateful to the man who bought her this."

"Sponge towels and horn combs! Watches!"

"What would the lady like? A book? Poems?"

Devon turned to her, "Just what I was about to ask. What, indeed, would the lady like?"

Catherine half smiled at him. A surge of emotion nearly closed her throat, it was so strong. What did she want? The problem was that what she wanted was for Devon to love her enough to risk anything, even the letters, for her. She wanted her father and brother to be able to live without fear in Scotland again. She wanted to be married to Devon and stay with him for the rest of her life. And none of those wishes was very likely to happen.

She reached out blindly to the booth in front of her, and picked up a cheap edition of a play, called *Romeo and Juliet*. "This," she said.

The next afternoon, Catherine had just tried on a new gown when Bess entered the room. Bess's red hair had been pulled back from her forehead and knotted under a crisp white and blue kerchief. Under the kerchief, her face was so pale the freckles stood out in bright relief.

Catherine took one look at her expression and swallowed the cheerful greeting she had been about to utter. Instead she cried, "What is the matter? Is it Devon?"

Bess limped painfully to the stool and sat down. She nervously wiped her hands on her apron. "No, not yer husband."

Her very hesitation filled Catherine with fear. "Please! What is it? I must know."

Bess picked her words carefully. "I canna betray ye.

Not when ye are of my clan, and my friend, as well. I know that ye saved me and my bairn. If ye had'na done so, we would have starved or been put into prison. But I do'na want to hurt the laird either." She sighed, and pulled out a leather packet from the folds of her apron. "I was given this."

Catherine was more mystified than ever, but she prodded, "Yes? Someone gave it to you?"

Bess gave a sharp nod. Finally she got out, "'Tis from yer father."

Stunned, Catherine reached down and picked up the packet. She longed to open it immediately, but she didn't dare unseal it in front of Bess, who was already so concerned about her divided loyalties.

Catherine clutched the packet to her chest and said, "Bess, please don't worry. It was kind of you to bring this to me. I can understand why you're worried about having done something to hurt Devon. Don't be. I can't believe that anything in this packet, no matter what it is, will harm Devon. Nothing could; his position is too secure. More—even if it could—I wouldn't allow it to happen. But my father could be hurt, and I could, by Devon or the king. And mayhap what you have brought me will save us."

Bess shook her head, still unsure. But she collected the dishes she had come to pick up, and then turned, and, after a long look, left the room.

Catherine waited until she was certain Bess had gone. Once she heard her footsteps fade away, Catherine yanked open the fastening and drew out what was within. Inside she found a dozen fine vellum letters tied together with an expensive, embroidered red ribbon. A ribbon with the king's seal on it.

Catherine stared at them open-mouthed. Before heaven, why had she been sent the letters that the king wanted so badly? It made no sense at all. Had there been a mistake of some kind?

But then she spied another letter, buried among the other ones, that had not been written by the king. This letter was written on cheap paper in her father's bold, round handwriting. Quickly, she drew it open and unfolded the paper, her eyes hurriedly scanning the words.

She read it once, then once again, still hardly able to believe what was there. Apparently her father didn't trust the king or the king's promise of an exchange. The only person, her father wrote, the king would not suspect of carrying the letters would be her. Her father bade her keep hold of the letters until the exchange. Then, if it went forward without any trickery on the king's part, she could hand the letters over to the king.

It was mad. It was reckless. It was so exactly the sort of thing her father would do.

Catherine put everything back into the packet and tied it to one of the petticoats she wore. Then she raced to the door, and flung it open. Two of Devon's men stood outside. She asked them to send Bess up to her again.

She sat down at the desk, blessing the fact that Devon had left his writing equipment out. There were a quill pen, sand, wax, and loose papers for her to use. She grabbed the pen and began to write to her father. Her father had to know that she didn't want to go back to him. There was no point in an exchange. She wanted to remain with Devon. And her father wanted her back only because he was afraid of what the king might do to her. But Devon would protect her from any real harm, she explained, so it would be far better for her father to use the letters, now, and not worry about her.

She was signing the letter when the door suddenly swung open. Devon stood in an arc of bright light.

Catherine shoved her hand over the letter she'd been writing, the blood pounding through her in uneven strokes. Was her sleeve full enough to cover everything?

If Devon noticed anything, he didn't mention it. He merely said, "Put on your cloak. The king has arranged for the exchange. We leave in a few minutes."

Catherine slid the letter she had been writing into her palm, and then, as surreptitiously as she could, she tossed it into the fire. It flamed for a moment, and was gone.

There was no chance now. Nothing she could do.

She could only hope that her father had been right to send the letters to her.

Chapter Eleven

A COLD, LATE AFTERNOON WIND SHOOK THE GLAZED windows in their panes and sent the red damask draperies fluttering. It made the edges of Devon's cloak dance as he paced anxiously from the window to his wife, and then back again. They waited in an anteroom just outside the king's bedchamber. In a few minutes, they had been told, the king would finish dressing and come and greet Devon.

Devon frowned. In a short time, he was supposed to give Catherine up to her father—and he simply couldn't do it. In the war between his duty and his love, his love had won. Before heaven, he was not going to let her go, not now that he had found her.

The only question was how he was going to prevent it. He had no idea, and wasn't even certain if it could be prevented. He only knew he had to.

Devon glanced at Catherine. She was frightened, but she'd marched into this room looking every inch the proud Highland lass, her dark hair swept cleanly under a flat blue cap, her straight-backed stride in sharp contrast to the painted and perfumed courtiers who had stared at them as they walked here. She was the only thing that looked real to him in all the grandeur of Holyrood, of rich brick and stone and walls so cut with tall windows that it almost seemed as if there were no walls. The rooms were all light, all shining rich materials and expensive furnishings.

Catherine stood with her hands clenched about the gloves she'd brought for their ride, and above the white ruff she wore about her neck her chin formed a mutinous line. He supposed she was planning on telling the king precisely what she thought of him.

A pity, but he couldn't allow that. He would have enjoyed watching her speak her mind, but this was not the time. Devon walked to his wife and bent so that his mouth rested against her ear. The two liveried servants who stood at the entryway to the anteroom couldn't hear when he told Catherine, "When you meet the king, be pleasant. Restrain any natural impulse on your part to call him names. And when he comes in, kneel before him."

Her brows flew together. "Kneel to the man who ordered—"

Devon sighed. There was no time to explain to her what only someone who'd known the king for some time would have learned—that the one thing King James needed was to feel that he was a man, and in control. He required that reassurance because, in fact, he was weak. Devon, who had been at court many times, understood well that a situation in which the king was made to feel ludicrous—as now with the letters—made him spiteful, and therefore dangerous.

He explained, "Cat, believe me, it wouldn't be wise

to do or say anything that might put James in a foul temper. He doesn't like women overly much in the best of circumstances. He can barely tolerate his own wife's company. Given your background and your father and the circumstances, he's bound to like you even less. And this is not the time to have him angry, not when the king is taking us to meet with your father. If ever you wanted James to feel forgiving and generous, this is the moment. Now. Be clever and do as I tell you."

She bit on her lower lip. "Do you really expect me to be polite to him?"

Devon cast a faintly exasperated glance at her. Again he leaned close enough to her so that the two servants couldn't hear his comments. "If you want to help your father, treat the king as if you were in awe of him."

Before she could protest any further, Devon cut off the conversation by moving over to the window. He stood by a cupboard with rondel carvings, his face implacable, his thoughts on how he could prevent Catherine from being taken away from him. Restively he picked up a gilt bowl enriched by chased enamel, and then set it down with a click on the polished table.

Catherine felt soundly put in her place. Devon had never spoken to her so curtly before. She played with the gloves she held, thinking that perhaps Devon was right about her kneeling to the king. "What is James like?"

Devon turned. He regarded her with wry amusement. "Does this strike you as the place to discuss it?"

It was the second time he had rebuked her, and she dropped her gaze from him and fell silent. She supposed she understood what was making Devon look so fierce. Behind them were the servants, and, in a few seconds, the king would come out of his bedchamber.

This was hardly the time or the place to engage in a frank discussion of the king's character.

Catherine dug her nails into the soft brown leather of the riding gloves. The king! James, who had ordered the marriage between herself and Devon, who had commanded Devon to burn down her family's castle, who had banished her father from Scotland. Resentment against him made her scowl blackly at the door he was going to walk through.

She felt no awe of the king. Once, she had met an English friend of her father's. The man had held his own ruler in a kind of fearsome reverence. All the Highlanders had laughed at such a daft reaction. To them, a king was merely one of many leaders. The head one, mayhap, but not necessarily the most important. Indeed, there was a laird on one of the outlying islands who claimed to be the head of all clans, and therefore of more importance than any king. Not that anyone listened to such talk.

It might have been different if King James were a man worthy of admiration. A Scot wanted a proud, hard, and loyal leader to follow. None of which described the king. James was the son of Mary, Queen of Scots, and Lord Darnley, and he seemed to have inherited the worst characteristics of them both. He was faithless and weak like Darnley. Some snide gossips even claimed the king had inherited his liking for pretty young men from Darnley, as well. And from Mary, his mother, James had obtained his propensity for enraging clergy and gentry alike.

As for loyalty—Catherine shook her head. Was there ever a weaker or more vacillating ruler than James? When Queen Elizabeth of England beheaded his mother, James made hardly a squeak of protest. Not many

Scots held fond memories of Mary, but it was thought a disgrace that James had no reaction to the murder of his own mother. There wasn't a man in the whole of Scotland who wouldn't have sought revenge for such a thing.

But James remained silent. He hadn't been willing to say or do anything that might endanger his chance of inheriting Queen Elizabeth's throne in the future—not to mention the allowance Elizabeth sent him at the present. James was middle-aged now, and he had survived kidnappings and plots and endless dissent from his subjects. He wasn't about to do anything that might upset his chance to be taken from the realm of the quarrelsome, independent, poor Scots, and transported to rich, fat England.

He'd spent his life waiting to hear that Elizabeth was dead and that he, her closest relative, would become king of England. James had been willing to make promises to Catholics and Protestants alike to obtain the throne of England. He had sprinkled Europe with his promises and his letters and his spies.

Not that anything he'd done or said had made Elizabeth name him as her successor. No, that woman was too canny and had sat upon her throne for too long. She'd seen too many other royal persons thrown down, and had lived through too many troubles herself, to permit the name of a successor to fall from her lips. She knew that her successor, once named, would become a rallying point for any dissenters in her realm.

Catherine sighed. Would the English like James any better than the Scots had, if they had him? James fancied himself a man of culture and literary accomplishments, and the English loved their poets and playwrights. She herself had thought it ludicrous that

James had published two works expounding the divine right of kings, especially considering the fact that he ruled a people who were as proud and freedom-loving as any in the world. Yet James had seen fit to write glowingly about the divine right of kings, as if this were Russia, as if they should all look up to him as the Good Father. Scots!

The door swung open, making the candle flames genuflect in their holders of engraved silver. James VI, King of the Scots, shambled into the room. His chest looked barrel shaped, partly as a result of the thickly padded doublet he wore to protect himself from assassins.

The king leaned heavily upon a pretty male servant. Below his heavy chest and arms, the king's bowed, spindly legs barely seemed able to support him. Some claimed James' poor legs were a result of the bad diet fed him as a child; others, maliciously, blamed it on the pox which Darnley, James's father, was supposed to have gotten by sleeping with persons of ill repute. However he had gotten them, James's legs had caused him problems and ill health ever since childhood. He frequently needed help to be able to walk.

"Devon," the king said. He had staggered to the middle of the room and waited until Devon walked to him and kissed him, as was proper, on the mouth.

When the kiss of greeting had been exchanged, Devon said cordially, "Sir, may I present my wife, Catherine Craig."

The king's head swung in Catherine's direction. She met his gaze with a steady curiosity of her own. James had a sparse brown beard which was now beginning to turn grey. He wore an expensive slashed and laced riding outfit of the softest brown leather, with a dozen gold chains and medallions glittering about his neck. And above his ruff, his clever-clown eyes were bright with dislike as they stared at her.

Catherine drew in a breath, and then knelt gracefully at his feet, her umber gown pleating about her like a fan. She thought, he hates me. He hates me because he hates my father. She kept her eyes on the Turkish carpet, almost afraid to raise her head again and look at his expression.

But James gestured for her to rise. Slowly, Catherine got to her feet. James spoke in English in an unpleasantly high-pitched voice, "Your father has caused me a great deal of trouble."

Catherine recalled Devon's remarks earlier about being polite to the king. Now she could see what Devon meant. Even though she scarcely knew him, she could feel the maliciousness in him. Speaking in a submissively soft voice, she said, "I am sorry, sir. My father was always a reckless man."

The king began a long, rambling discourse on her father's many sins, and the trouble the king had had with all the Highlanders. James finished by saying, "They hold to their barbaric language, they plunder one another constantly, they commit indecency after indecency, and never do they listen to my commands. It must stop."

Catherine hunted for something to say that might mollify him. "I daresay they'd change if they had a chance to hear you, sir. You speak most wonderfully on the subject." It was the most blatant sort of flattery, but it seemed to appease James, at least a little, for he nodded, and then indicated that it was time to leave.

Catherine trailed alongside Devon. As Devon had suggested, she'd tried to please the king. Yet it had been clear from his heavy scowl that the king was in anything but a pleasant mood. But surely that wouldn't affect the exchange in any way. Or would it?

Outside, they found well over a hundred of the king's soldiers waiting on the broad lawn to accompany them for the exchange. There were also horses for Devon and Catherine. As Devon helped Catherine mount, she asked him, "How far is it to the place where we're to meet with my father?"

Devon shrugged. "I don't know, but it must be close to Holyrood, since the king didn't decide to leave until late afternoon." His hand came to rest over hers, and his blue eyes locked with hers. "Cat, there is something I must say."

Around them, horses whickered; two of the soldiers were arguing. Catherine stared silently at Devon, wondering what was making him look so intense. His face looked dark against the background of heavy clouds and trees shaken by the wind. He hadn't completed his statement, and by now she knew that whenever Devon had something important to say, he seemed to wait a while, formulating just the right words.

She prompted him, "Yes?"

He told her in a low voice, "I'm not going to let you go."

She leaned forward, not really understanding what he had meant. Surely it couldn't be that he intended to try and keep her in spite of the exchange. "But what about the letters?"

"I can't explain any further. I just wanted to tell you again that I'm not going to let you leave me." The closer they came to separation, the more Devon knew how impossible it would be for him to ever allow her to go. He had no idea how he would prevent it. Just that he would. Damn the consequences. Damn the king. He wanted to keep her as his wife.

Once the king had been seated, the long group of horses were ridden away from Holyrood and toward the hills. The afternoon had turned dank and mournful. Damp clouds grew over the blue sky, and a fitful rain began, sprinkling grey water over the low, yellow hills. The few trees rose like ghosts out of the mists, grey, leafless skeletons. Branches swayed and clicked in the rain-swept wind.

Catherine noted that the soldiers surrounding her looked like moving pyramids, in their enveloping cloaks. She couldn't see whether they wore any armour, but she knew they'd all be unarmed. According to the terms of the truce they had to be. James rode in the middle of the troops.

He was cowering behind them, Catherine thought contemptuously. Her father would have had little patience with such cowardice. Then she shifted her gaze and peered anxiously ahead, wishing she could see farther. But the drizzle prevented her from seeing beyond a short distance. Wet drops slithered across her face and she impatiently batted them away.

At last they reached the king's forest, which was kept for hunting, and the horses plodded through thick, wet ground, kicking up black flecks of mud. It took only a short time for them to reach an open glen.

Waiting there, seated on their horses, were Catherine's father and twenty of his men. Catherine took one look at them, and her throat constricted achingly. Their cloaks were shabby and patched, their boots worn. Three of the men were even shoeless, with their long bare legs dangling from their plaids. She had an agonizing picture of what their lives would be, of them living as reivers in the Border country, poor and hunted, never knowing whom to trust or what place held safety.

Yet her father wore a diamond-bright smile. "Cat!" he called to her in a bold, loud voice. "Have any of these so-called gentlemen harmed you?" The wind flipped back his grey-black mane of hair, and the rain threw a glittering sheen over his weathered, energetic features. "If so much as a hair on your head is missing, kitty, there's not a man you ride with that won't be finding out tonight what heaven is like."

"I have not been harmed," she shouted back at him, craning her head to see him better through the line of soldiers in front of her. Since she had last been with him, Sheamus seemed to have grown older and smaller, but he still retained the well-remembered air of carefree bravado. She nudged her mount to a faster pace. Behind her, she could hear the muffled thunder of hoofs hitting mud, and the jangle of harnesses from the rest of the king's soldiers as they drew near. Devon rode at her side, his face as hard as stone.

Her heart began to beat in rapid skips. She didn't know quite what to expect of the next few minutes. Would she be given to her father, or would Devon prevent that from happening, as he had told her? And even if the king did demand that she go to Sheamus, what would she do?

Catherine glanced at Devon. She didn't want to leave him. Not ever. Not because she loved him—not exactly —but she was his wife now, and she did feel something for him, something she couldn't explain even to herself. Perhaps she could just tell her father that and then hope that he could leave, without giving up the letters. That would be best for everyone except the king. But she doubted James would allow it to happen.

To her surprise, the king's soldiers fanned out around Sheamus's group until they formed a circle of a hundred men. She wondered at their doing so, for it

189

seemed far too threatening a position for the soldiers to take when both sides were meeting for a truce. Once all the soldiers were in position there was a silence, with only the wind rustling through the low heather and grass. A cordon of the king's most loyal guards moved closer. In their midst, surrounded by a wall of men, rode the king.

When at last the king and his guards were close enough, the king asked her father, "Are you unarmed?"

Sheamus nodded. "Aye, as we agreed." He held up his hands for emphasis. There was nothing in them. "Will you give me back my daughter?"

In response, the king's high-pitched voice rang out, crying, "Now! Take them!"

There was an explosion of movement. One huge soldier lunged from his mount directly at Sheamus. The rest of the troops jerked aside their long, enveloping cloaks. Swords screamed from sheaths. Leather-covered shields jumped into place before their faces. Each one of James's soldiers was armed, and each one aimed his crossbow or pistol or musket directly at Sheamus and his men.

Catherine shrieked, "Father, it's a trick!" just as Sheamus uttered a low oath, and reached to his side for his own sword. But there was nothing hanging by his hip. Unlike the king, Sheamus had kept faith with the truce. One of the king's soldiers ripped Sheamus from his horse, and then kicked him to the ground. A basket-hilted sword flashed at Sheamus's throat before he had a chance to jump back up.

There was no other fighting. It would have been hopeless. Sheamus's men were too few and, surrounded by so many armed soldiers, in no position to fight. The only thing they could do was to call out, shouting at the king in loud and rude language at the idea of the king breaking a truce of his own making.

Catherine was crying out, too. "Why have you done this?" she raged at the king, the shrillness of her tone making her mount dance nervously beneath her. She could hardly seem to take in what had happened. Had the king no shame, no sense of honor? "They meant no harm to you! You would have had your letters!"

James had no reply for anyone. He didn't even glance in her direction. He was too busy ordering his men to search Sheamus and the others for the letters.

Catherine kicked at the sides of her horse to go and tell the king to his face what she thought of him. Before she could move, Devon flung his hands over her reins.

He told her violently, "There's not a thing you can do now. Leave it." When she continued to tug at the reins, her hair flying in dark curls on her forehead, her breath coming in gasps, he grated out, "Do you want your father killed? If you make James angry enough, I swear to you that is what will happen."

She went white. Breathing in the deep, loamy scent of the rain drenched forest, she tried to calm herself. Devon was right. There was nothing she could do, at least for now.

She could see her father staring at her from across the glen. Without question, he wondered about the letters. She let him know where they were by sliding one of her hands across her thigh. It reassured her to find the letters still tied securely to her petticoats with the king's embroidered red ribbon. Her father had been right not to trust the king, and right to send them to her.

A tall, helmeted soldier pawed through her father's pillion, looking for the letters. Catherine choked with anger at the way the soldier carelessly tossed her father's things upon the ground. Once the soldiers appeared satisfied that they weren't going to find what they were looking for on the men or their mounts, the king ordered everyone back to Holyrood. Sheamus and his men were forced to walk.

Devon told her gently, "Come, Cat."

She jerked her horse in the direction the others were taking. What would James do to her father? He'd done all this to steal the letters from her father. But he didn't have them, and she vowed grimly to do her best to use them to her father's advantage. Perhaps there was some way she could use them to get her father freed.

Not now, however. She couldn't bring up the subject of the letters yet. Not when they could easily pull her off her horse and search her. Later, when she had had some time to think the matter through, perhaps she'd come up with a plan. But in the meantime, what would happen to her father?

Catherine glanced in his direction. Sheamus slogged through the muddy ground, his head held proud and high. Her poor father. How furious and how humiliated he must feel. But surely the king wouldn't harm him in any way. Whatever James had planned for her father, Sheamus wouldn't be executed. At least not until the letters were accounted for.

Once they had reached Holyrood, Devon escorted her back to their bedchamber. Numbly, Catherine followed him to their room, but, once they were nearly inside, she asked, "Why did you bring me here? I want to find out what is going to happen to my father. Please. Let me go back to the garden."

Devon shook his head. "Not now." He swung open the door to their room. "I'm sorry, but there's nothing you can do for Sheamus. Your father and his men will be taken inside and stripped and searched methodically. You couldn't be present for that, anyway. Then they'll be marched to the old castle and locked up while, no doubt, James tries to think up some way to get the letters."

She flung off her cloak and gloves and tossed them onto a chair. "I hope the king is sick with worry! I hope they're sent to Queen Elizabeth and she names someone else to succeed her!"

Devon strolled over to the fire to warm himself in front of the hearth. He said calmly, "That would scarcely be of help to your father. Or haven't you realized yet that your father will be executed if those letters are ever used against the king?"

In the grey room, her eyes were stark and shadowed. Of course it had occurred to her. The king had ordered her father out of the country under the law of fire and sword. By that rule, if her father were caught again in Scotland, he was to be killed. The only thing keeping her father from being killed now was the fact that the king needed the letters. A cold, clammy chill crept up her spine. What was she to do?

She only realized Devon had moved to her side when his arms came around her. "I swear to you," he told her, his head buried in her dark hair, "that I'll do whatever I can to make sure your father and his men are well treated."

Catherine let her eyelids close. "Thank you." Strange, she thought, Devon had been right. He'd told her that she wasn't going to leave him and she hadn't. Then she tensed, as a terrible thought bolted through her. Yes, Devon had told her he was going to keep her by his side. But why? Before, he'd always claimed it was more important to see that James succeeded to the English throne.

There could be only one reason. Only one. Because

he knew what was going to happen. The king had told Devon that he meant to play her father false. She cried, "You knew! You knew in advance. Devon! How could you let the king betray my father?"

The blue eyes opened innocently. "What do you mean? I didn't help the king do anything except take you prisoner."

She jerked out of his arms, her umber skirt belling about her violently. All along, ever since she had first met Devon, she'd been fighting an attraction for him. She hadn't wanted to like him—certainly she never meant to trust him. Yet she'd allowed him to make love to her, and had come to—almost—trust him.

Her hand rubbed anxiously against her forehead. All she had to do was to dredge up the memory of her father being thrown to the ground and a lump tightened her throat. Her father might have many faults, but she loved him. And she vowed to do her best to try and free him.

But Devon had plotted with the king to capture her father! Devon had done that, to her. Her father had been right, apparently, when he told her that Devon was an ambitious man, a man willing to do anything to gain the king's favor. No doubt the king was paying Devon well for his services.

Her head came up and, slowly, she raised her eyes to him. She asked bitingly, "I would like to know what the king promised you to make you kidnap me and hold me as a prisoner. It is a matter that concerns me. What was it? Another estate? A title?"

Devon made an abrupt gesture with his hand, and the light from the hearth lit up his austere features, made them harsher suddenly. "Cat, what are you thinking?"

The door to their bedchamber squeaked open. The

king stood in the doorway. His grey-brown hair looked as if he had been running his hand through it, and the riding breeches were still stained with mud from their earlier ride. He breathed in hard, angry pants.

"Sir?" Devon said. "What is it?"

James leaned heavily against the jamb, his hands shaking from some emotion. "I have had them searched carefully. Horses, bags, clothing, everything. There isn't any trace of the letters. Not even one."

Devon shrugged. He said wearily, "Mayhap you should have let the exchange go through. At least you should have asked to see the letters before you ordered Sheamus and his men taken captive."

An angry flush darkened James's face. "Are you questioning my judgment?" He snapped, "It was a good plan, I tell you! The only problem was with Craig. He lied. He tried to cheat me by not bringing the letters with him."

Catherine had been silent long enough. She burst out with, "I'm glad you couldn't find them. And my father wasn't the cheat. You were! You were the one who broke the truce—"

Devon grabbed her by the arm. "Be quiet!" he thundered.

The king glared at them both. "I plan to have her put in prison, too. Both the father and the daughter. Mayhap then whoever has the letters will see fit to send them to me."

"She is my wife," Devon said sharply.

The king gave a high-pitched laugh. "That was what I came here to tell you. She is indeed your wife. And our agreement is not completed until those letters are safe."

As soon as she heard the king mention a bargain, Catherine's eyes widened. So. She had not guessed wrong. Devon had planned this with James, and the agreement, whatever it was, included some sort of a payment to Devon.

The king pulled angrily at his ruff of cloth-of-gold. "Do you hear me?" he said to Devon, who stood before him as still and composed as if he were carved. "I tell you our agreement has ended. You wanted a divorce. But you won't get it, not now. Your wife, you said. And so she is, forever. Until I have those letters."

James motioned to a servant, who came to help him walk. The king shambled away from their room without bothering to take his leave of them. Catherine stood by the fire, her hands loose by her side, letting the words and their meaning sink in. A divorce. That was to be the bargain.

She turned to her husband.

Chapter Twelve

"DIVORCE." SHE ROLLED THE WORD OVER HER TONGUE, savouring it, letting her anger build. After all the shocks of today, Catherine would have guessed she couldn't feel anything more. She'd have told anyone who asked that she'd been drained of surprise and emotion, that she was finally numb.

Wrong. Just around the corner, disaster had lurked like a tiger, claws drawn, just panting to prove how much she was still capable of feeling.

Catherine's fingernails dug into her clenched fists, leaving white half moons in her palms. Nothing, nothing at all, could have prepared her for her reaction to hearing that Devon had only been using her. The knowledge swept over her in waves of anguish and sheer, unadulterated fury. She felt smothered; she couldn't breathe. Had anything in her life ever been as painful as this betrayal?

Devon had planned all along to divorce her. All the

flattering things he'd said were lies. He'd intended, from the first, to cast her off. Even when they'd made love he'd known he was going to leave her. He'd never wanted her to be his wife. He'd lied when he claimed to love her, lied so that she would give in to him.

How could he have been so callous? Their lovemaking had been so sweet, so all-consuming. It had meant so much to her—more, perhaps, than she had been willing to admit, even to herself.

Hot tears pricked behind her eyes. She blinked quickly, vowing never to let Devon see how much he had hurt her. Later, when she was alone, she could cry. But not now. Not in front of him. For the moment, her emotions already raw from what had happened earlier in the day, all she wanted to feel was righteous, red, enveloping fury. She had more pride than to allow herself to break down in front of Devon.

The thought added a certain measure of steel to her words. "Well? Are you going to try and explain about this divorce the king mentioned?" She glared fiercely at him.

Devon stood by the window, with the glossy red brocade draperies a counterpoint to his dark blue doublet of tuft-taffeta. He had never looked more graceful, more reserved, or more calm. He said in a soothing voice that made her long to scream, "Cat, my sweet Cat, I want you to take a deep breath and listen to me. I know you're astonished at what the king said—"

"A classic understatement, surely." Suddenly realizing she was trembling, Catherine walked stiffly over to the fire and held out her hands, letting the heat radiate out to her chilly fingers. Her gown was still damp from the ride, but she scarcely noticed it, and didn't care that the edge of her petticoats clung soggily to her ankles.

"I don't want you to worry. I can explain—"

"Everything. But I don't need it explained," she said with deadly sweetness. She noted huffily that there were few things more annoying than raging at a person who was in utter control of himself. Devon looked as cool as a Highland stream in winter, cool and contained and even a little amazed at her reaction.

Why wasn't he uncomfortable facing her after what he had done to her? He should be squirming like a fish! No doubt he had planned to be far, far away once the news of their divorce was made official.

She said, "If you had plotted with the devil to ruin my life you could not have managed a more effective job. First you drove me from my home, and then stole our estates. Next you took me prisoner and seduced me with lies of how you love me. Then, just to make sure I was thoroughly miserable, you decided to divorce me. But even that was not enough for you."

"Cat, this is nonsense."

She stamped her foot. "Not content, you schemed with the king to take my father's life as well. Oh yes, it's all very clear. Never has anything been clearer to me."

Devon gave a groan. "It wasn't like that at all. Are you going to calm down and listen to me?"

"Ha!" she uttered scornfully. She couldn't believe a woman anywhere would be calm in a situation like this. Before heaven, it was a sign of saintlike restraint on her part that she had not wrapped her hands around his throat.

Devon suggested, "Perhaps if you sat down."

"I want to be standing up while we talk. It makes it easier to grab things to throw at you."

He took two strides in her direction, and she jumped back and nearly tumbled against the coiled-gold flames of the fire. "Now you nearly burned me. What do you

199

do when you're not lying to virgins and ruining their fathers? Steal from elderly widows? Kick beggers? Drown puppies?"

Devon grabbed her by the shoulders. He held her so that she leaned against the plastered wall. Catherine breathed raggedly, her milk-white face rosy with anger, her breasts heaving. His hands were hard against her shoulders, and he was so close to her she could feel the heat of his body, and see a sprinkling of remaining raindrops tinseling his doublet like gems.

When he spoke, it was in an urgent, low voice that might have sounded convincing if she hadn't already known what a liar he was. "Will you listen? I tell you, there's no point in your being upset. None."

Her cheeks burned. "Nonsense. Why not?"

"I asked the king for a divorce before I met you—"

"You admit it!" The words exploded from her mouth. Catherine hadn't expected him to be so blatant as to tell her the truth right away. She'd thought she would have to drag the story from his lying lips, sentence by sentence. Now that he had told the truth, a fresh jolt of rage shot through her. Jerking out of his arms, she whirled away from him, every inch of her a study of infuriated, betrayed womanhood. "You less than a flea upon a dog! You leavings of a worm!"

He smiled down at her with a very private, very fond smile. That caused her teeth to clench. "Don't be silly," he said mildly. "I tell you, I made the arrangement for the divorce long before I met you. It had nothing to do with you."

"Nothing to do with me," she echoed in disbelief. "I hope the king never gives you a divorce!" Catherine sucked in her breath when it struck her that if Devon wasn't divorced, she'd still be married to him. That was a possibility too ghastly to be considered for any reason, even the joy of spiting him. "I take it back. I hope the king gives us a divorce for I never want to see you again, much less be tied to you in marriage." She wailed, "How could you seduce me?"

His eyebrows shot up in amazement at her question. "With great delight," he replied chattily. At the memory, a grin of pure pleasure turned up the corners of his mouth. "I'm astounded you could ask such a thing. Haven't I told you you're the most desirable woman I've ever met? Not only did I enjoy making love to you before, I'd be glad to do it again, any time you ask."

She ground her teeth. "I hope you come down with the pox. No, with leprosy. Aye, leprosy, and guess which part of your body I shall pray falls off first!"

He burst out laughing. "Cat, look, sweeting—"

"Never call me sweeting!"

"Cat my adored—"

"That is even worse! Call me nothing!"

"Very well, nothing, I wish you'd calm down and listen to what I have to say. It's absurd of you to be so upset." When she opened her mouth to explain why she had every reason to be upset, he continued hastily, "Yes, I wanted a divorce. At the time, it seemed the kindest course I could take."

She made a noise that vaguely resembled a snarl.

"Kindest," he repeated with patient calm, "since it meant you would be free to remarry, too. But that was all so long ago, before—"

"You decided you wanted to sleep with me," she raged. "And then get a divorce. Oh, why didn't I listen to what my father said about you?"

"Rot. Will you be silent and let me explain? Why can't you try to be logical?"

"What has logic to do with any of this?"

"Not a thing," he shot back, "considering the mood you're in."

She blinked. How dare Devon say such a thing, considering what she had just learned about him? Catherine paced back and forth over the scarlet and cream Turkish carpet, her damp petticoat kicking up and down in a flurry of color and movement, her pulses thrumming. She wanted him to see how dreadful his behavior had been. She wanted an apology, wanted him to fling himself at her feet and cry that he'd been wholly in the wrong but that he had reformed. That he now saw how much he loved her. Instead he acted as if she were the one who was misbehaving! It was infuriating.

She told him roundly, "Trying to shift the blame won't work. The fact remains, you were the one who schemed to ruin my family and me."

He stared down at her, lines of exasperation etched around his mouth. "Did I? How?"

"By scheming with the king, of course." A thought struck her suddenly and she asked, "For that matter, what did you offer the king to make him willing to help you get a divorce?"

It did not amaze her to discover that Devon wore the look of a man who wanted to be anywhere at all but in this room. He ran a finger around his Flemish ruff as if it needed to be loosened before he choked to death. "We don't have a divorce, so don't speak as if it were already a fact," Devon snapped. It was the first time she'd seen him angry this afternoon. "By the cross, will you listen to my explanation?"

"No. And will you answer my question? You did have to bribe the king for the divorce, didn't you?"

Devon said reluctantly, "As a matter of fact, I did. Without a bribe it's nigh impossible to obtain a divorce. In return for help from the king, I was to find you and take you prisoner."

"It makes me wonder what the king paid you to accept the broken truce this afternoon with my father."

"Not a thing. Cat! This afternoon was sheer idiocy. If the king had mentioned what he planned to do, I swear to you I would have done my best to talk him out of it."

She said suspiciously, "Indeed, why?"

"Because of what was at stake. From the beginning, the king has behaved with incredible incompetence. If it had been up to me, I'd have given your father back his lands immediately and gotten the letters in return. The succession to the English throne is at stake. It was madness to wait, and barter and bicker the way the king did. At the very least he should have gone ahead with the exchange as planned. Or, failing that, he should at least have waited until the letters were in his hands to play your father false. I can assure you, I would have."

"Of that," she sniffed, "I have not the smallest doubt. You really don't like the king overly much, do you?"

He said, with a refined and elegant distaste, "James is hardly the sort of man who inspires friendship. No, I don't like him, although I don't exactly dislike him. But he is the best hope Scotland has, merely because he is the king, and therefore I support him. God's blood, sweeting, don't look at me like that!"

"I told you not to call me sweeting."

"Very well, my dear virago. Will you listen to my explanation? Have you finished with your fit of temper?"

"No!"

There was a pause, while they both stood staring at one another, both breathing hard, both frowning. Night had fallen outside, and, since no one had lit the candles, grey shadows latticed Devon's face, and surrounded Catherine, standing in the corner, in a shroud of gloom.

At last Devon said, his voice strained, "There is no point in arguing with you about this. You refuse to hear what I am trying to explain to you. Well, you're tired and the entire day has been difficult for you. Certainly the way your father was taken prisoner was a shock. I think it would be best if I left. Once you've had a chance to think about my words, I'm sure you'll see there is no point in being so upset."

She brushed aside a dark curl of hair. If this was a sample of his logic, logic was leading him astray. "I will not cool down. And I don't want you to leave."

A charming smile lit his blue eyes. "You'd rather I stayed to receive my full punishment, including the thumb screws and the rack? How sorry I am to disappoint you."

"I don't want you sorry I want you—"

"I know. Impaled and begging for mercy. Alas, it is not to be. I see no reason for continuing this scene." As if that ended the matter, he sat down gracefully on the stool and pulled off his mud-spattered boots.

"How can you think of leaving now?"

"Because I'm a base coward," he replied promptly. The mocking tone made a lie of his statement. He grinned at her, grinned in a way that, yesterday, would have made her feel an unsteady kind of glow in the pit of her abdomen. "And because it will only embarrass you, later on, to realize how wrong you are now."

"Thoughtful of you," she muttered. With a certain

wariness, she watched him untie his breeches. Really, he had no sense of the fitness of things. How could he stand before her, clad in nothing below the waist but his smallclothes?

Devon stepped closer to her to rummage through the cupboard, pulling out pairs of hose and then rejecting them. "I am always thoughtful of you. I've been told I am thoughtful of everyone."

"Whoever told you that was a prevaricating toady."

"It was my mother." He pulled out a pair of finely embroidered hose.

"It's wonderful the way a mother will love and flatter even the most unprepossessing child. Are you really going to leave me like this?"

"I never enjoy leaving you. But I'm afraid it's urgent I leave this time."

"To escape me," she fumed.

"No, because of something the king said. In your unseemly desire to snap at me you appear to have overlooked the one truly important thing that James said to us. Didn't you pay any attention?" He looked at her, the brows above his eyes dark and straight. "The king told us he intended to lock you up, as well as your father." Devon stripped off his damp jerkin and prowled through the cupboard for a new one.

She glowered at him. "Yes, I heard him. I intended to—"

"Growl at me about it after you'd finished with the subject of our divorce," he finished for her. Apparently he had found what he wanted in the cupboard, for he drew out a doublet that blazed with gems and pearls.

Catherine dropped her eyes so that Devon wouldn't see her expression. In fact, in the emotional upheaval of learning about the divorce, she had forgotten about the king's threat. Now the idea sunk into her like a despairing wail. She couldn't be sent to prison! Not now.

The letters were still tied securely to one of the points of her petticoat. If she were sent to prison, wouldn't someone take her clothes from her, search her? The packet was bound to be discovered if anyone searched her. Even if she wasn't stripped immediately, sooner or later the letters would be found. And then her father truly would be lost.

Her mouth went dry. "I—I don't want to go to prison. Isn't there anything that can be done?"

Devon adjusted a fall of Flemish lace about his wrist. "I would never allow such a thing to happen. I'll go now and talk the king out of it."

"How?"

He told her with a grim smile, "By managing to lose to James at chess, and by telling him, once he is flush with this unusual victory, that I have made you my wife in fact, as well as name." He added under his breath, "No doubt the king never even considered such a possibility."

"Oh." She could only hope that his plan would succeed. Although the thought of owing Devon thanks grated like a handful of rough stones.

Devon finished dressing. He made a low bow before her, sweeping off his plumed hat in a graceful manner. "Good evening, wife. I'll have dinner sent to you. The king will undoubtedly have posted guards at the door, so don't attempt to leave."

He reached for the latch on the door. Before he could leave, Catherine asked rapidly, "Please! When will you let me know whether or not I am to go to prison?"

"When I come back, of course. I sleep here, remember?"

He went away laughing at the mixture of confusion and irritation on her face. As he walked down the gallery, with the white wax candles shining from each of the chandeliers, Devon told himself he really should take her anger more seriously. He doubted she'd soon forget what had happened. But she'd misread his intentions toward her so completely it was almost comical.

He had forgotten about the divorce he'd arranged until the king mentioned it. About a year ago he had decided to end his sham of a marriage with Catherine so that he could have an heir. A divorce seemed the kindest thing for Catherine as well, since it meant she too would be freed of what had become a troublesome tie. The king had told Devon he would help him obtain a divorce in exchange for taking Catherine prisoner. Devon shrugged. Almost from the first day he met his wife all thought of divorce had faded from his mind. And now . . .

He stopped for a moment, breathing in the cold, empty air of the gallery, the room vast and echoing and lined by tall portraits. Now he knew he could never imagine his life without her. He conjured up her image in his mind, seeing the tumble of dark hair, the artless face, and the vibrant warmth of her. Even here, far away from her, he could feel a quickening at the mere thought of her.

He knew every inch of her, but that would never be enough. Love appeared to feed on love; it could never be concluded, never be surfeited by too much. Just as now he understood he could sleep with her every night of his life and still hunger for more.

What was he going to do, now that she distrusted him? He didn't blame her for losing faith in him. The broken truce today, and then the king's revelation about the divorce, had simply been too much for her.

He tried to think of some clever way to charm her back into a happier state, and failed utterly. He hadn't really known what she felt for him before this happened. Perhaps nothing. Had she cared about him at all, at least a little? And had the events of this day smothered that caring?

He uttered a low, violent curse, and swung up the stairs towards the king's rooms. He hoped the business with the **king** would be done with quickly; and guessed unhappily **that it** would not be.

In fact, it turned out to be very late by the time he came back down the same stairs. By then, most of the rooms of the castle were dark. Shadows lay flatly in the corners, and the candles sputtered low in their pans, stiffened wax hanging down like tears.

Devon was bone weary, his mind deadened by hours of wine and games and refined, overly clever, razor-honed arguments. It was a relief to walk into his own room again.

No lights burned in the chamber, but by the fire in the hearth, he found his way easily. His wife was already in bed. She wore a plain white nightsmock, and her dark hair fell lightly over the linen covering of the pillow. Her eyes were open.

He asked, "Have you been waiting up for me? What wifely dutifulness."

"I wanted," she told him austerely, "to find out whether or not I was to be sent to prison tomorrow. Duty had nothing to do with it."

"Ah." He noted with an inner wrenching how husky

her voice sounded. She'd been crying, and crying for hours, if her voice were any indication. For a moment, he wished passionately he could take her in his arms and hold her and talk to her until she felt better. But she wouldn't listen to anything he'd have to say. Not after today.

With a sigh, he said, "I can at least put your mind at ease about prison. You won't be going. James only suggested it because I criticized him. He's not interested in you."

She relaxed against the covers. At least the letters were safe for now. The tightness in her chest eased a bit, and she said, in a much more cheerful tone, "I thank you for keeping me out of prison."

Devon shrugged. "Have you thought any more about what I told you? I hoped perhaps that given a little time alone—"

"I am not going to forgive you!" she cried in a shuddery tone. "And now that you have imparted your news, I hope you'll go away and leave me alone."

"Catherine, I am very, very tired. I am going to sleep next to you. There's not another room to be had in the castle, even if I wanted to change. At any rate, I don't want to. I can't, if it comes to that. I swore to the king that I'd keep a close watch on you."

Catherine shifted beneath the covers. Her throat ached and her eyes burned from all the weeping she'd done. Endless hours of it, while he'd been away. She'd never felt so lonely or miserable in her entire life. She yearned to have it all over with. "What are you going to do to me, tomorrow?"

Devon untied the bow at the tab of his shoes and then pushed them off. "We're going back to Caldwell. It's winter, and although the weather has been unusually clear, sooner or later the snows will start, and then it will be almost impossible to make it through. So we have to leave now."

"I'm not coming. You don't really want me, not when you're planning to divorce me. I care nothing for your promise to the king to watch over me—"

"But I do," he cut in sharply. "Besides, you are my wife. Of course you will come with me."

She molded the pillow violently. His wife. It was a wonder he didn't choke on the word. She didn't want to go back to Caldwell with him. The very idea upset her. Suppose he had some idiotic notion about sharing a bedroom with her again at Caldwell? If he did, she'd soon disabuse him of it. She longed to force him out of this room, but was too afraid of making any kind of a stir. If it angered the king he might send her to prison, after all. But once at Caldwell, it would be a different matter.

If Devon could even make her go. She had every intention of trying to do something with the letters before they left for the Highlands. And if she could manage to trade her father's freedom for the letters, her husband could get the divorce he so longed for, and she would never have to hear a word about Caldwell or Devon again.

She asked, "What about my father? Did the king mention him?"

He slid off the embroidered hose. "I'm afraid there's little anyone can do for him. He and his men must remain in the old castle as prisoners until the letters turn up, according to the wishes of the king. I've seen to it that they'll be well treated. For the moment, it was the best that could be done."

When she made no further comment, Devon busied himself removing the last of his clothing. The slashed and ribboned breeches were tugged off and then his smallclothes. Once he was naked, he stood up and walked toward the bed.

Catherine slithered to the far end of the bed.

He pointed out dryly, "One more inch, and you'll fall off the end of the mattress." Then he pulled up the covers, and slid underneath.

"I suppose," she muttered, "that you're going to make unwanted attempts to seduce me?"

"I would certainly enjoy making love to you. Very much. If you want me to—"

She made a squeak of protest.

"I see. Well, just as I thought, we shall both have to go to sleep frustrated. Pointlessly frustrated. Goodnight, sweeting." He shifted in the bed until he was comfortable.

There was a silence, while the wind whispered against the panes, and the fire crackled at them from the hearth. At last Catherine heard Devon's steady breathing. He'd gone to sleep.

She remained unhappily awake, listening to the low hoot of an owl outside their window and the strange creakings and sighings of the castle. It didn't seem to her that she could go to sleep even if someone gave her a sleeping draught. She stared sightlessly into the dark, her thoughts as tumbled and worried as a snarled knot. She worried about her father and about the letters. And what would happen between her and Devon.

The light from the hearth pulsed over his face, and drew yellow lines on his straight nose and severe mouth. He looked graceful and sleek and utterly beautiful. She recalled the time when she had slid her hands over him, explored him just as he explored her. It had been like nothing else she had ever imagined. Her gaze dropped down to the gold wedding band on his hand.

She recalled the way he joked with her and the way he argued. She remembered the time they had ridden around his castle, and the wild dance they'd had together before they made love that night. She had never before had so much fun with another person, never felt so close to anyone. It was almost as if . . .

Her eyes flew to his face.

There was no longer any point in fighting the truth. She'd known it, but avoided it, for a long time now. The truth, hard as it was, was that she loved him. Catherine shook her head as if to make the terrible idea vanish. But it only took a stronger hold, grew in certainty. Yes, she loved him. She'd struggled against loving him from the moment they met.

She would have given anything to remain his wife, to love him and be with him and have children with him. But he'd never cared for her, no matter what he'd said the night they'd made love. The fact was, he wanted to divorce her. That hurt. The knowledge was as bitter and cruel as any could be.

Well, she simply wouldn't love him any longer. She would wrench out all feeling for him, force herself to fall out of love. He had betrayed her and her father, and she would not, could not stay in love with him. That was all there would be to it. Somehow, she would learn to dislike Devon.

Mutinously, she stared at him in the red-black light of the fire.

Chapter Thirteen

"GOOD MORNING, SWEETING."

Catherine poked one eye open. The morning air was clear as glass and very cold. White shafts of light poured through the parting in the damask draperies. And across from her, at the other end of the bed, Devon smiled down at her. She took one look at him and squeezed her eye shut. Then she rolled over and drew the blankets over her head.

"It's a waste of time pretending to go back to sleep," Devon pointed out pleasantly. "I shall still be here when you come out."

In response, Catherine curled into a tighter ball under the bedlinens. She didn't want to look at Devon. Surely he'd see her love for him. Once, he'd told her that her face was easy to read. Catherine knew he was right, and that she'd never been able to lie well.

Besides, the knowledge of her love was so new and

so strong, it had to be on her face like a brand. She felt smitten, blinded, as different as if she'd exchanged another body for her own. And even if she could fool him, how long could she look at him, know she loved him, and still keep up any pretense of disliking him?

She said, in a voice muffled by the covers, "Ever since I've met you, my sleeping habits have been erratic at best. Are you trying to wear me down by sheer exhaustion?"

"That all depends. Would it work?" When she shook her head violently, making the blankets sway, he added, with a chuckle, "Then I can't think why I keep insisting you leave bed so early. It's positively unreasonable of me. There's no getting around it, I am an ogre."

"How true," she muttered.

"Even at the risk of proving the words correct, I'm afraid we must rise. We're leaving for home today."

"Your home, you mean."

He told her sharply, "Caldwell is now home for both of us. You're my wife."

"Only until the king gives you the divorce you long for."

"There will be no divorce."

Catherine sighed. Last night, she'd discovered how much she loved him. It had been a bittersweet revelation, coming, as it had, with proof that he cared nothing for her.

She should never have grown friendly with him. Certainly she should never, ever have made love with him. What would her father say, if he learned about it? An unpleasant chill ran through her. The fact was, her father would be furious if he knew.

And now? She looked forward to going back to Caldwell with all the enthusiasm of the condemned contemplating the gallows. At Caldwell she'd see Devon constantly. It was too much to be borne. How could she force herself to fall out of love with him under those circumstances?

In fact, falling out of love with Devon was going to be nigh impossible. She'd grown sensitive to his slightest gesture, to the way he spoke when he was teasing, even to the faint rustling of his cloak when he walked. Waking up next to him, and looking up at him for that one second, she'd seen how warm he looked, how freshly arisen, with his brown hair still mussed and a faint shading at his jawline to indicate he hadn't yet shaved. She'd taken in the masculinity of him, the austere, crisp line of his mouth, and she'd longed—foolishly, insanely longed—to kiss him.

Devon's voice cut into her thoughts. "You look like a turtle hiding under its shell. But you're a good deal more vulnerable than a turtle." There was a dramatic pause. "I wonder, should I?"

She asked with deep suspicion, "What is it that you shouldn't do?"

There was no reply, but she could hear soft noises as he pushed the blankets back and climbed from bed. What was he doing? She listened carefully to the glide of his feet across the floor. Then there was another sound, much fainter. She strained to make it out. Splashing? Why would he be washing himself now? Then knowledge hit her. There was one excellent reason for him to be at the basin of washwater. Doubtless he was scooping out part of the fragile crust of ice that would have formed on the water during the cold winter night.

"Devon! Don't you dare—"

Her words came too late. The blankets were snatched off her and Devon, laughing, grabbed her by the waist just as she struggled to sit up. She tried to fling herself from the bed but was unable to shake off Devon. One of his hands came up and slid bits of ice down her nightsmock.

"Beast!" She didn't want to, but she giggled helplessly as he tickled her under her arms. "Stop! Stop this instant!" she cried through breathless laughter.

The world revolved dizzily as they struggled, legs and arms tangled and then untangled, the sheets coiling about them as they moved. The tiny ice shards trickled down her chest in wet, shivery lines, sharpening her senses deliciously. Laughing, damp and cold from his assault, she wriggled against him.

Then their noses bumped, and she went still. It was a shock for Catherine to realize her mouth was only a breath away from Devon's, that his leg was thrust between her own, that one of his hands had come to rest on the side of her breast. She froze, afraid of the weight of him pressing against her, and more afraid of the way her pulses hammered in sudden passion. It was far too dangerous to remain like this. He'd read her feelings for him all too easily this way. She had to get away.

Catherine said, "You've succeeded in waking me up. I think it's time we climbed from bed."

"Do we have to?" He smiled down at her with a persuasiveness that might have melted a rock.

Catherine could see he wanted to play more. His index finger stroked over the tip of her breast, raising it to a point. Frantic, she struggled against him, and hunted for something, anything to say that would make him leave. "I wish you'd move away from me. We have to discuss my father."

The sun must have gone behind a cloud, for the room grew suddenly darker and colder. Into what had become a tense silence, Devon uttered a low oath and climbed from bed. He eased on his doublet and breeches immediately. "Your father," he repeated. "What about him?"

Catherine sat up in bed. "I have to speak to him today."

"No."

She pulled the blanket up to her chin. Somehow, she had to be alone with her father. It was vital. She held the letters, so it was up to her to get her father released from prison. There didn't appear to be an easy way to accomplish this. She'd need soldiers to protect her during an exchange, so many soldiers that not even the king could break the truce. Her father would know how to contact people, and where to find the men who could help her. She had to see him before Devon forced her back to Caldwell.

Catherine leaned forwards. "Please, Devon. You can arrange it with the king. Let me talk to my father privately."

Devon picked up the gold neckchain with the medallion on it and pulled it about his neck. "I'm sorry, Cat. Couldn't you ask for something a little easier, a unicorn mayhap, or a pearl the size of a melon? Those I might manage. But a meeting with your father? No. Besides, we're leaving for Caldwell today so—"

"Don't tell me that there isn't enough time, for I know there is. It only takes half a day to reach the first stage of our trip, your castle. It's only for the second stage that we have to travel during all the daylight hours in order to reach Caldwell. This morning, we could easily spend with my father."

He was silent.

She argued feverishly, "Besides, it doesn't matter how long the journey takes. I won't go. I swear it. I'll scream and fight. I'll try to run off every chance I can unless you agree to let me speak to my father. Please, I have to—to feel certain that he is well. You can understand that. I can't leave until I know he is." She sat up in bed, with her face resting across her knees, and the dark hair sifted across her face so that Devon couldn't read her expression.

Devon considered her words while he was dressing. He tied each point with a mechanical carelessness. "And you're promising, what? That you'll remain with me in exchange for getting you in to see your father?"

"Well," she said, ever truthful, "at least I promise to be good until we get to Caldwell."

His fingers stilled in their task of dressing. For a moment, he was silent while he considered. At last he stated in a flat tone, "That's not enough. I want more than that. I could keep you prisoner, but it would be much easier on everyone if you remained with me of your own choice. Therefore I want your promise to stay with me for at least four months, without question, without any attempts to leave. And I want that promise from you upon your honor."

She frowned. Devon was asking a great deal. "Four months? Why?"

"It's long enough so that by the time it's over we'll be lovers again, no matter what you think I've done. In troth, I doubt you'll even be able to resist me for a full month." He smiled at her throaty sound of protest. "Now. Do you agree?"

Her lashes dropped. He knew perfectly well he had the upper hand. "Aye."

"Very well. In that case, I'll talk to the king and see if I can make the arrangements for a meeting."

She leaned back against the pillows, a feeling of triumph singing through her.

Only two hours later, she stepped quickly through the cobbled walk in the old castle, the breeze troubling the curls at the back of her neck. She thought Edinburgh castle looked just as grim, close up, as it had yesterday when she'd seen it from the street.

The castle was made from stones the color of gunmetal, with its buildings utilitarian and devoid of decoration. Nor had the soldiers kept it clean. Catherine held a pomander to her nose as protection against the combined reek of damp, ancient stones, moldy straw, and stale cooking odors. Above her, banners trembled in the wind from the Firth, and along the wall, the round eyes of cannon stared sightlessly downward.

It was not an ordinary prison. Common criminals were locked in the Tolbooths in the city. Those prisoners who stayed at the old castle were usually important to the king for some reason.

Her husband led her firmly in the direction of a door studded with brass nails. She avoided looking at him. She thought it was a vast pity Devon had insisted upon coming with her on this visit. Nothing she'd said had swayed him. He'd been determined to stay with her through her talk with her father.

Devon's presence meant it was going to be awkward to try to talk to her father about the letters. Very awkward. Yet somehow, through some subterfuge, Catherine knew she had to speak to her father privately. If only her father could tell her the best way to use the letters!

Devon flung open the door, and Catherine stepped within, holding her skirts up high so that the hem wouldn't brush against the dirty rushes. The chamber she entered was long and narrow. From the furnishings, she guessed it must be the residence of one of the officers at the castle. She skirted a cot snarled over with bed linen and walked toward the trestle table, which was congested with dirty pewter plates and empty bottles of aqua vitae. Next to it was a chair with cushions. Catherine pulled it out.

Devon's even, elegant tones stopped her. "I wouldn't sit down if I were you," he said.

She didn't glance up at him, although each separate sense she had was aware of Devon standing a few feet behind her. "And why shouldn't I sit down?"

"Because I'd be willing to wager whoever lives here is crawling with fleas and lice, and so is everything he owns."

Her gaze flicked over the chair. Perhaps it would be best to stand. "I hope my father's accommodations are better than this."

"The best my money can buy. Don't worry. I made sure he's well outfitted, comfortable, and properly fed." Devon's voice suddenly seemed very near. "When are you going to let me explain, sweeting?"

"We are past the point of explanations." Something brushed against her throat, and she jumped when she realized it was Devon, his fingers tracing a delicate pattern over the length of her neck. She kept her eyes locked upon the grey stone wall, painfully aware of the warmth that had flooded her body at his lightest touch. "Don't do that."

Two blunt fingers lifted a mahogany curl of her hair. Devon wound the curl about his fingers caressingly, slipping it around and around until his hand was held against the side of her neck, resting warm and gentle and heavy just below her ear. She could feel the slight callouses on his palm and the way the index finger played with the lobe of her ear, sending sparks throughout her body. She was frozen to the spot, unable to move, unable to breathe.

Devon whispered, "Why do you sound so afraid?"

"I can't imagine what you mean. Let go. You're pulling my hair." She attempted to put some bite into her words but knew she'd failed miserably.

He slid the curl from his fingers, but his hand remained about her throat. His voice, when he spoke, had all the warmth of honeyed wine. "I'd never hurt you. Never. I'm in love with you."

For a moment, she was painfully open to him, painfully sure of her own love and how much she wanted him to love her back. The note of emotion in Devon's voice made her ache to lean against him. She wanted to trust him, to believe that he loved her.

Before she had time to form a reply, the door to their room scraped open. Catherine whirled about. Her father stood in the doorway. Behind him stood two dozen soldiers, the men who had accompanied him here. For one stricken instant, she imagined the soldiers were going to come into the room. But Sheamus Craig stepped inside, and the door banged shut. The three of them were alone.

Her father wore the same clothes she'd seen on him yesterday. The one change about him seemed to be the chains he wore. But, to her relief, he looked as vital and energetic as ever.

Catherine darted forward and flung her arms around him. "Father!" she cried.

The loud greeting was for Devon's benefit. During all the ride up to the castle, Catherine had wondered how she was going to manage to talk to her father about the letters while Devon was in the room with her. The only solution she'd come up with was this, to whisper her message to her father while they were hugging in greeting.

In an urgent undertone that Devon couldn't hear, she murmured to her father, "Shall I try to bargain for your release with the letters?"

Her father stiffened in her arms. "No!" His whispered reply was low and fierce against her ear. "Swear to me you won't. The king would never bargain honorably with you, any more than he did with me."

Devon's voice, from the other side of the room, made Catherine fall silent. "It would be best if I heard everything you said to one another."

Sheamus Craig stared ferociously at Devon. "I'm telling my only daughter that I love her. 'Tis none of your affair, Macgowan!"

Devon strode forward, and grabbed Catherine by the arm, forcing her away from her father. Catherine felt near despair. She had to find a way to use the letters. But how? Devon wouldn't allow her to speak to her father.

Devon said cuttingly, "In point of fact, Catherine is my affair. And so are you. I vowed to the king that nothing untoward would go on in this meeting. It was my assurance that made the king grant your daughter leave to see you. I cannot allow the two of you to talk privately. I hope you understand."

"Aye."

The two men stared at one another in the smoky torchlight. Catherine had never seen them close together before, not since her marriage when she had been a child. Then, she'd thought her father the bravest man in the world, and his bold-spirited behavior far superior to Devon's iron composure.

Now, with a more adult vision, she saw how unevenly

they were matched, and how poorly her father fared in comparison to Devon. Sheamus stood with his legs slightly apart, his heavy grey-black hair circling his vivid, weathered features. The brown wool doublet he wore was old and threadbare, his leather belt tough and age-cracked. He looked every inch the Highland laird, and he wore his pride and bravery wrapped around him like a cape.

But Devon, dressed in silk, as immaculate and colorful as a spring plant, exuded a self-possession and intelligence that was harder and stronger, in its way, than her father's courage. Against Devon, with his court connections and his measured and thought-out response to every action, how could her father ever win? No wonder that in the clash between the two of them, her father had lost everything.

She frowned at the thought, hating this new knowledge, and feeling sorrier than ever for her father. Was it only the fact that she loved Devon that had made her realize this? Or had Devon's words about Scotland and the Highlands subtly changed her own beliefs?

No matter. At least she would never have to choose between the two of them. Once she'd discovered how little Devon really cared for her, her path was clear. She would have to remain with her father. In truth, that was the path she would have had to take, anyway, with her father in such trouble.

She looked up at Sheamus, who was shaking his head and saying to Devon, "I cannot understand why you let my daughter meet with me. Never would I have guessed you had a drop of compassion in your body." There was a rude dislike in his tone.

Catherine's gaze dropped. She studied her hands with great interest, hoping her father wasn't going to try to pin Devon down about why he had been willing to help her. The answer might prove most embarrassing to her.

But Devon replied at once, "I brought her here because Cat is my wife."

"Wife?" Sheamus seemed amused at his choice of word. "She's no more your wife than I am!"

Catherine grew aware of a mounting sense of disaster. Her features stiffened into polite, desperate composure. Any second now, Devon would flatten her father with the appalling truth.

Devon said, "We are married."

The stiff corners of Catherine's smile wavered. The situation seemed to be growing blacker by the instant. She breathed a little prayer that Devon wouldn't see fit to go into how the status of their marriage had changed.

Hope died instantly. Devon continued in a blunt tone, "She is indeed my wife. In every sense of the word."

There was a silence, a heavy, heart-pounding silence, while Catherine wondered if it wouldn't be too craven of her to hide behind Devon.

At last Sheamus turned to his daughter. "Cat," he asked in wild astonishment, "what is that man saying?"

Before she had a chance to pry her lips apart, Devon answered for her. Maddeningly, Devon wore the air of a man who had seen his duty and is about to do it, no matter how unpleasant. He stated patiently, "I thought I had been very clear. I mean we are now truly man and wife."

"You raped my daughter!" Sheamus's roar thundered through the narrow room. He banged his fist down on the trestle table for emphasis, and the plates rattled hysterically in reaction.

"Rape? Certainly not," Devon retorted, as his brows

snapped together and his voice grew cold. "She slept with me willingly. Very willingly."

Catherine's heart fell like a stone.

"Daughter!" her father yelled. "Before I kill this devil for telling such a lie, I want you to tell the both of us that everything the Macgowan has said is as base and false as he is!"

Catherine quivered before the sinister waiting look her father trained upon her. Devon had turned to her, too. She wondered in a frothing fury why Devon didn't bother to answer for her. Before heaven, he'd been quick enough with his replies before! Nothing short of a miracle would save her now. Unless she could find a way to bend the truth.

"No one," she told both men, "wants to see Devon Macgowan roasted over a fire more than I do! Sleep with him! I'd rather sleep with a hospital full of lepers! I'd rather wander through a trackless wilderness, alone and without sustenance—"

Devon cut in with, "But you've already made love with me, and that's what Sheamus was asking about, sweeting. He's not interested in anything else. As you well know. Now, tell your father the truth. It's necessary that he understand how things have changed."

"Aye, daughter," said Sheamus, through lips that had been drawn up to show the edge of his teeth, "tell me how things have changed."

Catherine vowed to strangle Devon in his sleep should she ever have the mischance to go to bed with him again. She longed to sink to the floor and hide, but the floor obstinately refused to open up a gaping hole into which she could fall. There was no way out now. She'd have to admit what had happened.

She sighed in a tiny voice, "What Devon has said is true."

Sheamus lunged toward Devon. Dodging him neatly, Devon jumped aside and shouted, "Stop!" When he had shaken off Sheamus, Devon walked to the back corner of the room and said forcefully, "You daft, reckless idiot! Didn't it strike you as sheer madness to try to kill me when I'm armed? For that matter, there are twenty men outside ready to rush in at the least sign of trouble. Now, will you listen? I'm here because I wanted you to understand that Catherine is under my protection, that she is truly my wife. You and I have always been enemies, but regardless of what you believe me to be, I've never wished you any harm—"

"No harm!" trumpeted Sheamus, red patches on his cheeks. "After what you did to my daughter?"

"I knew you'd be worried about Cat. But, as you see, there's no point in fearing for her safety. The king would never harm her now that she is under my protection. That was one of the things I came to tell you. The other is that our positions have changed, Sheamus. Catherine is my wife and you and I must come to terms. This mad war of yours has to stop." He drew in a breath. "But I realize you will need time to sort out all the things I've told you. We can come to an agreement later, when the business with the letters has been resolved. And now, Cat, I think it's time to leave."

Catherine shot her husband a look calculated to strike terror in his heart. "It certainly is time to go," she snapped. "I don't know if I could stand any more revelations."

"More revelations," Sheamus repeated faintly. He glared at his daughter.

"No, no," Catherine assured him without looking up. A merciful sense of unreality had numbed her. This was all to ghastly to be true. "None, father. I assure you."

"I want to know how you seduced my child!" yowled Sheamus.

"In the usual way," Devon said patiently.

Sheamus cried, "Catherine, you tell me!" He snatched at Catherine's hand and pulled her close to him.

And then, before Devon could walk closer to force them apart, Sheamus leaned over to her and whispered, "We'll speak of your behavior later. Now. You must write to your brother about the letters. He alone can bargain with the king because he can bring soldiers—"

Whatever Sheamus meant to add, Catherine had no chance to find out. Devon yanked her from her father's arms.

Devon stated coldly, "I told you. No private conversation." He stepped to the door and held it open for Catherine, while saying, "And however angry you are now, Sheamus, remember that I will be the father of your grandchildren."

Sheamus ground his teeth. "Catherine!"

She said in a rush, "No, truly, father." She lifted up her skirts to step through the door, and added as Devon led her outside, "Please, you are not to worry. I won't let him seduce me again. There won't be any grandchildren."

Devon made a low noise of dissent. As soon as they stood on the wide cobbled courtyard, he whispered to her, "Sweeting, you wouldn't really want your father worrying about your safety, would you?"

Catherine bit on her lower lip and prayed for the control not to attack him in front of witnesses.

She longed to tell Devon what she thought of his way of relieving her father of worry, but Devon—in a move that she could only think of as craven—avoided her throughout that day, and also the next. He spent most of the journey back to Caldwell with his soldiers. Catherine wondered if he foolishly imagined that she'd forget his behavior if he left her alone. Mayhap he thought that sooner or later she'd welcome him back into her bed with a glad smile and a clapping of hands.

She knew differently. By the time the long ride was over, Catherine had prepared a fine speech to deliver to her husband.

It was late when they finally reached Caldwell, with a cold wind blowing from the north, and the chimney smoke rising from the castle in grey feathers of vapor. Once inside, Catherine was led to Devon's bedchamber once again. She'd expected that. Much later, Devon strolled into the room. He moved toward the trestle table and tossed down his cape.

Catherine stood by the window, her hands busy closing the draperies. Although it was very late, and nearly everyone else would already be asleep, she hadn't removed her travel-stained dress and put on a nightsmock. She turned when he entered the room. Dropping her hands from the draperies, she took a deep breath and plunged directly into what she wanted to tell him, "I want you to leave. You cannot sleep here."

"But this is my bedroom," he pointed out reasonably. He lifted his head to look at her, and the pulsing light from the candles gilded his hair with the purest of gold and made the medallion he wore flame brightly. Above the medallion, his face was set and controlled, but Catherine had the oddest notion she saw something else there. She thought he looked nervous. Immediately, she dismissed the notion. How could any man as strong as Devon be nervous about merely speaking to her?

"Cat, I know you've reason to be angry with me. I hoped you'd come to see reason eventually. In fact, I've been trying to find the words that would convince you to see my side of things. I have a whole speech prepared. Will you listen to me now?" The blue eyes stared at her wistfully.

She steeled herself against that note of wistfulness and his bewitching presence. Whatever he did, whatever he told her, she couldn't afford to weaken and let him share this room with her. The idea of sleeping next to him, night after night, was insupportable. She'd somehow managed to conceal her feelings for him so far but she wouldn't be able to forever, not if they shared a bed. Nor could she make herself fall out of love with Devon if she and Devon were thrown together constantly.

Besides all those reasons, there was one more reason, a terrifying reason, why she couldn't share the room with her husband. She'd hidden the letters in this room. The letters couldn't be kept tied to her petticoats forever, so, desperate, she'd sewn the letters into an old gown she had no intention of wearing again. It hung in the cupboard next to her. In view of that it would be too risky to have Devon wandering through this room.

Catherine said definitely, "The only words I want to hear from you are those you give me in leave-taking. Devon, please believe me. It won't matter what you tell me, I'm not going to change my mind. I swore to stay at Caldwell, but not to share a bed with you."

He ran his hands over the chain at his throat as if it bothered him. "Are you upset because I told your father we made love?"

"Upset," she repeated with hollow disbelief. "You've ruined my life and nearly sent my father to an early grave from the shock of learning what I did! Upset!"

"I daresay that answers my question," he said dryly. "Will you leave now?"

He strode closer, until he stood only a foot away from her. She could see the intensity in him, the tightness in his body. When he spoke, his voice was low and urgent, "I am not moving out of this room, and neither are you. We need to settle matters, Cat."

She licked her lips. It was going to be harder to talk to Devon than she'd expected. The fact that they were alone together was a problem in itself. The candlelight lit his eyes and embellished the very air about him with warm amber. She could see the hollow at the base of his neck and the sun-browned skin of his chest before the doublet began. She knew what it felt like to touch him there, the roughness of the hair and the bone-hard flatness of his chest.

Unable to draw an even breath, she dragged her gaze from him and stared blankly into the shadowed corners of the room, where, unhappily, her eyes fell upon the bed where they had made love.

Devon didn't touch her, but his words were a caress. "I want to stay with you. I need to, and you know why. I've already waited what has seemed like an eternity to make love to you again." His voice grew dark and rich. "I've waited until I'm aching with need. Cat, I want you. Do you remember how it was?" He took a step toward her.

It had become impossible to draw a breath. She choked out, "I don't want to remember!" and ran to the door and flung it open. Outside was the antechamber which Devon used for meetings. Four of his closest guards slept there. The men gaped incredulously at her as she stood in the arched doorway.

"The Macgowan is leaving," she announced crisply. "Please help him remove his things."

The men stared, open-mouthed, at her. Then they gawked speechlessly at Devon Macgowan, friend of the king, chief of the most important clan in the Highlands, who was being thrown out of his room.

Chapter Fourteen

WINTER FINALLY ARRIVED IN THE HIGHLANDS. A BITING wind dragged through the pine forests and shivered the lake in front of Caldwell Castle. The burns were rimed with ice, and the water flowed, rushing and hissing, underneath. Snowfalls powdered the trees and laced the mountains with white.

Devon spent the long, dreary weeks hunting until, at last, even that became impossible. He went outside one morning to find that the weather had closed in upon them like a clenched fist, in stinging needles of sleet that cut faces like shards of glass.

Feeling restless as a caged animal, Devon strode back to the antechamber that had become his retreat since his wife had thrown him out of his bedroom over a month ago. Tossing his sodden, white-flaked cape into the corner, he moved to the window and flung himself on the huge chair in front of it.

Outside he could see his wife. She walked through

the courtyard with Bess. They were apparently on their way to the dovecote. Cat was talking in an animated way and smiling. She held the hood of her cape over the side of her face to protect herself from the wind and sleet, but already the blowing snow had spangled her hair like some exotic decoration.

Devon closed his eyes. Even then it seemed to him that he could see her.

It had become impossible to live here, to speak to her every day, and yet have to stay away from her at night. But he was no closer to convincing her that he loved her than he had been the day they visited Sheamus. Time after time, he'd made an effort to explain what had happened. She wouldn't listen. As soon as he began to speak, she'd storm out of the room.

His hands ran uneasily over the arms of his chair. She was friendly to everyone else and interested in what they were doing. He heard her ask excited questions about this woman's child, or that man's ailments. Her loving warmth extended to everyone she met. Except him. When she was with him, her face grew shuttered and closed. If their eyes met, she'd quickly turn her gaze in another direction.

The nights without her were worst of all. He'd lie in bed thinking how only a door separated them. The picture of her in bed with only a nightsmock covering her soft body nearly drove him wild. He'd remember that she was his wife and how much he loved her. Why couldn't he just go into her room? Hot visions of removing her gown and stroking her and kissing her until she was willing filled his mind. He could see himself toying with her nipples until they formed hard peaks, kissing them, playing with her and stroking her until her legs parted for him, and their bodies merged into sweet fullfillment.

Again and again he'd recall the way it had been to make love to her the one night they had spent together. The memory of her would grow so real he could almost feel the sweet silkiness of her body beneath him. He'd grow hard with passion, and it would take every ounce of his self-control not to get out of bed and walk into her room.

Sometimes during the day he'd have a chance to touch her. During dinner, when everyone was in the great hall, Catherine sat by his side. Frequently their arms would brush against one another. They'd break apart immediately, as if scorched. Or she'd lean closer to tell him something and a curl of her dark hair would sweep against his shoulder. At such times, desire would surge through him with such fierceness he could scarcely bear it.

His passion for her had been strong before they'd made love but now, knowing every curve of her, his desire for her was even stronger, less controllable. Yet even as the need for her pulled at him, he was aware of how the events in Edinburgh had hurt her.

He could see her position clearly, understand how she felt pulled in one direction by her duty and her love for her father. Devon sympathized because he had always felt a strong sense of duty and love for his own clan. That was the reason he held back. She needed time to learn to trust him again. If they were ever to make a sound marriage, that was the way it had to be. He couldn't force anything on her, not even his explanations.

And yet he didn't know how much longer he could go on like this, seeing her every day and wanting her, and yet having to hold back.

A knock on the door made Devon raise his head and

ask who was there. Mouse entered the room. "I came to see if ye needed anything. Are ye hungry?"

"No." Devon knew he sounded curt, but he wanted to be alone.

"Ye havena eaten today."

"Because I am not hungry."

Mouse stared down at him. Outside, through the window, Catherine and Bess were returning from the dovecote. They half ran, giggling, sliding across the ice and snow and hard packed ground, snow and sleet flying about them in mad circles.

Mouse said, "I think what ye really want ye canna have. Do ye think she'll come around?"

Devon's mouth firmed. "She will, if I have anything to say about the matter." He changed the subject. "And you? Is it my fantasy, or have I seen you standing near Bess suspiciously often?"

"Ah." Mouse cleared his throat as if something had gotten caught in it. For a man who resembled a giant, he could look very small and boyish when embarrassed. "She's a fine woman, very bonny."

"A good person," Devon agreed. He'd been very happy to see Mouse's interest in Bess. Ever since his wife's death, well over six years ago, Mouse had avoided women. It was time for him to find someone else. "But that doesn't answer my question. Are you going to court her?"

There was a long pause. Devon watched in fascination as a dull red spread over Mouse's cheeks. "I take it you're a little shy about courting her?"

Mouse was silent.

"It appears we both have problems." Devon leaned back in his chair and stared idly at the window. Glossy icicles hung from the stone overhang of the window and sheets of tiny crystals clustered about the iron grillwork on the glass. "Before heaven! This snow drives everyone indoors. We can't go out, and there's little to do inside. I feel—"

"What?"

"Smothered. Caged." In the courtyard below, the women had vanished. There was little to be seen outside. On one side of the flagstoned courtyard stood the stacks of brown peat and charcoal, and on the other, the stable and bakehouse. Everything looked mournful under its canopy of white.

Devon asked with a certain savage restlessness, "Have you ever wondered what women talk about when they're alone?"

"Men," Catherine said, with a shake of her head.

"Aye, they are a problem," Bess admitted, snagging the little man they were talking about, her baby son, who had just fallen down. Bess set him up straight again. The little boy pumped up and down on his stubby legs, and then set off again, lurching across the room.

The two women, having accomplished their early morning duties, had retired to Catherine's bedchamber. Bess spun by the fireplace, while Catherine had picked up a piece of needlework and was poking at it listlessly.

After glancing about to make sure no one else was in the room, Catherine asked softly, "Are you sure that my letter to my brother was sent off?" She had written to her brother in Ireland, just as her father had suggested. In her letter, she'd explained everything that had happened and begged her brother to be quick and do something to rescue their father.

Bess nodded. "It was given to one of our clansman, a

man I trust. He's a good member of the Kirk. Also he was traveling to Glasgow, so he was able to take it with him." She added scrupulously, "But I canna say when your message will arrive. 'Twill be difficult for him to find a person who could take it to Ireland. Few ships sail there, now that the English have invaded the island."

Catherine's hand paused in its rhythmic sewing. She knew how difficult it would be to get the message through. It might be weeks before someone could give her brother the letter, or even months. There were no regular mail services. Each letter had to be hand carried, by friends or sailors to distant places. And even after the message did reach her brother, Catherine couldn't guess how long it would take for her brother to find men who'd be willing to sail to Scotland to help her father.

So it looked as if she'd be at Caldwell for many more months. Catherine put down the needlepoint and examined it without seeing it. Months more of living with Devon.

Every night she had to sit with him at dinner. Every night she had to walk past him as she went through the antechamber to her room. She could feel the way his eyes followed her. His blue gaze caressed her whenever she was near him. It made her feel edgy, as if she were going to fly apart. Sometimes, lying sleepless in bed, she had the oddest fancy that she could sense him thinking about her. And she'd be certain he was thinking about the time they made love. Then she'd toss in bed, unable to rid her mind of the memory of that night. Images of the two of them together tormented her, making her skin flush.

Why couldn't she force herself to fall out of love with Devon? Didn't she have every reason to hate him? Yet at times she'd feel her love for him so strongly her throat would constrict and tears would come into her eyes. Ridiculous fantasies sometimes took hold of her. She'd imagine the two of them living at Caldwell as man and wife, building a life together, raising their children.

What was the matter with her? She knew Devon had betrayed her and her father. She'd heard from the king how he'd planned to divorce her. Shouldn't that be enough to drive him from her thoughts forever?

Bess said suddenly, "I am anxious about the laird."

"Devon? Why?" Catherine glanced up, and noted happily the glow Bess had attained since she came to Caldwell. Her red hair, so neatly combed and tied above her head, looked glossy, and the weeks of being able to eat enough had added roundness and color to her cheeks.

Bess spun serenely. Tufts and trails of wool dotted her gown and clustered about her feet like little woolly lambs. "He has changed since we've come back here. He's worked himself to the point of exhaustion. He's angry with people, sharp and fault-finding when before he was so calm. Forgive me, but I thought perhaps ye might be the cause of his change."

Catherine squirmed uncomfortably in her chair. So Devon's poor behavior was to be laid at her door, was it? It hardly seemed fair, even though she understood why Bess was so upset. Bess was conservative in her religious beliefs and conservative in every other way as well. For Bess, women were supposed to follow men without question. And if there was a problem of which man to follow, a woman was always to side with her husband.

Perhaps Bess could be comfortable, living scrupulously by such rules. Catherine shook her head, knowing that rules just weren't enough for her. Even back in the convent, she'd never managed to passively obey the rules. What did matter to her was people. And what mattered most of all was seeing that her family and those she loved were well.

Every time she remembered the way her father had looked in that glen, his pride and desperation, his bravado and his poverty, her heart would constrict with pity. Some of his men had even been shoeless! It must have been hard for her father to be so poor, to know that everything in his life that he valued had been taken away from him.

Now her father and his few remaining followers were in even worse trouble. It was worrying enough to think about how they might be faring in that dreary prison. What bothered her most was that, at any moment, the king might suddenly decide to slay them all. After all, by the law of fire and sword, if her father was found in Scotland, he was supposed to be killed.

Yet Bess seemed to think she should go back to live with her husband, should do so while her father's life hung in the balance. Why couldn't Bess see that the rules she believed in couldn't cover this situation? Yes, Devon was her husband, and he wanted her. But he was also a friend of the king, and he would side with the king in any matter concerning her father. Even if Devon had not betrayed the truce or tried to obtain a divorce, and even if she weren't furious with him, how could she forget that? Her father had no one to rely upon but her, for she had the letters which could set him free. And with her father in danger, how could she side with Devon?

Catherine said, "I have done nothing to Devon."

"Ye willna sleep with him."

Catherine felt a flush creep up her cheeks. She pulled a thread through the needlepoint without noticing she'd put the needle in the wrong hole. It was true that over the last few weeks, Devon's temper had been short. Twice she'd heard him yelling at his soldiers, an event so unusual that she'd stopped what she was doing and simply listened, open-mouthed.

Bess smiled suddenly, "I shouldna tax ye with this. 'Tis not very Christian of me to judge ye. Will ye forgive me?"

Catherine returned her smile, warmed by her words, and glad to leave the subject of her husband. "Goose, of course. But while we are speaking of men, I have been wondering about you and Mouse. He seems to like you, but he hasn't been courting you. Why?"

The thread Bess had been pulling broke, and a snatch of white down was caught by the draft from the window. It flew upwards, and Bess reached out to catch it, but it got away from her. "'Tis not for me to say," she said. "Well, mayhap he is too shy to speak."

"Isn't there anything you could do to encourage him?"

Bess looked shocked. "'Tis not a woman's place to do that. No, I shall just have to wait."

"I didn't mean anything alarming, like appearing in his bedroom without your clothes. Just be nice." But Bess had already shrunk back against her chair, bits of wool fluff trembling on her dress, clearly unwilling to listen to anything Catherine had to say. Catherine sighed. How Bess and Mouse would ever begin courting she had no idea. "Perhaps we'd best go downstairs," she announced. "We need to see how the pastilles are coming."

The pastilles, a kind of paste made from spices, were used to sweeten the air. When they were burned, the aroma of spring spices and flowers would fill a room. Catherine had been amazed to discover Caldwell didn't have any pastilles put down in jars. She'd immediately set to making some.

A short time later, she and Bess walked out of the kitchen, both of them sniffing at the pastes they had on wooden sticks.

"Mine canna be improved upon," Bess said, bending down to give her little boy a chance to smell it.

"I think mine needs some more sweetness." Catherine pushed open the door to the solar where she was going to gather some more herbs for the pastilles. Just as she was about to walk inside, a hand came down upon her shoulder, stopping her. She turned to see who had come up behind her.

It was Devon. He stood in the dim antechamber looking very alive and very male. He told her, with a smile, "Cat, the very person I was searching for. You can go, Bess."

Catherine was tempted to tell Bess to stay, but that would only cause Bess to have to choose between her friendship and her sense of duty, so she stood silent as Bess and her child left for the kitchen.

Catherine's eyes swept over Devon. He was on his way outside, for he wore his dark brown cape, and a wide-brimmed hat was pulled low over his forehead. Underneath the hat, his eyes looked very blue and intense. Bess had told her that Devon looked tired, and Catherine, studying him, had to agree. If she hadn't known better she might have guessed that he had just returned home after a long and arduous campaign. The skin was drawn tautly over his face, making it seem

241

more austere than ever. He looked thinner. She felt a sudden certainty that it was because she had denied him her bed.

Her voice was soft when she asked, "What did you need me for?"

"Interesting question. But you know the answer to it." One of his hands went out and touched her cheek, and then his arm dropped to his side again. "I thought you might be feeling as housebound as I am, so I wondered if you'd like to come for a walk outdoors."

She pointed out reasonably, "It's cold."

"Aye."

"And it's snowing."

"Yes. But I'm not planning on setting up housekeeping under a tree. Just spending a few minutes on a brisk walk to the lake and back."

"Brisk? Even if we ran like madmen, we'd be twin ice statues before we reached the lake."

"I promise not. Here, I brought your cape." He held out her blue cloak.

Catherine's eyes widened at the sight. In order to find it Devon must have opened her cupboard. The cupboard where she'd hidden the letters. Feeling almost queasy, she reached out a hand for the garment.

Devon slipped it over her shoulders, apparently thinking her gesture indicated agreement. Catherine was too upset to bother to explain otherwise. She felt him place the cloak over her and then she tied it together and drew on the gloves he held out. She knew he couldn't have found the letters, for otherwise he would have said something to her. Yet it still alarmed her to think of him in the cupboard. Silently, she allowed him to lead her to the door.

Outside, the chilly air made Catherine's skin feel as

though someone had tossed something cold and sparkling on her face. The sky was the color of a moonstone, a translucent white. The snow decorated everything in fresh white paint, the hill the castle stood on, the pine trees, the rugged mountains beyond. Icicles hung like strands of milky, shining pearls from every twig and bush.

Devon said, as they walked through the courtyard to the front wall, "I've noticed you've started to take on some of the household chores. I'd like to thank you. It was good of you."

"Many things have been neglected for years."

"My mother used to see to everything in her scrupulous way. I'm afraid that since she has taken to staying in England most of the year, to avoid the severe weather here, many of the jobs she did have been overlooked."

They plowed through the snow, their feet sinking into soft powder. Catherine spoke cheerfully to Devon. The topic of household chores was a safe one, and Catherine found, once she could relax, she enjoyed her husband's company. She explained various problems, and added, "Your tapestries will be ruined if you don't do something to mend them."

Devon's words came out in puffs of white smoke. "Is it that bad? Perhaps I should have some of the seamstresses tend to it."

"Later, I'm afraid. During the winter there's so much work inside none of the women would have any time for it." They had reached the bottom of the hill in front of the lake. In front of them, the water spread out as flat and deep blue as a bolt of velvet laid out on a table. Around the edges, the loch was ribboned in ice, and beyond that, the snowfall around the rim of the lake looked undisturbed. There were no tracks, no signs that men had been there. The powder lay as white as unbleached linen, fresh and perfect.

Catherine exclaimed, "It's lovely. I'm glad you brought me here."

"When I was a boy, I used to escape the castle and come out here to be alone."

She glanced at him. "Why did you have to escape?"

"If you had been the only child of those two loving, doting, zealous parents you would never have had to ask me why. My mother and father wanted me to be perfect in every way. For a while, I could tolerate the endless school lessons from my tutor and the practice in the tiltyard with my uncle. But sometimes I just needed to escape."

"It sounds trying. Did you resent them?"

He smiled. "No. Did I give that impression? It wasn't like that. In fact, I loved my parents. I didn't even dislike the schooling and the practice. I suppose I wanted to be the person they were educating me to become."

She tightened her cloak about her shoulders. It was very cold, but the chilly, clean air tasted good, and she found it exciting to talk to Devon. She'd spent the last few weeks avoiding him. "What do you mean? What did you want to be?"

He bent down and snapped off the brown stalk of a weed. Idly, he ran the stem through his fingers. "You'll laugh at me. I was full of the most adolescent ambitions. I wanted to be the perfect knight, like one of the knights in those tales of high chivalry, only I wanted to be braver and smarter than any of them. I knew I was going to be laird and it excited me knowing so many people would rely upon my judgment. I wanted to be the greatest chief that Scotland ever knew, the most important, the most influential." He threw the twig down. "But that was when I was a boy."

She pictured him as a little boy, fantasizing as he sat by the lake. It felt odd to think of Devon that way. She'd seen him in the role of the laird, powerful, clever, and eloquent, and she'd seen him as a man, passionate and physical. Now she had a glimpse into a softer, younger side of him. "Your dreams don't seem foolish. Only hard to achieve. Why do you sound as if you were ashamed of them?"

Twirling snowflakes fell through the air and came to rest against the hood of his cloak. "Because I am. After my father died I realized how vain and childish my ambitions were. In truth, I have to be strong because other people rely on me, not because I want to prove how strong I can be."

She thought she understood. "How soon after your father died did you see that?"

More snowflakes drifted down, dotting his face. He took her hand to lead her back to the castle. "I suppose that happened the year after I became laird. There was a dispute over a handfast union. The man died before the year was up, and the woman and her family claimed they should inherit his farm. The dispute between the woman's family and the man's over who owned his farm ended in a murder."

"How terrible." Handfast marriages were a form of trial marriage. The woman lived with the man for a year, and, if she became pregnant, the marriage became permanent. But such unions had fallen into disfavor since the Reformation, and now were entered into very rarely.

Devon said, "If I'd been here to oversee and to judge, the problem might never have resulted in a death. A quick decision from me about who owned the farm might have ended the matter. As it was, I was off at court, so the argument continued, and a man died."

"I see."

Devon's voice was level, but there was an underlying passion to it. "I needed to be at court at the time. It was vital for me to make alliances there. Yet I was needed at Caldwell, too. That lesson taught me, as nothing else could, how difficult and how important my responsibilities really were. My fantasies about becoming a perfect knight seemed childish by comparison."

Devon stared sightlessly out at the white landscape. The fact was, he'd been as conscientious as he could, had tried the best he could, and it hadn't been enough. No matter how hard he tried there were always bound to be some failures. There was no perfect knight, nor was there any real greatness, nor could there ever be, not when each decision had its dark side. He'd had a dozen successes, dazzling ones, some of them. And yet there had been times when he'd felt that he had failed, as with the murder over the handfast union.

He wondered if Catherine knew he was telling her something about himself that he'd never related to another soul. Not even Mouse had heard about his youthful dreams. Yet he wanted to share them with Catherine.

The snow fell in wild, clustered flurries. It skittered about Catherine like a dancing curtain. "You haven't told me the end of the story," she said to Devon, looking up at him through eyelashes that were starred with snow. "The ambitions you told me about. Have you really forgotten them?"

Even through the snow, she could see he was smiling. "Yes and no. I daresay I'm still idiot enough to enjoy besting the king in some matter, or winning some new concession for my clan. But it's a tempered ambition, and it hardly rules me."

She let him take her hand to lead her back to the castle, while feeling the strangest reluctance to go. She'd felt close to Devon here. She didn't want to go back to the castle and their separation, and back to trying to dislike him.

But Devon said insistently, "We've been out too long. Come, we'd best go inside before we're so covered we can't move." The snow sifted through the air, and fell, glistening, on his cloak.

They staggered through the deepening drifts. The air grew misty with snow, as if a cloud had fallen to the ground. It became hard to see. A blinding whiteness sheeted everything. Devon wore his high boots, which protected him against the worst of it, but Catherine had on her wooden patens. Snow slid down her legs and into the space between her hose and the shoe. Her body heat melted the flakes and icy rivulets streaked down towards her toes.

"I'm freezing," she told Devon. She looked up, through the endless white vista. At last. They had reached the castle. Above her, the grey stone castle walls flew upwards towards a crystal sky. "I've never been so grateful to see Caldwell."

Before she could plow forward again, Devon had picked her up in his strong arms. He carried her silently to the stable door, flung it open, and stepped inside.

Catherine came down, gasping, on the rush lined floor. The stable was dark, lit only by a peat fire which blazed from the brick hearth. The mossy, woodsy smell of the peat mingled with the odors from animals. The entire building was filled with musky aromas and rustling noises, whickerings, and warmth.

She asked, "Why did you bring me in here?"

"I've been trying to speak to you alone for weeks." He undid the ties at her cloak and swung it off her, white flakes dancing down as he did.

Catherine took a step back. "I'm cold. I want to go to the castle."

"It's hot in here." He took off his own cloak, as if to prove his point.

Nervously, she clenched and unclenched her hands. "Please take me back. I enjoyed our walk to the lake, but I don't want to be alone with you here."

"I know. You don't trust me. You don't believe a thing I say. But do you at least believe me when I tell you I want to make love to you?" His voice was dark and rich. In the streaming light from the fire, he looked like a painting done in gesso, the colors brilliant and jewel-like. There was the flash of gold in the chain around his neck, the gilded brown hair, the deep blue of his eyes. Lightly, his hands came down upon her shoulders. "Well, Cat? Am I telling the truth about desiring you?"

"I—perhaps. It doesn't matter, since I don't want you."

"Now you're the one who's lying." His eyes challenged her to disprove the statement. "You might be angry with me, and you might mistrust me. But I know what we shared. I know you wanted me then."

"Devon, I have to be loyal to my father. Don't ask me to do anything that would jeopardize that loyalty."

His hands on her shoulders tightened. She must have washed her hair with perfumed rosewater, for he could detect its vague scent. There was another scent that clung to her as well, a clean fragrance that belonged only to her, and it stirred memories of the time he'd

248

held her naked in his arms. It was heady, being alone together, being this close to her.

He'd prepared a speech for her. But now that he finally had her alone, he hardly knew what to say. All the wonderfully logical arguments he'd wanted to present to her had vanished from his head. It didn't seem to matter.

Nothing seemed important now but her. All he was aware of was the fact that his heart was pounding violently and a wild excitement flowed through his veins. His desire for her was so strong he could scarcely bear it. She moved, and the side of her breast brushed against his arm. He gave a groan, picturing how soft her breasts had been, how sweet to kiss. He ached to taste her and hold her and make love to her. With a quickening of his breath, he stroked her shoulders. One of his hands reached up and cupped her chin, lifting it. Her mahogany hair spilled backwards.

She spoke his name like a sigh.

"Sweeting?"

Catherine said faintly, "Let me go."

"As soon as I've kissed you."

"Kiss?" She shivered. "No." But she didn't sound as if she meant it.

He said huskily, "I love you," and wished he could think up something more persuasive to say. He'd usually found it easy to persuade people. Why couldn't he seem to find the words to explain to her just how much he loved her, how deeply?

Catherine's nearness jumbled his thoughts. He stared down at her, thinking that she was nothing like him. She didn't hide her feelings or plan every action carefully. In many ways she was just the opposite; she rushed at things while he thought them through. She was impulsive and warm while he had always felt separated from other people because of his responsibilities. The differences intrigued him.

He hadn't even realized how lonely he'd been until he met her. Looking at her now, with her lips parted, he wished he could find some way to tell her that she meant everything to him. That he couldn't bear to be estranged from her.

But all he could seem to do was to bend closer, bringing his mouth down upon hers. She shuddered at the first light touch of his lips upon hers. Her body leaned in closer. He could sense the building passion in her, feel her pulses race beneath his touch.

Suddenly she broke free. She pushed away from him, and stood for a second in the dusky light of the stables, her chest jumping with the force of her rapid breathing. "No," she cried. "I don't want you!"

Grabbing her cloak, Catherine ran outside. The stable door flapped open, and a gust of cold wind and snow flew in.

Devon remained behind, with his hands flung outwards. He drew in a low breath. Surprise ran through him like a hot liquid. She'd wanted him. Maybe she didn't love him yet, maybe she didn't trust him, but at least she wanted him. That hadn't changed, no matter how coldly she treated him.

It wasn't much, but it was more than he had expected. It struck him that the day was lovely. Grinning, he strolled outside and shut the stable door.

He knew now what to do.

Chapter Fifteen

CATHERINE PRESSED HER CHEEK TO THE ICE-COLD GLASS. Peering past the castle walls, she could see that the forests were a sharply defined pattern of dark and light, with deep purple shadows slanting over a landscape of crystal white.

She sighed. The weather had been like this for weeks. No one could go anywhere; the roads were impassable. They were all trapped inside, all of Devon's troops, all the stableboys and chambermaids, everyone.

The unpleasant conditions reflected her mood well. She felt emotionally wrung dry and utterly miserable. Yet at least she thought she had achieved one goal. For, although she knew she still responded to Devon in a physical way, she thought that she had managed to fall out of love with him. She faced him day after day, and had managed not to be seduced back into his bed. That was one proof. The other was that she was managing to speak to him without giving away her feelings.

But no matter how often she told herself that she no longer loved him, she found it had become nearly impossible to deal with Devon. Not that he had done anything specifically to upset her. Yet ever since their visit to the stables, he had changed in some odd way. The hard, restless edge he'd had was gone, and in its place, there was a cool certainty about him. Now, oddly enough, he acted as if he were in control again, and sure of victory with her. But she couldn't see why.

Nothing about his behavior was alarming. He was affable to her, friendly. He made no remarks to her which he couldn't make in front of other people. She couldn't even complain that he had tried again to drag her off into a dark stable to try and kiss her.

Yet he was always there. Like a wild animal stalking its prey, Devon refused to leave her alone. He seemed to have focused all that measured, careful intelligence of his onto making sure that she was never away from him for very long. In the kitchen, he stood behind her asking if he could have one of the French biscuits the cooks were sugaring. If she was in the loft under the roof overseeing the sorting of the apples and vegetables, he wandered up to see what was going on. As if he didn't know the stored and dried fruit had to be sorted through once a week for signs of spoilage!

Once, when she was seeing to the brewing of the ale, she turned to find him at her elbow. She snapped, "Do you always have to be so close to me?" He only smiled down at her, one of those slow, careful smiles that always made her stomach contract. It was maddening.

Life became a series of skirmishes with her husband. Only not quite skirmishes, for there was nothing hostile about their encounters. Yet somehow Catherine felt besieged. As the days passed, it began to seem to her that the very air she breathed had grown stifling, that a breath-robbing element had charged the atmosphere. If only she could manage to stop thinking of him, stop feeling!

She was so desperate for a diversion, she plunged into cleaning projects. If it hadn't been for Devon's constant presence she might even have enjoyed herself, because she loved setting things straight and working with other people. She even, to the astonishment of Devon's steward, threw herself into the household account books to begin an inventory.

One day, Catherine was in the process of totalling the figures when her husband strolled into the antechamber where she worked. She glanced up at him.

It was one of those pale winter mornings when the light that poured through the windows seemed bleached. Catherine sat at a high oak desk, dabs of ink on her fingers and apron, a dozen lists strewn about her feet, pouring over an enormous set of books. Her white batiste undersleeves had been covered with folded linen to protect them from stains, and a rose-colored velvet beret snugly capped her dark hair, holding it away from her face.

Devon stood in the doorway for a moment, assessing her. "You look the very picture of the proper housewife."

She flushed. The last image she wanted to achieve was that of a good wife.

A high-pitched barking made Devon look down. He gestured at the half-dozen small, brown puppies tumbling bonelessly about the floor. "Would you like me to have them removed? They're not supposed to be in here."

She smiled down at the puppies. One of Devon's

hunting hounds had given birth to a litter in this room. "No. I like having them here. They don't bother me."

"Good, then."

A puppy had started to tug at Catherine's shoe, digging sharp little teeth into the thin leather. She shook it off gently and said, "I've discovered that for a man as careful as you are about everything else, your accounts are in complete disarray."

He shrugged. "My steward is always complaining about the same thing. I don't have the time to sift through things properly."

"But you can't order supplies without knowing exactly what you have. You can't plan."

"I know," he admitted with a smile, clearly amused by her vehemence. "That's just what the steward says." He walked closer to her desk and touched the smudge of ink on her nose. "I didn't think anyone could have fun adding up long rows of numbers, but you look as if you're enjoying yourself."

Catherine once again picked up the quill and twirled it between inky fingers. "I am. I used to watch my mother do these things when I was a little girl."

"I suppose you wanted to be just like her."

"Yes," Catherine admitted. "She seemed so important. She ran the household, managed the servants, checked expenses, and even, whenever my father was away, oversaw the entire clan. She distributed land and settled disputes among the clansmen. We all relied on her."

Devon nodded. Although some laird's wives tended only to their household problems, many of them saw to much more complex tasks. Some even took charge of the entire clan when the laird was away. Apparently Catherine's mother had been like that, and Catherine would wish to be the same way.

He felt a sudden ache to have Catherine see how well they fit together. He'd be glad to share his responsibilities with her, and she'd be the perfect mistress for Caldwell. If only she would open her eyes and really see how things were.

He pointed out, "I've always wanted a wife who could work with me."

"Then no doubt you should find a wife to work with you after our divorce."

"Divorce, when I already have what I want? No." She peered up at him through the dark fringe of her lashes, her expression mulish. A fitful sun, white behind the haze of clouds, threw pale golden light upon her face, turning it luminous. Devon bent over and lifted one mahogany curl that rested on the side of her cheek. "I like what I already have."

"You don't have me."

He regarded her with a wry smile. When he spoke, it was with a certain sardonic humor underlining his words. "I am all too aware that I don't have you. No one knows it better." His eyes swept over her. "How long has it been since I met you? Over three months? And in that time, only one night of making love. I've never been the most celibate of men. The waiting for you to give in has been . . . let's say it's been difficult. No one could be more aware than I am that I don't have you. At least not often enough. By heaven, not nearly enough. If you continue to deny me access to your bed, I may be forced to take drastic measures."

She cocked her head to one side. "What drastic measures?"

There was a moment of tense silence, while Catherine, alarmed, noted how his lissome body leaned toward her. She was half afraid he was going to gather

her up into his arms for a kiss. But at last he broke the
tension with a joke. "What drastic measures? Baying at
the moon, gnashing my teeth, and falling, whining, at
the foot of your bed." He laughed softly. "Would that
help?"

The look upon his face, not his words, made her
heart pump faster. She felt an urge to be somewhere,
anywhere, else. Devon leaned toward her slightly, his
body tense, an obvious sensuality quickening his
breathing. One of his large hands came down and
touched her on the shoulder and a bolt of pleasure shot
to her abdomen. She jumped to her feet, with every
intention of leaving. Reaching out, she shut the household book.

There was a pause. At last Devon said, "Very well. If
it bothers you so much, we'll drop the subject. I'm
afraid you're cross this morning." He asked soothingly,
"Did someone get you out of bed early? I know how
you are about sleeping late."

She sat down again and stared stonily at the quill
pen. It was true that she hadn't gotten enough sleep,
but not because someone had awakened her too early.
She simply hadn't been able to fall asleep. Not that that
had caused her to be cross, as Devon suggested. The
fact was, she wasn't cross at all; he was being provoking.

She said, "I thought of it as a perfectly delicious
morning, a morning made by angels. The birds sang,
and the trees were wreathed in shining golden leaves.
At least until you sidled in and started talking about
divorce and the like."

"You were the one who brought up the subject of
divorce."

She sighed the sigh of one who has been sorely tried.

"Have I annoyed you again? Perhaps we should make another start." His hands brushed restlessly over the oak table and stopped when they reached the book of accounts. "What about the inventory? Surely that's a safe topic."

He pulled up a stool and sat down. He read through her notes carefully, one leg crossed negligently over the other, the books upon his lap. Catherine went back to the scribbling she was doing, but covertly, she watched him.

After a few minutes, she guessed Devon must have found some notation in the book that interested him, because he read over a few pages very slowly, as if he were memorizing their contents. Then he kept going back, returning to them, as if there was something else he wanted to check.

At last, having read through what she had finished so far, he laid down the book in front of her and said, "I want to ask you something. You've done everything to put Caldwell into proper shape. You've cleaned, inventoried, investigated, and generally done everything a wife should." His voice grew sharp as a sword cutting through glass. "Why?"

Catherine couldn't think of anything to say. She could scarcely admit she found his presence so disturbing she'd been driven to find work, any kind of work, to do. "I was bored. I needed something to fill up my time."

"Something to fill up your time would have been to start a new tapestry for yourself. This goes far beyond that, far beyond what any woman who was bored would care to do."

"Nonsense." She refused to look up at him.

"I kept asking myself why you would be doing this.

Then, reading through here, it struck me. There's only one possible reason. It's because you know in your heart you're going to stay here at Caldwell."

Catherine's head jerked up, her ruff trembling with sudden movement. "That is nonsense."

"Is it?" Devon's blue eyes were intense. "This inventory system of yours is going to be nearly impossible for anyone else to follow. You've set it up for yourself, for next year. Think, Cat."

She stared at him blankly. "I don't know what you mean."

"Look down at what you've done. Those notations there," he said, pointing at some of her writing. "Do you think anyone but you will know what all those words mean? They're one word scribbles. I could never logically figure out what they refer to, could never guess at it. Neither could my steward. Look at them. They're your notes to yourself, Cat. Meant for no one's eyes but your own, for next year's inventory. Admit it."

She went white. Before heaven, was he right? She ran her eyes over the telltale notes, and knew, sickeningly, that at least one of his accusations was true. Her jottings wouldn't be comprehensible to anyone but her. Why hadn't she thought of that? "I'm sorry," she said. "I should have been more careful to put down explanations. Not that the notes mean anything. I'm not going to be here next year to oversee any inventory."

He looked down at her, the lift of his eyebrows telling her that he didn't believe her.

Just then, the puppy's mother loped into the room, stepping with muddy paws on some of Catherine's household lists. Catherine gave a cry and bent to retrieve her papers. By the time she raised her head again, she found Devon standing by the dogs. The mother had laid down to let the pups suckle, and the little puppies were at her teats, making furious, wet noises. Devon picked up one squirming puppy and petted it.

"They're sweet, aren't they?" she remarked, glad to talk to him about something other than her notations. Hoping, in fact, he'd forget the whole subject.

"Yes." He ran a finger down the animal's soft, brown back, before placing it down next to its mother. "I like babies of all kinds. I'd like some of my own, in fact, if my wife would grant me access to her bed." With that he turned, and walked from the room.

Catherine went back to the accounts, squinting owlishly down and rewriting her notations.

That night, her bedroom door swung open just as she had pulled on her nightsmock. She turned quickly to see who was there.

Devon sat in the room beyond at a table, his long legs sprawled out in front of him, a book in his hands. By the complete surprise on his face, she knew instantly that he had nothing to do with the opening of the door. She must not have shut it completely, and the wind had swung it free.

For a moment, the two of them remained where they were, while Catherine's blood surged through her in heavy, wild beats, and she felt almost dizzy with emotion. She could see every part of him with a sharper eye—the severe cut of his jaw, the earnest eyes, and even, his lawn shirt which, having been half pulled off, revealed the strong breadth of his chest and the brown hair laced over it. The distance between the two of them seemed both vast and yet only the length of a heartbeat.

Her mouth went dry.

What might have happened between them she never knew, for at that moment, one of Devon's men entered his room. Quickly, shaking off the strange heaviness of her limbs, she walked to the door and shut it.

The small battles with Devon continued as the weeks passed and February ended. By the end of March, the skies had lightened, and the snows came less frequently. The ice on the burns began to break apart. A few sprigs of green poked through the white drifts in front of Caldwell, and the castle took on an air of expectancy.

Catherine could feel that expectancy racing through her, as well. Every day she woke up wondering when she'd hear from her brother. Surely the letter had reached him by now. He could even have had enough time to organize men to come to Scotland. Mayhap he'd come to Caldwell to take her and the letters to her father. How she wanted to leave!

But with time still heavy on her hands, she began yet one more project—the tapestries. As Catherine had told Devon before, the tapestries were in sore need of repair. Many of them were centuries old, and very beautiful. But they had been neglected for so long that the colorful tourneys they portrayed had faded, and some of the mythical forests, with fantastical creatures like unicorns sporting in them, had begun to fray about the edges.

She cast about for women to help do the repair. There were only a few seamstresses at Caldwell, and those few were usually busy cutting and sewing cloth for the laird and his retainers. Nor were any of the other maids unoccupied.

She had nearly decided the tapestries would have to wait until she walked into the gallery one day and saw the line of pallets that Devon's soldiers slept on. It struck her that none of Devon's soldiers had anything to do but sit and eat until spring.

An idea spurring her on, Catherine went to find her husband. She discovered him in the solar. He was staring out at the white landscape outside. Beyond the window, a few delicate snowflakes drifted through the still air.

Devon must have heard her coming for he turned about. "My lady?" he said, in his most rich, elegant voice. Even though it was daylight, torches had been lit to help keep the plants in the solar warm. Around him, a dozen pots sprouted with green herbs. "How delightful to discover you coming to find me. Your usual tendency is to run in the opposite direction."

"I have something to discuss with you."

"Better and better," he said with relish. "What about? Cheer me up by telling me it's something personal."

She eyed him with suspicion. Whenever Devon was in that bright, teasing mood, she was always afraid he'd start talking about them going to bed together. "I hate to disappoint you, but it's about your tapestries."

He raised his eyebrows in curiosity.

She explained, "They need repair. At first I didn't think I had enough people to do the work. Then I remembered the Countess of Shrewsbury—"

"Has she volunteered to do the work? Good of her, considering how far she'd have to travel to help."

"The Countess will stay in England, where she belongs." She added scrupulously, "In truth, I am not even sure she's still alive. Never mind that. It was your soldiers who gave me the idea."

"I thought you said it was the Countess."

"You're teasing me."

"Aye." He grinned unrepentantly.

"Well, don't. Before heaven, you are the most provoking man. As I was about to explain to you, the Countess used to make all of her husband's soldiers sew tapestries for her."

"Did she now? And what did the Count have to say about all this, or was he even consulted? If it's the same woman I'm thinking of, I doubt that she cared what he said, consulted or not."

"Devon," she stated firmly, "please control your desire to make a joke of everything. I don't know and I don't care what the woman told her husband. The point is, she managed to teach the soldiers how to do needlework. It struck me that with all of your soldiers wandering about with little to do, and with the tapestries in such sad condition, why shouldn't we have them mend the tapestries?"

"Why shouldn't we indeed?" he murmured. "I like that 'we', Cat sweeting. It fell so trippingly from your tongue."

"It's lovely that you're so easily pleased. Does this mean I can go and tell your soldiers they have to help me with the tapestries?"

"Cat, you don't need to come asking me things like this. I've given orders that you're to be obeyed instantly. That applies to my men as well. The only thing they won't help you do is to escape. And they won't aid your father in any way. But you don't need my permission for repairing anything." He added flatly, "Why should you? You're my wife."

"Oh." At least she knew now why everyone had jumped to do whatever she wanted. It hadn't occurred to her before that Devon had told his clansmen to obey her. Now she saw that he would have had to say something to them first. "Good, then." She felt the oddest sensation, a sort of awkwardness. Devon was staring at her, and she mumbled her thanks in a voice that seemed tight and thin.

As she walked away, the picture of Devon stayed in her mind. She could see him as clearly as if he stood in front of her, the long, hard shape of his legs and the wary blue eyes, so warm when they fell on her. He'd been kind to her, telling all of his clansmen to obey her. Another man would have had a guard trailing after her, would have refused to let her do anything. But then, Devon was always kind.

Catherine sighed. Something had to happen, and soon. Why didn't her brother write her? It seemed as if she'd been waiting forever. Every day, no matter how many times she assured herself she no longer cared for her husband, she found it more difficult to deal with Devon. Teasing, elegant Devon. His eyes followed her, and his remarks, so frequently laced with a dangerous passion, struck a responsive chord in her. She had to leave!

Instead, unable to do anything else, she taught thick-fingered men how to hold a needle and sew. A few days later, to her relief, Devon went out hunting. The weather had cleared, and meat was needed on the table. She watched him leave, riding off with his men into the woods. Catherine smiled in happiness to see him go.

She expected him to be out all day, and so she wasn't surprised when sunset came and he was still not home. But then dinner was served, and cleared away, and still he hadn't returned to Caldwell. At last, apprehensive about what could have happened, she went to find Mouse. She discovered him in his bedchamber, sitting at a low pine table and playing draughts with another man.

As soon as Catherine entered his room, she announced, "The men who went out hunting today haven't returned. We must send someone out to look for them. They must be lost."

Mouse didn't look alarmed. He shook his head slowly. "There's no need for ye to worry or for us to search. They are all skilled in woodcraft."

"But anything could have happened to them! We must go out and hunt for them!"

Mouse said ponderously, "Ye must consider. It is dark. We canna find anyone in the dark. More, we'd be risking the lives of the men we'd send to look. At night, 'tis far too easy for a horse to stumble and fall."

"But what about the people who are out there! Anything could have happened to Devon. He could be hurt, dying. Perhaps another clan—"

Mouse had been holding the dice. He set them down on the inlaid board carefully. "No, ye must not worry about that. The only clan nearby who would have harmed the laird was—" He cleared his throat, and added hastily. "But that's over."

She supposed he'd meant her father. Catherine twisted her hands anxiously. "But it's snowing outside! We have to save Devon! Please!"

Mouse climbed heavily from his stool. "Lass, will ye listen to me? The laird isna in trouble. He knows each crook and crag of the land close by. He is an expert rider. Even if something did hurt the laird or one of his men, there are a dozen other riders to help."

"But why isn't Devon home, then?" She bit on her lip, not at all reassured by Mouse's words.

He shrugged. "They may have gone out too far. Mayhap they thought to spend the night in one of the shieling cottages. It has happened before." Mouse and the man across from him stared at her impatiently, as if they thought her foolish and wanted to get back to their play.

Turning on her heel, she raced from the room. Although she asked a dozen different persons, from the stableboy to the tackman, no one seemed concerned about Devon's absence. No one wanted to help look for him, and, in a sense, that reassured her. But not completely.

Since little could be done while it was still dark, Catherine went to her room. She didn't even attempt to sleep. The night seemed endless, each hour an anguished and measured torture. At first Catherine paced back and forth, so worried for Devon's safety that she felt sick. The forests were dangerous. The men could have encountered wolves, or outlaws of some sort. They could be freezing outside, with no protection against the snow and cold and wind. Devon could be injured, even dead.

The more she thought of it, the more she was able to conjure up possible disasters that might have overcome Devon. She flung herself on her bed, and sobbed until she couldn't cry any more. She couldn't bear it if anything had happened to Devon. Of course she hadn't fallen out of love with him. Of course she loved him. Nothing else mattered but him.

At last Devon's German pendant clock, dangling from its jeweled chain, showed that sunrise was near. Catherine dressed and ran down to the stables determined to oversee the arrangements that were being made to send out a search party. She insisted that a horse be saddled for her, too, even though Mouse frowned.

Before anyone left, however, Devon returned. He and his men rode in with snowflakes dotting their cloaks. They seemed surprised at the commotion their absence had caused. Devon swung off his mount, and walked over to Catherine. "I hope you weren't worried about me."

"Of course I was. Where were you? What happened?"

He shrugged. "We came across Red Sandy, one of my tenants. The roof of his cottage had collapsed under the weight of the snow, and he and his family were desperately trying to save their animals and belongings. We had to stay to help him make repairs." He gave a laugh. "It was a memorable night. We spent the entire evening battling the snow and wind and the hole in the roof."

She hovered between a desire to throw her arms around him and a ridiculous and illogical urge to be angry with him. She didn't get the chance to do either. Mouse called to Devon, and her husband strolled over to confer with Mouse about some household matter.

Catherine, left stranded in the stable, with the saddled horses about her and a dozen of Devon's troops gaping at her curiously, turned, and went back to the castle. She was still shaking with emotion. She thought, although it didn't make any sense, that somehow this had been another skirmish, and that she had lost, and lost badly.

After a breakfast which she took alone in her room, Catherine went downstairs to oversee the mending of the tapestries. To her surprise, the galleries were empty. She found Bess at the end of one room, and asked her, "What happened? I told Devon's troops to be here today so that we could do more work on the tapestries."

"'Twas the laird's orders. He told the men they had to clean their weapons instead. That's what they'll all be doing."

Catherine was surprised that Devon had rescinded an order of hers. "I'll speak to him about it when he wakes up."

"He's not asleep. I saw him go out to the old hot house a few minutes ago. I think they keep weapons in there; he may have taken some men over to collect them."

Catherine lifted her eyebrows. Devon should be in bed. He'd been out all night, and he must be exhausted. She decided to go and speak to him about the tapestries, and, while she was there, suggest he go to his room for some rest.

She threw Bess a quick thank-you for the information, and ran out of the gallery. A few minutes later, her cloak wrapped around her, she made her way outside and through the blowing snow toward the hot house.

These houses remained in a few castles. They had originally been built by Vikings, during the time centuries ago when the Vikings had invaded Scotland. Hot houses were small stone buildings in which a man could sit in front of a blazing fire, sit and sit until he was boiled and red. Why the Vikings had found that enjoyable Catherine had no idea.

There was no lock on the door. Flinging it open, she darted inside, the white flakes flying about her, blinding her for a moment.

Once she had adjusted to the light of the hot house, Catherine froze in astonishment. Bess had been wrong. Devon hadn't come to check on any weapons. There were none in this building. There was only a fire, and Devon. He was naked. And alone.

She drew in a long, unsteady breath.

Chapter Sixteen

CATHERINE STOOD ROOTED TO THE FLOOR.

She stared with wide eyes at Devon, at the strong, perfect body flushed with heat from the fire. He was only a few feet away from her. Heat had tinseled his naked body with moisture, making it shine like polished stone.

She grew aware of how small the building was, only one cramped room. One wall was taken up by an enormous fireplace filled with burning pine logs. The fire blazed, infusing the chamber with a suffocating, almost tropical warmth. A large wooden tub brimming with scented water had been placed in front of the hearth. Steam rose from the tub, curling through the chamber in soft white shoulders of vapour. On a wide ledge next to the bath a dozen furs had been spread out, and the silver and brown hides shone glossily in the red light.

No hint that there was an outside world entered into

the room. There were no windows, no ventilation save the fireplace. Catherine found it hard to believe that beyond the blooming heat of this room the snow lay thick on the ground.

"Catherine." Devon took a step toward her.

When he moved, whatever spell had kept her motionless was broken. She turned to leave.

Just as her hand fell on the latch, Devon, with a sinuous movement, placed himself between her and the door. Catherine was walking forwards, so she fell against him, her chin coming to rest on the flat, bare expanse of his chest. She jerked back quickly, a dewy patch on her jaw.

He said, "How pleasant to see you."

She told him in a rush, "I came in here by mistake. A complete mistake. I didn't realize you were inside." She didn't care about the tapestries now. Let his soldiers run off and play with their idiot weapons, let the entire castle rot and crumble to dust. Let Devon stay awake until he dropped. She didn't care. She only wanted to get away. "Will you please move aside so that I can leave?"

He smiled in a way that made her instantly nervous. "Not this time, I think." His hand came down, slamming the latch into place. "This time, I'm not letting you get away from me. I've waited a long time to have a chance like this with you, Cat. I think I've waited long enough."

She didn't want to know what he was talking about. "Actually," she announced with a bright cheerful gush, "I did want to speak to you about the problem of the tapestries."

"A fascinating topic," he agreed. "You must be hot in here. Let me undo your collar."

"My collar will stay where it is." She backed up from

270

his outraised arms. "It's never felt better. It could only feel better if I were outside."

He remained stolidly in front of the door, smiling. There was no way past him short of pushing him aside. And that would involve touching him.

She was not going to touch him. A little wildly, Catherine tried to remember her father. She should never be alone with Devon. It was too hard to keep up any pretense of not wanting him in a situation like this. Willing to say anything, anything at all to avoid a personal subject, she cried, "You may not have your men back. The tapestries need repair."

"So they do," he said soothingly. "And my men can help repair them, too, in between practice. Why don't you sit down on the furs and we can discuss just how often they should help you? I must tell you, I am susceptible to bribery."

She did not sit down and she was certainly not going to ask what he would accept as a bribe. "Are you really going to hold me here as captive, stewing me to death in this wretched oven?"

He pointed out considerately, "You'd be quite comfortable without your clothes."

"I knew you'd say that," she said with a discernible snarl. "Doubtless you are harboring some idiotic notions of seducing me."

"Doubtless."

Catherine kept her eyes steady on his face, but inside she quaked. "Bess," she lied quickly, "was coming right after me. She'll be here in a moment. I think I'd better—"

"Bess isn't coming after you. I arranged for you to come here to me, and to come alone. There won't be any interruptions. As I told you, I've waited long enough. It's time for us to talk."

271

Catherine's heart sank like a stone. To think that her own friend, Bess, had conspired to make this happen! "I don't think I want to know the topic of conversation you had in mind."

Devon said huskily, "The topic is you. Do you remember when we first met? The first time I saw you, I was amazed. I'd remembered you as being a little girl. It was a shock to realize what you had become. There was a line from a poem that stuck in my mind once. Something about someone being as lovely as a summer's day. You're like that, fair and warm and soft like a summer day. I wanted you then. I'll always want you."

"I want to leave!"

"You can't."

Catherine blinked. Devon had always been so kind to her before. She had heard him use that same tone with other people, but never with her. He had sounded implacable. She knew with absolute certainty that he meant what he had said. He was not, under any circumstances, going to let her walk past him. There was another change about him, not easy to define, but it was almost as if he'd come to some decision, and, having reached it, he was going to follow it to the very end.

He said, "I cannot wait another day. And I damned well can't wait one more night."

He put his hands at her throat, and slid his fingers into the tie of her cloak. "You'll suffocate in here unless you at least take this off." The cloak tumbled downward. Catherine stood in her russet gown, the bodice pulled tightly over her chest, the skirt full and sweeping the brick floor with bands of embroidered cream. Under the tidy cap of her dark hair, her face was lightly colored from the heat. A delicate shade of rose tinted her cheeks.

He said, "Don't you think it's time you stopped all this ceaseless work and faced what you are running away from?"

Catherine swallowed. How did he know she'd kept herself busy so she'd have less time to think about him? In one sentence he'd laid bare her careful ruse.

His lean body was garlanded with moisture. One of his arms reached out to touch her throat. "It's been close to three months since we've come back from Edinburgh. I've deliberately stayed away from you because I knew you needed that time to learn to trust me again." Without waiting for her comment, Devon drew off her collar and tossed it aside.

She took a step back, eyeing the collar lying on the floor next to his naked foot. Her hand went to her throat, where the pulse echoed the frantic pace of her heart. The oddest thought struck her that all those little skirmishes these last few weeks had led her to this moment, almost as if they all had been planned, like a war, to lead to this final confrontation. "I still don't know if I trust you."

"Don't you?" he asked sharply. "Cat, you are painfully honest. It's what I have been counting on. I want you to tell me again, while looking at me, that you don't trust me."

She kept her eyes on the floor and said, "You are on the king's side, and my father's life is at stake."

"I suppose that means you do trust me, but you wish you didn't." He stared down at her and said fiercely, "I need you."

She stared at him. All her effort these last two months to fall out of love with Devon had been a crashing failure. She still loved him. She'd realized how much last night, when he had been missing. How could she stop loving him? It seemed as if loving him had been burned into her, grown patterned and instinctive like breathing. It would last all her life, and could never be changed, or altered.

He said, "I'd never intentionally hurt you." Curving his palm against her neck, he toyed with the dampening tendrils of her hair.

"I have to think of my father."

"I had nothing to do with your father's imprisonment, and the king never said anything to me about breaking the truce." His voice was soft. "I had hoped you knew me well enough by now to judge the truth of it. Have I ever lied to you before, or given you any reason to think I'd cheat at a truce?"

She opened her mouth and then closed it silently. She wanted to tell him that she didn't believe him—but she couldn't. The fact was that Devon was the most decent man she had ever known, the most honorable. Again and again he'd proven that. She would have admitted what an honorable person he was from their first meeting if their past and her father's words hadn't blinded her to what he was. Devon might have helped the king drive her father from Scotland, and he may have chosen to side with the king, but he was in no way as faithless as the king.

She looked up into his face, and knew with sudden, absolute clarity that she couldn't deny him. "No." Catherine drew a shaky breath. "I suppose I do believe you." A swimming sensation of relief ran through her. Just to be able to admit to herself and to Devon that she believed him made some cold, hard knot inside her come unbound.

Devon's fingers thrust into her hair. The pins that

held her beret in place clattered to the floor, and the beret followed immediately after.

Catherine found that breathing was becoming extremely difficult. The heat, the moist air stifled her. As his fingers wended through her hair, tumbling the silken mass about her shoulders, she told herself to move away from him. Her legs refused to obey her. "But even if that's true, my duty to my father and my clan would never allow me to live with you. Devon, please. You know how impossible it is."

"I don't want to come between you and your obligations. I swear to you that I'll try to see that it never has to come to a choice." The light darkened before Catherine's eyes as his shadow fell over her. His head bent down toward her.

She turned her head just as his lips descended, and his mouth grazed her cheek.

"Don't pull away from me, Cat. I want you, and I am going to have you." His words were thick and drugged with passion. Devon cupped her flushed face between his hand, and tilted her head up so he could stare deeply into her eyes.

She listened as he repeatedly told her of his need for her. Wild words, hungry words that made the color of her cheeks grow rosier. A raft of different sensations swept over her. Devon's hands caressed her as he held her chin, and she felt the slight callouses on his hands, tickling her, arousing her. There was an herbal aroma in the air from the steaming spiced water in the wooden tub. The aroma mingled with Devon's own clean male scent.

Devon's thumb massaged the sensitive area just below her ear. He said, "My other self, my wife, I swear I'd never leave you. How could I? I love you."

She trembled. "Devon, please."

The thumb dropped to her neck. "How could you imagine I would divorce you? How could you imagine such a thing? I will never let you go. Could not fathom a life without you." His lips were inches from hers, and she knew without question that he was going to kiss her. There was nothing she could do to stop him. She didn't want to stop him.

The firm line of his mouth lowered gently upon hers. There was no insistence in his touch, no aggression. His kiss held nothing but love, and, perhaps, a questioning. She knew he was waiting for her to respond, to show if she wanted this to continue. Through the beating confusion of her senses the only response she could make was to reach up with her fingertips and cling lightly to his shoulders.

At that small sign of capitulation, he deepened the pressure of his mouth almost imperceptively, until she could scarcely bear the pleasure that vibrated through her. Devon outlined the curve of her mouth with the tip of his tongue. Catherine didn't know if the tiny sound that escaped from her throat was in protest of his gentle assault, or a moan of delight.

Devon began a slow, sensuous onslaught. His hands stroked down the length of her arms, sending tingling sensations radiating along her body. He kissed her until she was breathless, kissing her chin, the soft curve of her cheeks, her throat, her forehead. His fingers made small circles at the nape of her neck, and then grazed downwards to tenderly caress the full swelling of her breasts.

Devon lifted his head to say huskily, "Let me love you. I've lain in bed night after night, wanting you, thinking about how it would feel to do this." His hand held the curve of her breast.

Catherine found herself trying to struggle out of a

rapturous cloud that threatened to envelop her completely. If she didn't stop him now, she'd be helpless against the aching need his words and caresses had aroused in her. Mayhap it was too late already. Even as she fought the fires within her, her fingers curled against his hard arms. "Devon, try to understand. I can't give in to you."

"But do you want to?"

She shook her head, and the threads of crimson in her dark hair caught the light from the hearth and shone like bits of captured fire. "I—I don't know."

Devon pulled her against him. "Yes you do, Cat." His mouth came down again, this time with a desire that brooked no opposition. He kissed her deeply, with a profound, desperate passion, a passion too long denied. His lips clung to hers, and then his tongue probed at the damp parting of her mouth.

Catherine shivered. For what had seemed ages, she'd wanted him, had loved him. Now, in his arms, his mouth moving seductively over hers, she could only bend her head back in acceptance, allowing him to deepen the kiss. When his tongue entered the honeyed interior of her mouth, she pressed her body against him, feeling his hard body pushing deeply into the folds of her dress.

Devon's voice whispered against her ear, "Deny that you want me."

She was silent.

He gave a low groan, and sensuously kissed her again, his tongue thrusting into her mouth, its erotic rhythm echoing the culmination of love. Catherine reveled in the sheer physical pleasure of his kiss. She felt lost in desire. The steamy warmth, the furs nearby strewn out like booty from an ancient Viking's hoard, made the room seem like something timeless, something apart from the real world beyond the door. How could anything be wrong between them in this place?

Once again, he spoke against her lips, "Tell me you want me."

Catherine's response was little more than a raggedly drawn breath. "Yes. I do. Make love to me."

His hands drew her closer, placing her hips snugly against his. She was instantly aware of his arousal, and it excited her to know how much he wanted her. He whispered to her, "You can't imagine how much I've longed to hear you say that you want me." While his fingers untied the points of her bodice, he said, again and again, "I love you."

Suddenly it felt to Catherine that as if some great burden had been lifted from her. For the first time in months, she felt really free and happy. She laughed delightedly because his fingers tickled as he removed her clothes. It was heaven to be with him again.

Devon undid her bodice and skirt and let them slip to the floor. Catherine now had nothing on save her petticoats and shift. Her skin, after the long sunless winter, was fair as new cream. Against it, her dark curls shone like coal. He brushed out her hair with his fingers until it fell in waves to her shoulders.

They moved to the fur-covered ledge. Devon removed the petticoats and they dropped to the brick floor in a rustle of white linen. He kissed her shoulders and bare arms and Catherine sighed in contentment.

Only her shift hid her body from him, and that, too, he took from her. Once she was naked, Devon lay back with her on the furs. The furs felt like silk beneath her. She brushed her legs against them, stretching, all of her senses alert.

The fire in the huge hearth sent red waves of light over Devon's body as he lowered himself to the ledge beside her. She reached out to touch him, stroking her hand over the breadth of his chest, then curling her fingers into the tracery of brown-gold hair between his nipples.

But her hand fell away as he began to kiss her throat, and then the underside of her breasts. Roving, his fingers drifted across the full swelling of her breasts until they had reached the dark centers. Already, her nipples had tightened in desire. He brushed his hand over the rosy peaks, caressing with loving delight until she trembled. Then his mouth came down to tease at them provocatively, his tongue rasping over the tips again and again, drawing circles over them, sucking on them. The nipples rose, grew even harder. She called his name, helpless, lost in passion and love.

Devon stroked each separate part of her with exquisite sweetness, his hands sliding over the line of her shoulders, the curve of her hips, and down to the straight sleekness of her legs. He said, "I dreamed of doing this to you. I would lie in bed at night tortured by your nearness and thinking of how much I wanted to do this to you." His fingers raised again to hold her breasts. "Waiting has been torture."

His movements had become quicker, bolder, as he stroked down to the triangle of dark curls between her legs. She could hear the harsh stridency of his breathing, as harsh as if he had been running a long distance. Alive to each new sensation, Catherine wanted to tell him how he made her feel, and her hands, unknowingly, came down to the center of his desire and touched him there.

He seemed to be scarcely able to bear the thrill her gentle fingers gave him. At last he had to push her aside, tenderly. Urgent now, he pressed damp, heated kisses down her abdomen to the core of her femininity.

She parted her thighs and let him fondle her in such a private, erotic way that it brought a blush even as she cried out at the warm tingles that radiated outward from her abdomen.

"Devon, please. Oh, I cannot bear another moment."

At her words, he moved up to position himself over her. She felt his hard member probe at her and she drew in a breath of anticipation. Then there was a movement that brought their bodies together, fused them. An aching jolt of sheer pleasure raced through her. She clung to him, shuddering, as they began the primitive rhythm of love. His lips pressed down upon hers, claiming her, while their bodies grew damp from exertion. They touched, felt, as one. Heartbeat by heartbeat, they moved together until Catherine, in a white incandescence, met the final completion. A second later, Devon gave a stifled cry as he, too, found his satisfaction.

Afterwards, they lay in one another's arms without speaking. The fire heaped heat and stillness and laziness upon them, drugging them with its warmth. It took Catherine a long time to drift back to reality. At last she lifted heavy eyelids to look at her husband. Devon stared dreamily into the hearth, the white vapor from the wooden tub trailing a silver mist above his head. For the first time in weeks, she thought, he looked completely relaxed and happy.

He lifted his head. "I meant what I said about never letting you go. Tell me that you know we will always live together."

The smile on her mouth faded. "Devon, please don't ask me to make any promises to you."

The arm around her tightened. He said in a curiously

hoarse voice. "I love you. Whether you know it yet or not, we will make a fine life together."

She smiled, but didn't answer him. The fireplace smoked and the spring-time spices from the scented tub rose in the air to tease their nostrils. Catherine, nestled next to her husband, fell asleep.

For a long time afterwards, Devon gazed down at her. They had resumed their lovemaking. For the moment, nothing else mattered. But what about later? He had no idea what would happen between the king and Sheamus. The letters might never be found. Or they might be used in a way that enraged the king. Although Devon would do his best to prevent it, the king might, at some point, grow angry enough to order Sheamus's execution. What would Catherine do then? And, although Catherine had let him make love to her, how much did she care for him?

He shoved the thoughts aside. He had stalked her and won her, had planned his war with her carefully. Even the fact that he hadn't come home last night had been planned. Now he wanted only to savor the fact that they were lovers again. He didn't want to ask himself whether she loved him yet. Instead he let his mind drift to what he would say to her once she awoke.

His thoughts were cut short by a knock at the door. Devon looked up, and swore softly. He couldn't imagine who could have disturbed their privacy. He flung a cape around his shoulders and strode to the door, which he opened only a crack, so that whoever was outside wouldn't be able to see Catherine.

On the snow was a man Devon had never met before. The man wore clothes grimed in sweat and dirt, and his hands looked calloused and sore. He said, "I've been riding all day and night to deliver this to you." He held out a letter with a red seal and two ribbons hanging from it.

Devon accepted the letter and dismissed the messenger. As soon as the door was shut, he tore open the letter and scanned the words inside.

The noise must have awakened Catherine, for she stretched and climbed from the fur-strewn ledge. "What is it?" she wondered.

Silently, he handed her the letter to read. She took it from him with a smile, her mind still on their lovemaking. But as she read the message, the color drained from her face.

The note was from the king. It explained that Elizabeth, Queen of England, was ill and near death. No one expected her to live through the next few days. The knowledge was not yet public, but soon would be. King James commanded Devon to appear at court. There was no further explanation, but Catherine could well imagine what furious plottings were going on. The king would be frantic to have himself declared the new ruler of England. He'd want Devon's advice about the succession.

She read the letter again, this time with a thrum of apprehension. The letters her father had stolen must be used, and now. There was no more time, no chance to wait for a reply from her brother. Once James was named the ruler of England, publication of the letters could do no more than embarrass him. Therefore there would only be the briefest of times—from now until the English named James ruler, if they did—when the letters could be used to free her father.

And that meant she would have to be the one to use them. Without a troop of soldiers to protect her, without resources at all, she somehow had to blackmail the king into releasing her father.

Catherine looked up at Devon, who was staring at the wall, his brow wrinkled in thought. She said, "Devon, please. Take me with you to Edinburgh."

"Are you sure? I'll be attending an endless round of talks with the king about the succession. I won't be able to spend much time with you."

A sharp edge entered her voice. "I have to go." She searched for a reason, and said quickly, "If the king is named the next English ruler, he'll be in a magnanimous mood. It might be the one time I could petition him to set my father free."

He hesitated, then said, "Very well. In truth, I have no idea how long I'll be away. I'd rather have you with me."

She smiled at him, relief surging through her, and then bent to pick up her clothing. They'd leave immediately.

Catherine threw on her clothes and rushed up to her chamber while Devon assembled the men he'd be taking with them. Once inside her room, she drew open the doors to her cupboard and tossed out the dresses into her traveling box, not caring if they were sadly wrinkled. What concerned her at the moment was the letters. Would it be safest to leave them sewn inside the old gown, or would somewhere else be better?

Chewing on her lower lip, she considered the problem. Her clothes would all be in the traveling box, which had no key to it. Anyone could go through her things. But no place seemed safer, and tomorrow she could either wear the gown or sew the letters into one of her petticoats. That way, the letters would be safe. Satisfied that it was the best she could do for now, she folded the dress into the bottom of the box, and then went to oversee the packing for Devon.

Soon afterwards, they set out for Edinburgh. It was

late March, and although the weather had warmed a little since winter, the sun was like a wan, daylight moon in a sky of shaggy clouds. Cold sunlight, garlanded with shadows, fell through the pine forests onto ground still dusted and patched with snow. Riding was treacherous, yet they had to move quickly over a road alternately slippery and lush with mud or glazed hard with ice.

It was well after dark before they reached Devon's keep. Devon told her, as they walked up the narrow spiral stairway to their room, "I don't like taking you out on that road."

"I was fine," she reminded him, and then forgot about his words as he shut the door to their room and took her in his arms.

It was barely dawn when Catherine climbed from bed. Devon must have been up for some time, for he had already dressed.

He smiled down at her and said, "I'm leaving you here. I can't take you out on the roads today. It's raining, and it's just too dangerous. If I hadn't wanted you with me so much, I'd never have been fool enough to agree to bring you."

"But Devon, I have to see the king—"

He had his back to her as he shaved. The blade flashed in the light. "You can see the king. You'll just ride to Edinburgh at a saner pace than we will. I'll leave some men behind to escort you."

Catherine dragged out her traveling box and flung it open. It was nice of Devon to be concerned for her safety, but she had to go with him. She drew out the gown with the letters from the bottom of the box. "I'm going with you," she announced.

Devon turned to stare at her naked body. When she glanced up and caught his eye, he explained. "I like looking at you." Flinging on her shift, she suddenly found the clothes she was to wear in a wild tangle in her hands. "Here, you'll rip something," Devon said, and reached forward to help her.

Catherine gave a little gasp of panic. He was reaching for her gown, the one that held the letters. She snatched at the dress just as his hand came down upon it. There was a dreadful ripping sound, which rang in Catherine's ears like a tocsin.

Spilling out of the dress, and out from the red ribbon that had held them, the letters danced gracefully, silently, to the floor.

Devon stood still, staring at them.

Chapter Seventeen

DEVON GAVE A LOW, INCREDULOUS LAUGH. "OF course." He reached down and picked up the letters, turning them over between his fingers. "Of course. How like Sheamus. I should have realized it earlier. Your father never meant to play false with the king. Yet when Sheamus and his men were searched, no one could find the letters. I wondered why, and now I know. Because you had them." He looked at her. "When did your father give them to you?"

Catherine didn't know what to do or say. She turned wide eyes at Devon while her hands uselessly gripped the gown, the skirt bunched between her fingers, the torn hem hanging starkly down. In a pool beneath it lay the handful of white letters and the red ribbon that had tied them together.

Devon shrugged. "Your father must have found a way to give them to you in Edinburgh."

She nodded stiffly, while her wits chased various

possibilities for protecting the letters. None that were feasible occurred to her. Of all calamities! Why hadn't she put the letters elsewhere? Now nothing could be done. Her poor father. She had failed him again. Devon owed allegiance to the king; he couldn't just ignore the fact that he'd seen the letters. He couldn't give them back to her and forget the matter. Still, she had to at least try. "You told me you loved me. I would hate to have my father hurt by—"

He interrupted her, saying softly and distinctly, "Do you trust me?"

She stared at her husband. Behind him, she could see the cheerful rumple they had made of their bed last night, the pillows pushed together, the blankets twisted tellingly into the center of the mattress. They'd made love. Catherine said, "Yes."

He walked closer to her. "Then give me the letters. I swear your father won't suffer for it."

"Why? What do you mean to do?"

"I'll use them to force the king to set Sheamus free."

His words stunned her. Whatever she had expected, it hadn't been that Devon would help free her father. "You'd do that?"

"For you? Cat, do you need to ask?" He looked down at her with eyes that were clear and without artifice, eyes that held nothing but love for her.

"Devon." The word was choked. She realized she could hardly speak. It was one thing to know he loved her, and quite another to understand how much he did. He was even willing to risk the king's anger to help her.

Before she could find her voice, he explained, "I'm the only one who could be of any value to your father now. You can't. Nor could any of your father's agents in Edinburgh. There isn't time enough for you to find the men you'd need to help your father. I'm the king's friend. I have access to him that you don't. More, I have the power to force the king's hand, if it should come to that. He needs me in the Highlands. I am the one laird he can be certain of in an emergency."

Slowly, she nodded. Everything Devon had said was correct. "Take them. Do what you think best."

He smiled at her. The air around them suddenly seemed to have taken on a crystalline brightness, as if rarefied by happiness. Even the hiss and spatter of the rain outside couldn't drown the sudden flare of light that seemed to shine within their room. "Could you go and tell my men to be ready in ten minutes?" When she made a movement toward the door, he added dryly, "But put on a gown first. I'll help."

She laughed when his hands came down upon her. They spent an amusing few minutes dressing her, with Devon wasting as much time kissing her as he did tying the points of her dress. Afterwards, her skin feeling fresh and tingling, Catherine headed for the door again. She stopped just as her fingers reached for the latch, and turned to ask her husband, "Why can't I go with you?"

"I thought we'd decided that. It's raining, and there's still snow on the ground. The roads will be slick as glass. My soldiers are accustomed to it and you're not."

"But it takes only about four hours to ride from here to Edinburgh. I remember that from the first time we came," she countered. Catherine longed to go to hear Devon talk to the king.

"When we came before, the weather was clear. And no matter how short a ride it is in terms of distance, I doubt even my men can make it today. Doubtless we'll stop at an inn, and reach the city by midmorning tomorrow."

Catherine shrugged. Perhaps Devon was right. She

felt too cheerful to worry about it now. Swinging the door open, she ran on light steps down the narrow stairway.

Devon left shortly afterwards. She watched him from the window of the keep. A rain-dazzled mist clung low to the ground, as insubstantial as new-loomed silk, and the line of helmeted men and horses rode into it, turned into shadows, and then melted away. At last, when the silver fog had swallowed them up completely, she went to find Mouse, whom Devon had left in charge of her escort.

She discovered him in the stables, seeing to the grooming of his horse. The stables reeked of homey smells, of animals and damp wool blankets and straw. She stood just inside the doorway, her hood pulled low over her face because she'd run out through the rain to get here, and asked him, "When will we be leaving?"

Mouse looked up. He was alone in the building except for the horses. Because he was so tall, even the chestnut gelding he brushed seemed short in comparison. "I canna say. As soon as this rain lifts."

Catherine considered. "I suppose Devon told you I wasn't to go out in bad weather, no matter what."

Mouse smiled but said nothing. The only sounds were the endless needling of falling drops against the building and the shifting movements of the horses.

Catherine turned to leave. Then it struck her that, since she was alone with Mouse, now was the perfect time to discuss Bess. Catherine couldn't bear that two people so obviously meant for one another were apart. She worried that both of them were so shy they would never manage to tell one another their feelings. Besides, she felt so wonderful that she wanted everyone else to be happy, too. "Mouse," she said in a friendly way. "What do you think of Bess?"

Mouse rolled his large, mild eyes down at her.

She asked a bit too emphatically and loudly, "She's nice, isn't she?"

"Aye."

"Well, then." There seemed to be nowhere to go from there. Catherine grew aware of a certain awkwardness at Mouse's solemn silence. Perhaps she had strayed into too personal an area with him.

For a few minutes, Mouse continued to smooth the brush over the horse's glossy coat. Then he cleared his throat and said distinctly, "Ye can set your mind at rest. I'll be speaking to her shortly."

"I'm so glad." Catherine threw him a blinding grin.

She was still smiling by the time she sank into the cushioned chair in her bedroom. Propping her hand on her chin, Catherine thought that everything looked as if it would turn out just as it should.

Then her eyes narrowed when she spied a splash of red cloth caught in the iron grating. It was a ribbon, a brightly colored ribbon trembling in the draft from the fire. Curious, Catherine reached forward to draw it out, and then held it up to stare at it. She knew immediately what it was. There had only been one ribbon she'd ever seen with so much gilt embroidery and seed pearls set against a crimson background. And only one with the king's arms on it.

It was the ribbon that had tied the king's letters together.

For a moment, shock bolted her to the chair. Then she jumped forward and grabbed an iron tong to sift through the powdery ashes. Smoke rose in a grey cloud, and the flames from the fire leaped out as she whirled the tong through the hearth. The heat burned her cheeks, but carefully, bit by bit, she discovered one white, scorched fragment of paper after another. They were tiny, but enough to convince her that Devon had burned the letters.

A wave of horror nearly buckled her legs. Devon had burned the letters. He'd asked her to trust him, and then he'd burned them. Then he couldn't have left to bargain with the king about the letters, as he'd said. He must have gone to tell the king the letters were destroyed. How could Devon have done this to her and her family? As soon as the king learned that the letters were gone, there wouldn't be any reason to keep her father alive. Devon . . .

But she couldn't take the time to think about her husband now. If Devon did tell the king that he had burned the letters, what would then happen to her father? Catherine passed a hand before her face. She'd seen enough of James to guess he was capable of having her father slain out of sheer willfulness.

Panic gripped her. She couldn't let the king hurt her father. Somehow, she had to prevent it. Perhaps there was some way she could stop Devon in time and talk him out of telling the king anything.

What was it that Devon had said about his journey today? That he and his men would most likely have to stay at an inn somewhere in the Lowlands, and that they wouldn't be reaching Edinburgh until tomorrow morning? Devon had left only an hour ago. She could saddle a fast horse and ride after him.

Then an idea sprang at her. She wouldn't go and stop Devon. Instead she'd travel to Edinburgh and talk to the king herself. Maybe, just maybe, by using the ribbon and by bluffing, she could blackmail the king into freeing her father.

Having made her decision, Catherine wrote a quick

note to Mouse explaining that she'd gone after Devon. Then she snatched up her cloak, and, holding tightly to it and the ribbon, raced down to the stables.

To her relief, Mouse was no longer in the stables. He had, however, left behind his brown cloak. She picked it up. With Mouse's huge cape sheltering her instead of her own elegant blue one, she'd be taken as a man by anyone who noticed her. At least if they weren't too close.

The rain whirled about her as she started down the road, and mud clots and bits of snow flew from the gelding's hooves. The ground was white with snow, and silver rain fell in sad drops. The only traces of color were in the tan spider's web of bare trees and the stark, skeletal weed fingers poking through the snow.

She ignored the miserable conditions, setting her chin into the wind and leaning forward. It was bound to be a wretchedly unpleasant journey. But somehow, she had to see it through. She had to. Her father's life might depend upon it, as well as the lives of the men who had accompanied him to the exchange.

Yet it sent a thrill of fear through her at the idea of riding all the way to Edinburgh alone. She didn't know the country well, and wasn't at all certain of the roads. In the forests, she might meet wild animals, and there were reivers, the wild outlaws who roamed the Lowlands and stole from every traveler they came across.

The one thing she sternly refused to think about was Devon. The thought of him was so painful, so wrenching, she couldn't bear it. Later, after she knew why he had done it, she would consider Devon and the consequences of his action.

She rode until her hands were cold and stiff and her legs and back ached from the ceaseless rhythm. The churning movement of the horse beneath her drummed into every bone in her body, and her dark hair twisted and slapped about her cheeks in time to the rocking of her mount. Twice she passed people on the road, but they were on foot, and she clattered past as quickly as she could. Rivulets of water melted tearfully down her nose and along her cloak. Water slicked the reins, and fell in a shining drizzle through the netting of tree branches above her. Mud and the fluted fragments of dead leaves dotted the hem of her cloak.

After a while, the trees thinned and then disappeared completely. The countryside rolled out in broad, waving lines of hills, wet and dreary and covered in snow. Few shrubs except low, papery bracken and wiry heather poked through the wet, glistening powder. It frightened her that there was no shelter for her, nowhere to hide if there was some danger.

It was soon after she passed the crossroads village, that she saw the men. Catherine had been careful to skirt the village. Apparently despite the care she had taken, she must have been seen, for five men rode after her. They were pressing their mounts hard, and the clatter of hoofs on ice shattered the air. She swerved her head to look at them, fear bolting through her.

The men had to be poor, for they wore little other than their plaids. None of them had footwear of any kind, although they all carried weapons. She had no difficulty guessing what they were. Reivers.

They wanted to strip her of whatever money she carried. What would they do if they found out she was a woman? Catherine spurred her horse, wondering frantically how she could escape. Was her mount too tired to maintain a gallop, if she pushed him to it? If she couldn't outrun them, there didn't appear to be any way to escape. There was nowhere to hide, not in this endless, rolling country covered in scrub and heather.

She rounded one shallow rise, and realized her horse was winded. His pace had slackened. She glanced behind her. The men were gaining on her.

Then, just over the rim of the next hill, she spotted a castle. A castle meant people, people whose presence might scare off the reivers. With a goal in sight at last, Catherine urged her mount again, pressing her heels into his sides, trying to make him give his best.

At last Catherine, gasping, reached the castle walls. She turned to see what had happened to the reivers. In a cloud of snow, they had swerved about. They were now heading in the opposite direction.

She had escaped. Catherine sagged forward, laughing, while her gelding, anxious for the stable, began to amble in that direction. She nosed him in the opposite way, but not before she had spotted a familiar, white-faced mare in the stables. Didn't one of Devon's soldiers ride a horse that looked like that? Perhaps Devon and his men had stopped here.

That meant she'd still have a chance to get to Edinburgh ahead of her husband. Catherine felt fresh and impatient again, sure that she could make it.

Nevertheless, it took her all day to reach the low, pleasant country near Edinburgh. By the time she reached it, after skirting a dozen villages and castles, after stops to give her horse a rest, it was sunset.

She still had a few miles to go, and it was getting dark quickly. She ached to be inside. Peat smoke from the cottars' chimneys nearby scented the air, and, in the fields, there was the soft, homey sight of a few cows cropping at the wet grass. The setting sun painted the homes she passed with pink, giving the illusion of heat within. Catherine clenched the wet reins unhappily, all too aware she wouldn't find heat or comfort for some miles yet.

At last a midnight blue leaked across the sky. Shadows lengthened, and she began to gallop into a darkness as black as pitch, like a blind man traveling on a blind mount. Her teeth started to chatter, as much from fear as from the bitter cold.

A tree branch slashed at her hood. Suddenly, about her, spikey branches clawed out at her. Catherine guessed she was passing through a copse of trees. She slowed her horse immediately, letting the gelding pick his way through. Roots like traps thrust out at them. A fog, dense but insubstantial, turned every tree into fantastic sculptures of ogres.

She was shaking by the time they were out of the trees, her breath ragged. Then she realized the gelding was trotting through a farmer's field. Alarmed, she cried out. Where was the road? Had she missed it in the trees somehow? She gave the gelding its head, hoping it would find a way back to the path. Instead they seemed to be wandering farther and farther off track, ranging closer to the cottages.

She nudged the animal up a low hill. If only the moon would come out, she might be able to see something. But there turned out to be no need for moonlight, once she reached the top of the rise. Below, through the mist and the dark, she could see a far-off glow of lights. Edinburgh. Relief left her nearly giddy. She'd made it.

Catherine was too happy to care when she was stopped at the gates of the city and made to explain her business. It took at least an hour to argue her way to Holyrood. Luckily, once she was there, she was able to convince the guards to bring her to their captain.

She faced him with as much determination as she could muster. The captain, a middle-aged man with a lined, scarred face which surrounded two surprisingly merry brown eyes, took one look at her, and said, "Ye're the Macgowan's wife."

She smiled. "Yes. I'm glad you recognize me. Please, I must see the king immediately." She reached inside her pocket and handed him the red ribbon. "Give this to the king, and tell him who sent it. Explain that I seek an immediate audience."

The man shrugged, and went off to do as he was bid. Catherine remained behind in the captain's stuffy little chamber. The waiting was unbearable. Every second she expected the captain to come back with news that the king refused to see her. What would she do then?

She brushed futilely at her dirty skirt, skittering flakes of mud and bits of twigs and leaves onto the floor. Mentally she was going over the words she wanted to speak, planning an argument so convincing the king would set her father free this very night.

The captain returned, and informed her that the king would see her. Catherine followed him down the gallery with a thumping heart.

As they walked through the rich, glowing rooms, the captain leaned closer to her, and said, "From the look of ye, I take it ye've been riding hard. But ye'll be the second one, lass, to arrive with the message. The king has already heard the news."

Catherine blinked. "What news?"

"Ah, then. Ye havena heard." With the relish of a born gossip, the man related, "Robert Carey arrived but an hour ago. Robert Carey of England, mind, the Warden of the Middle March. He came staggering in, his head bloody, his clothes but reeking rags. He insisted on seeing the king, too. Claimed to have an important message." He paused dramatically and looked up at Catherine. Above his riveted body armour, his eyes gleamed.

Catherine walked forward stiffly. Around her, she could see the signs that told her that something special had occurred. Holyrood blazed with light. With complete disregard for the cost, every room had been lit by scented beeswax candles. The galleries and chambers were filled with people, dozens of people, all murmuring, all alert, all wearing expectant faces. Whatever the news was, it must have run, like the streaming light, from bracket to bracket, person to person, shining over the colorful assembly like the glittering chandeliers.

She asked, "What was this news?"

But the captain had no time to tell her. Already, they had finished the climb to James's apartments in the northeast tower. Almost ill with fear, she watched one of the servants pull open the door to the king's rooms. She stepped inside. The door shut behind her with a soft snap.

At the other end of the long, narrow room, King James sat alone in a finely carved walnut chair. Catherine guessed he must have been roused from his bed, for he wore a deep crimson robe decorated with gilt thread, and underneath, a nightsmock. A nightcap hung loosely down his hair.

Catherine walked slowly across the long room toward him. Blindly, she passed by a half dozen high-backed chairs, and a handful of tiny, embellished tables. The king watched her as she walked, sipping as he did so from a goblet of the finest Venetian glass. His clever-clown eyes were bright with curiosity.

Catherine knelt before him, and said, "Sir, please forgive my disarray. I've traveled hard to reach you in time."

"In time to give me back my ribbon."

She swallowed, not at all sure by his noncommital tone what his mood was. "If you recognized the ribbon, you must know I have the letters you seek. Set my father free and restore his lands, and I promise you I'll bring you the letters, burned to cinders."

"Indeed, madam?" James fingered his goblet thoughtfully. "And what if I don't?"

"I—" she didn't know what to say.

The king smiled at her confusion. "I have just learned that Queen Elizabeth is dead. Before she died, she indicated that I was to be proclaimed the next ruler of England. So why should I care about your letters?"

She stared at him, stricken, not knowing exactly what to say. If it were true that the Queen had named him as her successor before she died, would the king care if the letters were published? Still, they might at least embarrass him, or they would, if they still existed. And she had no intention of telling him that they had already been burned.

Catherine picked her words carefully, remembering what Devon had told her about the king's vanity. "I have no wish to do anything that might make you unhappy, sir. You are my king, and, as such, you command all my loyalty. But I also owe loyalty to my father. If you free him and his men, I swear to you, you will never have cause to worry about the letters again." There, that managed to hint that she might try to do something with the letters without actually being nasty about it.

"This appears to be the day for threats," James told her dryly. "Your suggestion is remarkably similar to your husband's, except he brought me one of the letters for his proof of possession. I wonder, which one of you is to be believed? Devon, what would you say?"

298

Catherine whirled about to see the person the king spoke to. Her mouth dropped as she spotted what, in her haste to reach to the king, she had failed to see when she walked through the room.

From one of the high-backed cushioned chairs by the hearth, Devon raised a glass of wine at her in a salute.

Chapter Eighteen

"DEVON!" SHE SAID, STUNNED.

He held up his glass. "Your servant, my lady."

She opened her mouth and then closed it. Before heaven, how should she act? What should she say? From the king's words, she assumed Devon had come here for the same purpose she had. The knowledge delighted her; but that feeling was overshadowed by the fear that she'd inadvertently blundered by rushing in here and talking as if she held the letters.

Devon rescued her. "No doubt, sir," he told the king, "you're wondering how we can both claim to have the letters."

The king stared into space and laughed. "Indeed."

Devon answered smoothly, "I have the letters, and my wife, of course, knows where they are hidden."

The king took a long drink from his glass. For the first time, Catherine noticed the unnatural brightness of

James's eyes. He must have had a great deal of wine in celebration over the news that he was to inherit the throne of England. James said in a slightly slurred voice, "It doesn't matter. The entire affair is over." Again he drank deeply from the flagon. He remarked, as if his mind couldn't stay with one subject for long, "I wonder what the English are thinking, knowing they'll have a Scotsman for king."

"You're no longer solely a Scotsman," Devon pointed out quietly. "Doubtless most Englishmen are wondering what you're like."

"What I'm like," the king repeated. The yellow candlelight flickered over his exquisite robe, the drunken line of his mouth, and highlighted the thin, weak leg which poked out of his robe.

Devon rose from the chair. "I believe we've kept you long enough, sir. My wife and I will retire for the night."

"As you wish." James laughed again, and the gold thread on the chest of his robe flashed. "Your wife seems to have a few questions for you."

Devon took Catherine firmly by the arm, and led her from the room. A soldier escorted them through the warren of galleries and rooms to a bedchamber. It was a small chamber, neat and trim, with such luxuries as Italian bronze sculptures and silver candelabras.

As soon as they were inside and alone, Devon said, "You never cease to amaze me. How did you persuade Mouse to bring you here today? Did you promise him Caldwell?"

"Caldwell is still in your possession."

"You relieve me greatly."

Catherine smiled automatically. She wasn't at all sure of what had taken place between Devon and the king before she arrived. "Devon, I'm burning with

301

curiosity. What happened? What about my father? Is he free? And what did you tell the king?"

Devon held up one hand. "One question at a time."

"My father first then."

"He's free, and so are all of his men. Sheamus may already be walking through Edinburgh looking for an inn free of fleas, something I suspect he won't find."

Catherine sank down onto a stool because her knees would no longer hold her. She'd been tense all day. Now, with her father safe, a sweet loosening untied every knot in her body. Her voice was the softest of murmurs. "Thank you. I know it was all your doing. But how did you accomplish it?"

Devon stood over her. His hand reached out and brushed aside a damp curl from her forehead. "All the rest I suppose you can guess. I brought with me one letter which I took to be harmless. I burnt the rest, because I thought they could be damaging to James succeeding to the English throne; so damaging I couldn't even chance carrying them here. The harmless one I took with me to prove to the king I had access to the rest. With it, I blackmailed James into setting your father free."

"But how? I thought he'd already been named king of England."

"Not quite," Devon said dryly. "The messenger came of his own accord. He wasn't sent by the government. That delegation, if it is to arrive, won't be here for a few days. So there was still time for—as I put it—blackmail."

Catherine asked anxiously, "Was James angry with you?"

Devon strode to the hearth to add more coals to the fire. It had blazed low, giving off little heat. "No. Tonight, nothing would have made him angry. He'd just received news he'd been waiting all his life to hear. Besides, he can't afford to be annoyed with me now. He's leaving for England within a week, and he'll make England his residence. He has to have someone he can trust in the Highlands."

"Oh yes." She lowered her eyes and stared with great interest at her muddied skirt. Devon had answered all her questions, had proved beyond a doubt that she should have trusted him from the first. Guilt curled in her abdomen. She squirmed, feeling small and in the wrong for not trusting him enough.

"Now let me guess about why you are here," Devon said quietly. "You found the burned letters and assumed I had lied to you. So you came here, ribbon in hand, to deal with the king yourself."

Miserably, she nodded.

"Cat." He moved, and his shadow, long and blue, fell over her silently. "Don't look so unhappy. I cannot bear to see you sad. Nor is there any need. Ever since we've met, you've been caught between me and your father, between your duty and your liking for me. It hasn't been easy for you." He touched her forehead with light, caressing fingers. "I don't blame you for coming here. I just hope, from this time on, you'll trust me."

"Devon." She faltered on the word, cleared her throat, and went on. "I swear to you I'll always trust you, from this moment until the day I die."

He told her dryly, "Before God, I've given you reason to. Any man who asks to have Sheamus Craig for his neighbor must be mad with love."

She raised her eyes. "Neighbor?"

"The king has restored your father's lands."

She jumped up and threw her arms around her husband. "Devon!"

"Your father and brother can even rebuild Cree Castle, if they can find the funds. I daresay they'll manage that somehow, no doubt illegally. So you see, we should have no more problems." He added in a mutter, "Except the trouble of living near Sheamus."

She carefully ignored his last comment. "I'm so glad. Do you know Mouse told me he planned to start courting Bess? Isn't that wonderful?"

Devon, who was far more intrigued by the interesting proximity of his wife's body to his own, murmured, "Wonderful. How did you pry the information out of him? Hot tongs or other exotic tortures? For that matter, how did you talk him into escorting you here when I gave him a direct order not to leave until he was certain you would be safe every step of the way?"

Catherine reflected that it might not have been such a fine idea to bring up the subject of Mouse. "Actually . . ."

"Actually, what?"

"I came alone."

There was a dramatic silence.

She said in a rush, "Don't be alarmed. As you see, I am quite unhurt. She hurried into her explanations, beginning with finding the ribbon and ending by saying, "I'm sorry I came."

His brows were locked together. "You rode here alone," he said, enunciating each word with crisp displeasure. "Cat, do you have any idea of how dangerous that was?"

"Of course. I've never been brave, so—"

He laughed. "What? Why did you say that?"

She gazed owlishly up at him and admitted, "I've just never been very brave, the way my father is, the way I wanted to be."

Devon stared down at her. "Sweeting, you are

indeed brave. Mayhap you don't have the recklessness of your father, but I don't count that a fault. It's nothing but clear thinking on your part." When she didn't look completely convinced he added, "You ran off into the forest to escape me, you rode here alone, and you think you're not brave? Catherine!"

"That was duty, not bravery." But a smile tugged at her lips. Perhaps she did have more courage than she thought.

"Then may you have less duty and no bravery at all."

"You just want me safe."

"Of course. I love you." He smoothed his hand over her hair. "I hope you'll never have to face anything as chancy as the ride to Edinburgh again, even though I know in our life together there may . . ." His voice trailed off.

She prompted him. "In an entire lifetime, what?"

He pushed aside the cap she wore and unpinned her hair. The dark curls, tangled fetchingly, clung in damp tendrils to the back of her neck. "It has occurred to me that I pushed you into staying with me. I'd been alone for a long time. For years, I must have wanted you without even knowing what it was I wanted. When we did meet, and when I fell in love with you, I know I pushed too hard."

She shook her head, not understanding. "What do you mean?"

"I've been willing to do anything to keep you with me. What I never really bothered to ask myself was whether you wanted to stay with me."

"I've already told you I intend to live with you as your wife. I told the truth," she admitted frankly.

He kissed the base of her throat. "Yes, I know you told me that. But only after I seduced you and then spent an entire two months trying to convince you that you couldn't live without me. I wanted you. But I never gave you a chance to consider, to weigh the choices. No, more than that. I know I didn't want to give you that chance."

She laughed, and shook her head. "Devon, I wanted you every bit as much as you wanted me from the first day we met. I'd heard all those stories about you from my father, but it was soon clear to me that you weren't anything like the person my father told me about. I kept telling myself I couldn't trust you, that I had to dislike you. But I never was able to."

"Then, are you sure you don't want to try to reconsider?" he asked, with the determination of a man who has seen the moral path and is bound to take it. "I could easily talk the king into giving us a divorce if you wanted one."

"Divorce!" The very word alarmed her. "Certainly not."

His arms came around her. "You don't know what it means to me to hear you say that." His fingers slid over her, untying the points of her dress, undoing the fastenings. "I want you as my wife."

"So I see," she said, as her sleeves and bodice fell to the floor.

"I love having you as my wife. And this is the very best part." Her skirt came undone.

She stepped out of it. "Of what? Of being man and wife? Or of undressing me?"

"Of anything." He worked enthusiastically on her petticoats.

As soon as he had reached her shift, she spun away from him, and said, "I think one of the best parts is hearing the words. Tell me again, Devon."

He had pounced on her and was firmly bent to the

task of removing her shift. "Hm?" he said distractedly. "Oh, you mean you want me to say I love you."

"Not like that. With more feeling."

She had shaken off his hands. He sighed, and said, "Very well. I love you madly."

"Better."

"I will always love you." His fingers returned to her body, and grazed enticingly along the smooth length of her arms.

"Nice, but surely you can say more. You do have a reputation for being most eloquent."

"Not when I have a nearly naked woman in my arms," he pointed out ruefully. "Then my mind is on other things."

"Any naked woman?" she wondered in what could only be termed a dangerous tone.

"Only you." He touched the tip of her mouth. "Only you." His voice thickened, growing as smooth and heavy as velvet. "Is this what you want to hear? That my life was empty of everything but duty. And then you came, and there was joy and love. Do you remember long ago when you told me I was lonely? You were right. I needed someone like you in my life. No, I didn't mean that. Not like you. Only you, could ever be right for me. It seems a miracle that I ended up married to the one woman in the world I would ever have wanted to marry."

"I'm certain you didn't think so at the time."

"No. It was only one more thing I had to do for my clan. I certainly didn't expect to learn to love you." He untied the ribbon of her shift and swept that last piece of clothing from her body. The bedroom was unlighted except for the rosy glow from the fire. Catherine's body, dappled with alternating patterns of shadow and gold, swayed toward him slightly.

"At the ceremony, you scared me," she admitted. "The thought of setting up housekeeping with someone so old and so—"

"Old?" he repeated, wounded.

"Before heaven, to a twelve-year-old girl you were ancient."

"I was twenty at the time, and I don't remember creaking in a single joint."

She teased, staring up at him under her lashes, "But you looked so to me."

He pulled her firmly against him. "I want to make love to you. Urgently. But first I need to know something. Nothing made me happier than the moment when you handed me the letters. I hoped . . . does it mean you've come to care for me, at least a little?"

Catherine raised her hands to touch his chin. His face, austerely drawn in the wavering firelight, shocked her. His brows were locked together, and there were two finely etched lines about his mouth, the ones that meant he was under some kind of strain. He looked anguished. He looked as if her answer would mean the difference between happiness or pain for him.

She thought, her heart pounding within her, that if she hadn't loved him before, she surely did at this second, knowing how much she meant to him. How strange that he didn't know the way she felt about him. Why couldn't he read it in her face and eyes and speech? But then, she too, had been blinded, not knowing how totally she could trust him, and how much he loved her.

"Devon," she told him, the tips of her fingers running lightly and quickly over his mouth, "I love you."

The words hung like stars in the air.

She repeated, "I love you, and I have for months.

The only thing that held me away from you was my feeling of duty to my father. But all that time I've loved you, ached for you, wanted you. I want you for my lover, and the father of my children. I want to have you beside me all my life."

He gave a muffled groan, and circled her with his arms, pulling her against the warmth of him. Behind them, the fire sizzled and smoked, a ruddy blizzard of light. Catherine slid her hands over her husband, feeling that she had never been so perfectly content in all her life.

Together they moved into the blue, languid darkness of the corner of the room, where the bed rested. Catherine found that at last there were no more words, and no more fears. There was only Devon, and the moment. Her lips met his in a kiss that was as much a promise for the future as it was a seal of love.

HISTORICAL ROMANCES

Next Month From Tapestry Romances

A LOVING DEFIANCE
by Joan Johnston
CAPTIVE HEARTS
by Catherine Lyndell

POCKET BOOKS

Home delivery from Pocket Books

Here's your opportunity to have fabulous bestsellers delivered right to you. Our free catalog is filled to the brim with the newest titles plus the finest in mysteries, science fiction, westerns, cookbooks, romances, biographies, health, psychology, humor—every subject under the sun. Order this today and a world of pleasure will arrive at your door.

POCKET BOOKS, Department ORD
1230 Avenue of the Americas, New York, N.Y. 10020

Please send me a free Pocket Books catalog for home delivery

NAME _____

ADDRESS _____

CITY _____ STATE/ZIP _____

If you have friends who would like to order books at home, we'll send them a catalog too—

NAME _____

ADDRESS _____

CITY _____ STATE/ZIP _____

NAME _____

ADDRESS _____

CITY _____ STATE/ZIP _____

368